122

PRAISE FOR *X*

"Davis is an astounding writer, seemingly unconstrained by taboos and waist-deep down in the maw of life, examining what the rest of us shy away from—never more than here in *X*, the rare book that can thrill and entertain, while simultaneously causing you to question everything about how you're living."
—Torrey Peters, author of *Detransition, Baby*

"OH OH OH I FINISHED IT AND THREW MYSELF DOWN THE STAIRS."
—Leigh Cowart, author of *Hurts So Good*

"Hardboiled style meets dyke drama in the clubs and play parties of queer Brooklyn. In an atmosphere of creeping fascism, Davey Davis gives us a fascinating protagonist. When not making a mess of their life or wasting it on true crime podcasts, Lee is an amateur sadist obsessed with finding the mysterious X, mistress of the craft to which they aspire. *X* is both a delight to read and a penetrating study on the intimacy of violence and the violence of intimacy." —McKenzie Wark, author of *Reverse Cowgirl*

"In *X*, Davey Davis presses down hard on all of our bruised places until we beg for more. In their taut, electric prose, Davis performs a skillful sleight of hand: keeping our eyes on the noirish tale of a pain slut's growing obsession, while just out of frame fascism slowly creeps into daily life. *X* will leave you wet, hard, and implicated." —Morgan M Page, *One from the Vaults* podcast

"Filled with clever and thoughtful turns of phrase, and drawing on traditions of noir, camp, memoir, and erotic thrillers. Davis depicts the trans/nonbinary/queer subculture of Brooklyn as an all consuming underground network of friends, playmates, lovers, and clients, with occasional forays into office jobs, self-absorbed on the edges of a larger society of official cruelty. They unflinchingly draw taut the tightrope between ego aggression and political passivity that so many live on."

—Sarah Schulman, author of *Let the Record Show*

X

ALSO BY DAVEY DAVIS

the earthquake room

A NOVEL

Davey Davis

Catapult
New York

This is a work of fiction. All of the characters, organizations, and events portrayed in this novel are either products of the author's imagination or are used fictitiously.

ISBN: 978-1-64622-093-9

Cover design by Nicole Caputo
Book design by Laura Berry

Library of Congress Control Number: 2021947154

Catapult
New York, NY
books.catapult.co

Printed in the United States of America

1 3 5 7 9 10 8 6 4 2

"Fantasy" is not just a thin wish but a logic that names a value.

—LAUREN BERLANT

Unnnnnnnnnnnnnnnnnnnnnnnnnnnnnnnnn . . . nnnnnnnnnnnn . . .
Ak-k-k . . . nnnnnnnnnnnnnnnnnn . . . Hhhhh . . . Unnnnn . . .
nnnnnnnnnnnnnnnnnnnnnnnnnnnn . . . K-k-k-k . . . nnnnnnnnnnnnnnn-
nnnnnnnnnnnnnnnnn . . . nnnnnnnn nnnnnnnnnnnnnn . . . Ch-ch-ch . . .
nnnnnnnnnnnnnnnnnnnnnnnnnnnnnnnnnnnnnnnnnn—nnnnnnnnnnnnnnnnnnn . . .

—SAMUEL R. DELANY, *HOGG*

X

####

"I just want to try it," said Venus. "It's not that deep."

"Not that deep," I repeated, rolling my eyes. We were in the parlor where the ladies bring their clients before taking them down into the dungeon. I wasn't a client, exactly, but she and I still had to negotiate.

Venus laughed. "You're cute, too. I like it when cuties can't breathe."

A Lynndie England fetish, I figured. And here I was to play bottom for her—a political prisoner, demeaned for the Polaroids. Abu Ghraib must have really been something for the right kind of American preteen.

But Venus denied any connection to all that. This very specific kind of discomfort that she was going to put me through, she said, had nothing to do with the world outside the dungeon. She had a wide mouth that curled into a moue when she wanted things. "Not political," she insisted. "Just sexy."

Impossible, but I wasn't about to argue with a femme who had me over a barrel. A real candle in a brass wall sconce (convenient, I thought, for when energy savers swept through Manhattan) flickered in time with the music easing from a hidden speaker: Hibari Misora covering Nat King Cole like honey on a comb, her contralto melting away into a sissified version of "Siboney" that I'd never heard before. No one except for Venus and me, and the anons paying for the camera footage of our time together, would know what I was willing to do for the information I wanted. And this was my only lead. I was lucky Venus wasn't asking for something much worse.

"Fine," I said. "I'm in." How bad could a waterboarding really be if you could get up and walk away afterward? *Waterboarding.* Sounded fake. But real life always feels less real than the news feeds. *Sueño,* lisped the speakers. *Te espero.*

"Great," said Venus. She stood up, tugging at the hem of her graphite bodycon. No stockings, no leather, no latex, no beat except for some mascara and a few strokes of the eyebrow pencil. She hadn't gotten dressed up for me, which I knew to take as a neg. "Let's go."

When I learned that X used to work in this dungeon, I asked Camille if she knew any of the girls, and of course she did. She gave me Venus's number, and I texted right away. Would she be willing to answer a few questions about someone I was looking for, someone we both knew?

who, Venus asked.

id rather talk about it in person, I countered; it's hard to tell if someone is lying over text. I waited a half hour, but she didn't reply. I texted again. *so when can i come see you.*

Another half hour, and nothing. Fuck her, I decided. Then I thought about X. It's always fine until I think about X. I tried again. *happy to pay.*

you are? This time, her response was immediate.

i mean, I was quick to text, *maybe not your normal rate.*

Then there was nothing. I figured she'd written me off and gone back to her video game or whatever—any smart girl would have—but the next night, when I was just lying there, staring up at Camille's ceiling, my phone lit up beside me.

send me a pic.

I was annoyed, but I never miss a chance to show off. I sent her one from last year, when I was less pale and skinny. A few moments later, my phone lit up again.

work trade?

I smiled at Camille's ceiling. If trade plays their cards right, they never have to work.

I gathered all the cash I could, plus a few twenties on loan from Camille, and went to meet Venus at the dungeon. I would make up the rest by letting her do whatever she wanted to me, to torture or tease me to her heart's content. That's where the waterboarding came in.

"You're into some weird stuff," I said. Whatever happened to good old-fashioned corporal punishment?

"My desires are unconventional," she replied, smirking over her shoulder. Her arm snaked over her head, gels tapping against the door frame she led me through. Five inches taller than her natural height, she jogged down the stairwell ahead of me like a champ.

Below the soundproofed parlor, I could hear the building's age. The thin walls and petrified floors popped like knuckles. Sounds escaped locked doors as we passed by: a man moaned; a woman laughed; wind rattled window. The whole effect was like those CDs they play at Halloween stores, the banal music of the oubliette in whining minor key. God, pain is corny.

At least Venus is sexy. I expected her to interrogate me, or strangle me with an American flag, but all she did was spray from the industrial-grade nozzle and tell me how cute I was. She laughed when I fought the restraints, which made the weight-lifting bench we dragged in from the Wrestling Fantasy room wobble, but she never let me tip over.

Were our roles reversed, I doubt I would have been so kind. Her pretty skin is unmarked, her eyebrows no match for spit or tears. Even if her idea of a good time is a simulated drowning, it's not so bad. Is there a Hallmark card for when you want to thank someone for not raping you with a cattle prod?

"You made it three seconds longer that time," Venus informs me.

The towel slides off the bridge of my nose, and I can see her again, though the water still burns behind my eyes. My lungs expand and contract, swift as spooked birds. I take another breath, pushing out my chest as far as it can go against the restraints, and it feels good, even though it hurts.

When she unties my hands, I touch my face. Skin cold as rubber under my fingers, all of them numb from Venus's bad bondage. Head still burning, I cough up water as she moves on to my legs, then block one nostril with my thumb, hook my index finger around the other hole, and blow. Some mucus, mostly water. More coughing. For the first time in weeks, I don't feel congested. "Basically a neti pot," I say. I laugh at my own joke and start coughing again.

She rolls her eyes. Her hair is big and shiny and ombré, like Venus Xtravaganza. Maybe that's her namesake.

When I sit up, everything inside my head slowly shifts, like a lava lamp. My nasal cavity is raw and I can taste copper, but no one ever says anything about waterboarding causing nosebleeds. Most people don't even know what waterboarding is, exactly, or at least I didn't, not until tonight.

Venus expands something on her screen. "You okay?" she asks absently.

"Yeah. You know, I think I'm a natural," I say. Now that I'm no longer bound and struggling, she seems more interested in her phone. Am I really that boring when I can breathe?

She smiles and flicks a piece of that golden hair out of her eyes, the strand jerking like a tawny snake. With a peek behind her to make sure the lid is down, she takes a seat on the toilet. Every move she makes—her ass slides back over the creamy ceramic like cakesitting porn—is dainty. "Well, I have no one to compare you with. Maybe you're not even any good." She laughs like Mariah Carey, though I don't know if it's herself or something on the internet that she finds funny.

"Anyway." She sighs, shoving her phone down her chest and into her bra. She flicks her hair again, allowing her head to follow the course of her mane away from me and toward the little clock on a shelf beside the door. Hair dramatics are a useful trick for covert timewatching. "Now you. Who you digging up dirt on?"

The way dungeons turn over, I knew it was possible that Venus had never heard of X, but tonight I'm lucky. When I say her name, the syllable crunching like a bad word, Venus is suddenly standing again.

"Her?" she demands, gilt-nailed fingers lost in ombré. "Why do you wanna know about her?"

"It doesn't matter. Why did she leave?"

Her mouth rolls, her face thinks. "I don't know exactly. But it had to do with a manager."

"Did X do something?" I ask. "Or the manager?" I'm relieved that she doesn't pry. Maybe it's good that Venus finds me boring.

More rolling, more flicking of the hair. Her babysoft feet pace the tile, most of it still dry. The water she drowned me with has disappeared into the drains along the walls of the sloping bathroom, which looks like any other you'd find in a rich white lady's house except for the walk-in shower with three heads, dripping like a pack of hungry dogs. Her shoes—size 6½ US— are a bird's nest of black vinyl next to the toilet. Towel around my neck, I take my phone down from the counter, where I left it to keep dry, and open my Notes app.

"Let me put it like this: That manager was asking for it," says Venus.

Even when I'm not eye-level with them like I am now, Venus's legs look bigger and softer and prettier than they do in her Cyte stories. In most of her carefully paywalled photos, she's staring down at the camera, her hip stuck out like Nomi Malone thumbing for a ride. But she markets herself as a switch—there are a few shots where her sneer is replaced with an over-the-shoulder simper, and a slender gloved hand presses a riding crop into the crease between her ass and her upper thigh. She has that nice laugh. I bet she has a nice scream.

Water runnels through my eyebrow and I note its course, the cool it leaves behind. I can't get distracted. I want to know everything Venus knows. Anything could be a clue. She screws up her mouth as she talks, crinkling her lips like a candy wrapper.

"Yeah, she was buzzed back then, too. She usually wore a wig in session. A nice one. Very expensive."

"She went by a few of them, but that was the one I heard the most. Can't remember the other ones."

"It's been like a year, you know? I don't remember everything. Trauma brain. But I do remember that she was a Leo. I think. Definitely a fire sign. Or like maybe an air sign."

When I run out of questions, I put my phone back in my pocket and massage the headache between my eyes.

"You good?" Venus asks.

I nod, digging my thumb into my eye socket. To be expected, I guess, when you huff a gallon of water through a towel. "I'm done."

Prim as a straight girl, she scoops up her heels, pulls a ratty pair of fleece-lined moccasins from the cabinet under the sink, and slides her golden toes inside. No more feet. That's when I know for sure a quickie is out of the question. The thought of jerking off alone in Camille's shower later, maybe while glaring at a mold spiral, makes my head hurt even more.

"I'll walk you out," Venus says, glancing at her phone again. "I have a client."

The front door closes in pneumatic silence behind me. Liquor store neon flickers to the left. Scaffolding cages a black storefront to the right. It's dark, and I don't see anyone on the street. I check my phone. Twenty-seven degrees and no messages. The icy wind brings my damp hair to life on my forehead. My emptied sinuses sing in the cold. I start for the train.

I don't know what I was expecting from tonight, but it wasn't this. I feel tired and creepy and horny. Worse, I bottomed for nothing. I asked Venus every question I could think of, but she had nothing useful for me. No address, no phone number, no aliases. There were a few details, the kinds of things you need to know about a girl so you can describe her to a client over the phone, but it was stuff that I already knew (shoe size) or that could have changed since Venus saw her last (no tattoos). Nothing she said was unbelievable, but I find it all a little hard to believe. She talked like she was hiding something. I keep my eyes trained on the ground, patrolling for ice on the littered pavement of Midtown.

I'm almost to the 1 when I feel my phone moving in my pocket, and for an instant, before I remember that she has neither my number nor any reason to use it, I wonder, with a stirring of hope, if it's X.

Syd's name glows atop my messages. The hope falls down a flight of stairs. But then I remember—Syd is responding to a text I sent over a week ago. I'd given up on them. But now, suddenly, I have another lead, right when I thought I was out of luck. Hope staggers to its feet.

sure, Syd says. *where should we meet?*

####

When I wake up, my whole body hurts. It was gonna hurt anyway, but sleeping on Camille's couch doesn't help. Ten days after X, the bruises are uglier than ever, but less tender, at least. I pull some clothes on over my long underwear and check the fridge. Nothing in there except a can of something and a plastic bottle of primordial ketchup. Time to go.

I arrive late on purpose, but I still end up sitting at a wobbly corner table for a full seven minutes before Syd strolls into the grimy Bushwick café. It takes almost seven more for them to order and receive their drink. I watch them pocket their change instead of tipping, a bold move for a trust fundie.

"Thanks for meeting me here," they say, collapsing into the chair as if they own the place. There's a grey veneer across their teeth, like the skin that grows on soy milk when it's been out on the counter all morning. Without taking a drink of their coffee, they set down their cup and push it away, as if to give it a little privacy. "We haven't hung out in like forever."

Syd is so fucking fake. Ever since I've known them they've spoken slowly, under the hipster pretense that lethargy is the same thing as intention. They often find ways to bring up the two years they spent sober, even though those two years were five years ago now, and they haven't gone a day without using since. They think that just because they've had EMDR and gone on a pricey peyote retreat that they're enlightened, but they're as authentic as Camille's nose. Unlike with Camille's nose, everyone can tell.

"Yeah, it's been a long time," I say. I know why I'm here, but what I haven't figured out is why Syd agreed to join me. They must want something, but what? As we trudge through small talk (Climate change. Always climate change.), I try to figure out a way to ask them about X. Before I can, they surprise me with their own question.

"So listen, you know Margot, right?"

"Margot Kuhl?" I can see her full name in Helvetica Neue, flanking a thumbnail of a Revlon'd mouth and knockoff Moschino sunglasses.

"Yeah," says Syd. "I think I've seen you two around."

As if they caught us fingering each other on a blanket in Prospect Park, when the truth is that the night we met, Margot posted a string of pictures that neither of us remember taking. Nothing too damning, but she deleted them the next morning, a sure sign of gay mess. Didn't matter. They were up long enough that Syd, or someone who knows Syd, could save them for dyke drama reference.

Margot's blackout fuckups have never panned out in my favor. I don't know how well Syd knows X, or if they've seen each other recently. If I could have figured it out with Cyte or Instagram or whatever, I obviously would have by now. Cracking open my phone is a lot easier than rolling off the couch an hour early to meet some secretly rich asshole in a café roughly the size of a hall closet for a cup of scalding imitation coffee. But I haven't found X online anywhere, not a trace. It doesn't help that X, the porniest letter, happens to be the world's worst search term. So here I am, sitting here with Syd, who I've long tolerated but never liked. At least now I have a bowel movement to look forward to, but of course there's an OUT OF ORDER sign on the fly-spotted bathroom door.

And Syd isn't wrong, about seeing me and Margot around. I do know Margot, or I did, but it's not something I feel like getting into with Syd, of all people. Not that my relationship with Margot is privileged information. It was just one of those things that happen in this small, gay world.

"Yeah," I say. The surface of my coffee is as greasy as a pesticided orange peel. The caffeine was a mistake. Now I'm even more attuned to the singed feeling in my nasal cavity. "Margot and I were hanging out for a little while."

"Oh yeah?" says Syd.

"Yeah." Conversations with Syd have always been like this. It's probably why we've never fucked—most people wait until the morning after to get boring. Not Syd. Every exchange happens at half speed, every statement and interjection followed up with a needless pause for confirmation, plus careful posturing to be sure everyone can see their incredible jaw definition. Their fakeness makes my skin crawl. It's probably the worst possible conversational juncture to pick up my phone, but I want it so bad my fingers flex. There's nothing worse than being bored, and Syd is as dull as a butt plug.

But I have to be polite. If Syd knows anything about X, then I need to know it, too. And if finding out means not being a bitch, well, I can do that, for a little while. I take a deep breath, exhale slowly, blocking out the hum of the café, the screech of a bus on the corner. Think about a beach with no trash on it. Think about sinking into a queen-size bed all by myself. Think about my lungs before I smoked my first cigarette, pink as a pair of popsicles. Nothing on my phone I can't see later. Nothing on the internet ever dies, though you never know what might end up shadowbanned or paywalled tomorrow.

"So how do you know Margot?" I ask. Syd and Margot are regulars in the gossipy game of telephone Camille is always playing, but I want to hear how they describe their relationship.

Syd sighs. They're dressed like a housepainter, but their fingers and ears are all silver. "I mean we're dating," they say. Their cup is still almost completely full, the coffee rippling like a full binder. "Were dating. I don't know anymore."

Personally, I can't imagine seeing a breakup with Margot as a bad thing.

"We haven't really talked about it," they go on. "But we haven't really talked at all in like a month. Maybe longer."

"So what happened?"

"It's just . . ." They fiddle with the dangliest of their earrings with one long, soft finger. They attempt a grimace. "It's just so many things."

God, leave it to Syd to make a lesbian breakup sound boring. "Yeah," I say, making a point of thoughtfully nodding my head. Most people are too self-absorbed to tell the difference between apathy and empathy, which is convenient in situations like this one.

The front door slams behind a customer, and Syd's cup—it's almost brimming, really—trembles in its aftershock. I wonder if they're ever going to drink it. "You probably heard what happened with Margot and me, right?" they ask.

I haven't—that news hasn't made it to Camille yet—but I need to make their stupid problems seem important. "I heard a little," I say. I draw out my words, as if I'm being forced to admit something. "Heard some things here and there."

Their coffee shines like a nightlight. Their coffee looks like it tastes better than mine.

Syd shakes their head. "The last time I saw her, she said I stole all her drugs. Which isn't true, and I told her that, but she didn't

believe me." They push soft black hair behind their ear, tick-
ling the silver. It's too bad they're horrible. They're lanky but
puppyish, like a young Keanu. Primo blowjob material. "Then
she left. I haven't heard from her, but she was telling people, our
friends, that I stole all her drugs, that I have a problem. And she
told them I like tried to drug her and stuff."

"Damn," I say.

"Yeah. She said that I was an abuser and that that was one of the
things I like did to control her. She told people that she saved
my life when I OD'd. I've never OD'd."

"Wow," I say. Liar. Everyone's OD'd, though not everyone is
still alive. And if you're dead, you OD'd or you killed yourself. Or maybe someone killed you. I finish my coffee. It tastes
good but fake, so it actually tastes gross. I'd settle for shitty
real coffee over chemicals designed to mimic the world's fin-
est Kenyan peaberry any day of the week. I look at Syd's cup.
There's a subway ad campaign I like that says BLACK OPIUM
over a perfume canister glittering with coal fragments and
rose gold. That's what Syd's coffee looks like.

"I've been so stressed out," Syd says. The grimace is back. "Everyone believed what she said about me, so most of my friends
aren't fucking with me right now. I had to quit my band. I missed
all this work. I almost lost my job." Syd works for a nonprofit,
where they help launder money for big corporations. From what
I remember, it's not all that different from my job at a big corpo-
ration, where I help launder money through nonprofits.

"That's hard," I say. I can't think of anything less hard than Syd's stupid life.

"It's been pretty lonely." They sniff, and for a second I think they're going to squeeze out a tear, but their hand levitates to rub the corner of their eye and then returns to their side, coffee untouched. (What do you call a Bushwick queer's nostrils? Their k-holes.) I wonder what would happen if I just picked up their coffee and chugged down those shards of gold and carbon. I wonder what would happen if I took Syd by the throat and squeezed.

"Anyway." Syd eases back into their chair and sighs, their breathing free and easy. The undertipped barista knocks the portafilter against the counter. Someone in the café is blasting trapchata from their phone. "I knew you and her had a thing or whatever. A while ago."

Finally, we're getting somewhere. I screw up my mouth and nod, blinking a lot. It might help to look a little contrite about dicking down their stupid girlfriend.

"Her friends won't tell me where she is. I was hoping you knew," Syd says. "She owes me money. And she took some of my things with her the last time she was at my apartment. She took one of my guitars."

There it is. Now I know what Syd wants—why they texted me back, why they're here—but I don't have anything to offer in return. For one thing, I haven't seen Margot, online or elsewhere, in ages, and I don't know where she is or what she's doing. Even if I did, I'm not sure I'd tell Syd. Deciding who is the least worst in a strung-out couple is a skill I've never claimed to have. It's entirely possible that Syd is lying—that they *had* been abusive, that they *had* been drugging Margot, that they deserved every-thing she'd done to them, and much more, if indeed it had been done. If I was going to rat out an abuse victim to their abuser, I'd have to have a really good reason.

Time to change the subject. I smile and sit up in my chair, as if my train of thought has all of a sudden been hijacked by a real bright idea. "You know, it's funny you're looking for someone. I'm looking for someone, too."

"Oh yeah?" says Syd.

"Yeah," I say. I pause, clear my throat. I want to sound as casual as possible. "Do you know X?"

For the first time this morning, Syd displays what looks like a spontaneous feeling. The surprise on their face is hilariously amphibian: big eyes, downturned lips. "X?" It comes out too fast, created in and launched from the front of their mouth.

"You do." It's all I can do to keep the exclamation mark out of my voice.

"I mean we've met," they admit. Their face has returned to its normal blankness, but when their fingers seek their cup, a sheet of coffee wraps over the brim. "Like once or twice." I know they know her much better than that, but the admission is promising, nonetheless.

"I'm trying to get in touch with her." I'm so good at hiding my excitement I wonder if it's even there. "I need to talk to her before she exports."

"She's exporting?" Coffee drips from their fingers. They don't seem to notice.

"You didn't know?"

"No." Syd frowns. "Why would I?"

"Can you connect us? Do you have her number?"

Syd frowns harder.

"Can you—"

"Listen, before this goes any further, I need to talk to Margot," says Syd, putting up a tinseled palm. They sound impatient, like I'm waitstaff with the gall to ask them to repeat their order.

Now my jaw is as tight as theirs is. I should have expected this from Syd. I try to head off my irritation, remembering the stuff that therapist taught me. Deep breaths. Planting my feet. The mantra: *beach, bed, lungs.* I try to imagine what my face looks like when it's expressionless. What does it matter if I'm being extorted by this asshole who was never my friend, anyway? All the more reason to extort them right back. I feel my heart slowing, although the tempo quickens slightly when the light catches some silver along Syd's snappable little collarbone. Sometimes I think my body doesn't know the difference between horny and angry.

I take another deep breath, bottle my sneer. Getting mad won't change the fact that they have the leverage here, not me. "I'll ask around about Margot." I should stay and chat for a while, pad this meetcute with more socializing so both of us can feel better about it later, but I just can't. I'd rather be early to work than spend another second with this cunt. I stand up and grab my bag.

"I'm late," I say. "Talk soon, yeah?"

Syd doesn't respond, eyes on their phone as they crane their arm behind them to drop their cup in the trash. I think about the wasted coffee all the way to the office.

I'm always finding ways to kill time at work, but when I go for one of my hourly trips to the bathroom, I'm even slower than usual.

My desk is toward the back of the office, which means no one's watching as I shuffle to the foyer. The glass door is heavy enough that I have to lean rather than push. I really should start hitting the heavy bag every once in a while. How do the body fascists motivate themselves when every news cycle shortens the time line between now and mass extinction? Tweaking lab mice, spinning homosexually while the world burns. What would be the point of getting fit? To live longer, so I can work myself to death over a longer period of time? Retirement's as extinct as bluefin tuna. I walk a little more slowly.

When I return from my first bathroom break of the day, Aisha swivels her chair toward me, smiling hard.

"How was your weekend?" she sings. The dog shifts his legs on her lap as if he wants to get down, but she holds him firmly in place, rubbing his skull as if searching for a latch.

"Fine." I sit down and put in my earbuds.

Aisha thinks we're friends because we work next to each other for like fifty hours a week. We have the same title (analyst) and do the same job (analytics) for a 501(c) shat out by a Bezos subsidiary for the purposes of, I don't know, tax evasion, probably. Everything we produce—Excel sheets with words like STATUS, PROGRESS, and QUALITY in the titles—is stored on a server somewhere, never to be opened, or else deleted and then rewritten by workers with identical job functions before being forwarded on to a marginally higher level of development, and so on, for eternity. It's mindless, and yet neither of us would have been hired without college degrees. I wonder if her parents are proud of her.

The earbuds don't phase her. "Do anything fun?" she demands.

"Not really." Petra and I were together for almost three years, but in all that time I never once mentioned her to Aisha. For all Aisha knows, I'm a monk.

"Same," she says. When she laughs, her upper lip pulls up into a wet snarl. "Me and Triskit stayed out of the cold and watched movies." Aisha has been loudly single for as long as we've worked together. She says she's waiting for a guy who's as nice as her dad. I pity straight women.

We both look down at Triskit. When she pets his head, Aisha pulls the skin back, and his eyes pop out like one of those plastic dolls you win at the carnival. He watches me in a way that's unsettlingly direct for a dog.

The radiator rattles like someone's handcuffed to it. I think it's gotten louder since I started working here, or maybe it's just that there are fewer of us in the office now, so there's more space for the noise to echo. Layoffs and no-shows are only replaced half the time. For every computer with someone sitting in front of it, two are unattended. In the kitchen, the industrial-size fridge opens onto lukewarm plastic shelves stocked with a handful of bagged lunches, a shriveled carrot, a rancid carton of hemp-based creamer. The anti-union propaganda curls along the edges, the white space between the words darkened with blue-inked doodles. The toaster oven is busted, though the coffee maker still spends its days drooling brown syrup. There's a rule about bringing animals into the office, but it's never enforced. Thus, Triskit.

I avoid his eyes, looking away from him toward the white-frosted windows above our heads. X would never set foot in a trap like this, but beyond that glass is an entire city of hiding places.

"Yep, we're total party animals," says Aisha. She takes Triskit's little front paw and waves it in my direction. He's still looking at me with his black-and-white-cookie eyes.

####

The night I met X began at Camille's apartment, where my hostess was already waiting for me when I got off from work.

"Hey, dollface," she said. She was sitting on the ground with her laptop on the coffee table, using the screen as a mirror while she did her makeup. She always springs for surveillance-camera jammers like ReflecTec, but she slathers it on like the cheap stuff, as if the bottom of the tube were miles away.

That's how Camille lives her life. Rectangles of black market cow butter warm on the counter, the faded yellow chunks hacked into blades of breadcrumb-flecked basalt. Posh Taiwanese lingerie, stained with blood and hot sauce, hangs from the lampshade. Everyone fancies themself a plant parent, but Camille's a plant empress, her army of philodendrons gleaming like lizard scales, the Monsteras soaring over the hardwood that she never sweeps and leaves strewn with the decorative cushions that outnumber us fifty to one.

She picked up a tube and twisted the wand free. "Mail stolen again," she announced. Her mouth hanging open as she began to apply her mascara, she sounded like she was talking through a toilet paper roll.

"Shit," I said, but it didn't matter to me. Even though I'd set up Camille's place as my forwarding address when I moved in a few months ago, I almost never got anything. "You working tonight?" I dropped my bag on the floor by the table and trudged to the refrigerator. On top: no cereal. Inside: no beer.

"Here." Camille appeared at my side, Swanson wreathed in weed smoke, the lashes on one eye shivering like a hummingbird. She reached through the ketchup and kimchi and takeout cartons for a hidden bottle and put it in my hand.

"My love," I said.

"I'm headed out in a bit," she said. "That thing is tonight."

"What thing?"

"That thing you said you'd come to. That warehouse thing." She took the beer from my hand, cranked it through the bottle opener stuck on the freezer door, and swigged, looking me up and down. "You better get a whole lot sluttier, or I'm leaving without you."

####

One time Mom went on a weekend trip with the professor. She called a babysitter, but accidentally gave her the wrong dates. We didn't learn this until after the fact, of course.

Mom wasn't home when I got back from school on Friday, but that wasn't unusual. I went to play with the foster kids next door like I always did. I remember we were bouncing a rubber ball against the back of the building, bored out of our skulls, when a dog came nosing around from the parking lot behind the complex. The dog was white with brown spots, like a cow. The stump of its badly docked tail wagged sideways.

We lured it toward us, bouncing the ball back and forth, *monkey in the middle*, but every time the funny dog was just about to catch it, we chased it away from us. We did it over and over, drawing it back and then chasing it again, laughing harder every time. I remember I twisted my ankle when I kicked its haunch and lost my balance, but I was having so much fun I hardly felt it.

The apartment was still empty when I limped inside, so I turned on TCM. It was almost time for the late-night movie (*Dancing Lady*, with Joan and the King) when I started to wonder if something was wrong. There was no phone—there was only Mom's cell, and she had it, wherever she was. It wouldn't have mattered anyway. I didn't have anyone to call besides her.

I spent the weekend locked in our apartment by myself, watching movies. It wasn't that bad, except for early Sunday morning, when something, I didn't know what, woke me up. I stood in my bedroom doorway, listening. The apartment was as silent as the street outside. It took me a minute to realize what was wrong. I couldn't hear Mom's white noise machine.

I crossed the carpeted hallway to her room. The machine wasn't on her night table. She must have taken it with her, I realized, along with her phone and purse and the carnation-pink cashmere sweater the professor got for her when he went to Tahoe with his family over winter break. I was alone in the apartment, without anything to make noise with me. I curled up under a cotton throw on her bed and stayed there, looking around in the dark, until the window began to turn grey.

When she came home later that evening, Mom called the babysitter to bitch her out for her own mistake. She promised me it wouldn't ever happen again, and it didn't.

####

In the weeks after the breakup, I was a mess. My nose ran constantly. My eyes swam. I couldn't sleep, but I couldn't really stay awake, either. When people talked to me, I'd get distracted, thinking about Petra. My Cyte photos showed me bruise-cheeked and open-mouthed, too thin in a gross way, or else bloated like a low-tide condom. I wouldn't have wanted to be seen with me. I don't know why Camille did.

But Camille has always been a good friend. My best friend. Like she never got on my case for being depressed, no matter how long it took me to get around to washing the dishes. (Though she did grumble about me putting off changing the dead light bulb in the kitchen. "What's a butch good for if not for that?") She cheerily ignored my silences and drunk tantrums, dragging me with her to raves and export fundraisers, though I almost always found an excuse to slink off and skulk in a corner, or French exit back home to the couch where I'd lie awake for hours, scrolling through my phone, jerking off and smelling my fingers.

Breakups are usually pretty easy for me, but after Petra, I was barely alive.

I got to know Margot when things between me and Petra were starting to go south. I think that's why I cruised her, despite knowing her reputation was muddled at best. Some tops liked her for a while. Others only needed to play with her once to understand what they were working with. "I never cut up someone I can't trust," another sadist once told me, "and I wouldn't trust Margot to repark my car."

Under normal circumstances, Margot would have been a nonstarter, but after another screaming fight with Petra I was feeling reckless. With my girlfriend at home sniffling and texting her best femmes from our bed, I went to an action to find someone to take my mind off things. I remember it well because it was one of the last before they started to really enforce that new ID law, the one that made it a felony to protest without special state authorization. The cops were getting aggressive, and I was thinking about calling it an afternoon when Margot and I just so happened to squat behind the same SUV for a piss. It seemed we both wanted to empty our bladders in case we got tased before we got arrested.

"It's you!" Margot cried, pointing, but I didn't recognize her until she pulled the bandana down from the bridge of her nose.

We laughed as we hiked our jeans back up over our asses. She was so sexy—the sweat beading the gem above her Cupid's bow, her skinny legs. Maybe Margot was just misunderstood, I thought, admiring the eyelets of scar tissue on her arms. Her marks were the same light brown as her eyes, which were big and jittery above the temptingly black fabric. Perhaps I was a little desperate.

Caught up in our own momentum, we ended up protesting outside the jail until early in the morning. For some reason, the cops dropped all charges (organized anarchy, black identity extremism, etc.) and let everyone go home, though they'd given the street medics plenty of work to do. Someone had been permanently blinded, or so the rumor went—the Cyte video going around was inconclusive. Of course, a few people had been picked up for deportation processing. They'd be shipped off before anyone could inform their families, let alone organize legal aid.

Margot and I wouldn't find out about any of that until the next day. We were too busy dry humping on the train. We went back to her place, a town house–style apartment off the Myrtle G with an apple head chihuahua guarding the front door.

"Is that yours?" I shrieked, taking a flying leap over its head. We barely made it to her room alive, laughing like hyenas.

Her block wasn't scheduled for an energy saver until the next day, but the power went out while I was undressing her. We tried to make do, but candles, Margot said, made her feel lonely. She had a painless orgasm and fell asleep on my arm. Somehow I got out of there without waking her, jonesing for a real fuck.

When she texted me the next morning, I ignored her. Petra and I had made up with a little late-night sodomy, christened with blood, and were on our way to brunch with our friends.

####

In the dream, Petra was murdered before I knew that I was the one who killed her. I won't say how. Heartless people ought to have their hearts removed, but that's not how I did it.

Her mouth sags open forever, and then I'm awake. Headache. Thirsty. We haven't shared a bed for months, but somehow I always find her in mine, even if it is a couch. I wonder if she's still at our old place or if she's moved on. I wonder if she's ruining someone else's life now.

I still haven't swapped out the bulb in the kitchen, but down in my insomnia, where it's always too early for coffee and too late for light, I appreciate the dark. Opening the fridge is like being interrogated by Laurence Olivier. I squint and grab the lone can in the back corner, pop it open, and, without moving from where I stand, chug all 150 negative calories. The label on the can says FATBURNER ACAI COCKTAIL. I realize, too late, that it's alcoholic.

When I moved out of my place with Petra, my things bagged up in Irish luggage, I crashlanded with Camille, who, like me, keeps her fridge almost empty and her Juuls mostly charged. Plus we're like the only dykes in the world who hate cats. She'd just kicked out her most recent boifriend, and there was a couch for someone who didn't mind being woken up when she got in late, and I didn't. It's not like I was sleeping, anyway.

One night Mom got home from work to find Marcus's mom waiting at our front door. I knew she'd been out there for a while, but since she hadn't knocked or anything, I just kept watching *The Awful Truth*.

Marcus's mom was angry. "She's been bullying Marcus again," she told my mom, which was true. He was bigger than me but harmless, the kind of kid you shove because you know he won't shove you back. He would watch you hurt him, big oily eyes shining, a grin smeared over his lips. It was like he wanted you to do it.

I turned down the TV and crept to the open window. Unlike her son, Marcus's mom was loud and bossy. "She's always picking on him," she told Mom. "She gets the other kids to do it, too."

"I'm sorry," said Mom. She sounded annoyed. "I've talked to her about it." She didn't like interacting with the neighbors, but she respected Marcus's mom, a mother of three with two jobs and no man. She never left the house without a full face of makeup, which Mom also respected, even if it was topping off the cheap pantsuits she wore to her job at a bank.

"Well," said Marcus's mom, "it's still a problem."

"I'm sorry," Mom said again. Her keys jingled impatiently.

"Listen, I have to ask. Do you ever discipline her?"

"Well," said Mom. People usually thought Mom was unfriendly, but the fact that she even talked to Marcus's mom when she obviously didn't want to was proof of her politeness.

"You know," said Marcus's mom. She had lowered her voice. I muted Ralph Bellamy and leaned my head against the wall. "Do you spank her?"

She didn't mean any of that spare-the-rod stuff, Marcus's mom explained. When she hit Marcus and his brothers, she could justify it with a truckload of evopsych, the kind you now hear from MRAs and people who think owning a dog that knows how to roll over is some kind of moral victory. Kids need structure or else they act out, Marcus's mom said. But if you correct them with loving discipline, they will respond with compliance. "It's just psychology," she told Mom, her voice still low.

I don't think Mom was convinced, but she let Marcus's mom go on for a while, sometimes in a whisper I couldn't hear. Just when I had decided to go sit back down in front of the TV,

Mom's keys crunched in the lock. I raced to my bedroom. The front door opened and closed, and then, a few moments later, my own door creaked inward.

"Guess you heard all that," said Mom. The skin on her face was shiny. Her purse was still slung over her shoulder.

"Oh," I said. How had she known I was listening?

"You have to stop doing that," said Mom, stepping inside. She sunk a shoulder and hung the strap of her purse on the doorknob. "Being mean to that kid."

"I didn't do anything," I lied. I kept my voice flat, but I was excited. Mom almost never came into my room. I wished it were cleaner.

She took my hand and pulled me toward my bed. "I'm going to spank you now," Mom said. She sounded very formal. She wasn't looking at my face. I figured she wanted to do it just so she could tell Marcus's mom that she had.

"Okay," I said. I thought she was going to put me over her knee, but she turned me around so I was facing the bed. She pointed at the comforter, and I put my hands down on it, sticking my hips out behind me. With pincer-shaped fingers, she repositioned my body a few inches to the side, then stood behind me.

I tensed, waiting for something to happen. When nothing did, I peeked behind me. She was standing with her hand in the air, as if about to wave at a friend walking toward her on the street. She had no idea what she was doing. When she caught my eye, I whipped my head forward again, stifling my laughter.

"Okay," she said. Her voice was resigned. "I'm starting."

I jumped when her hand landed on me, but it didn't hurt at all. She hadn't hit me very hard. In fact, it sort of tickled. Now I couldn't hold back. When she hit me again, I started to laugh. She did it again and again, harder and harder each time, her aim traveling between my lower back to the tops of my thighs, and the harder she hit me, the weirder I felt. The weirdness made me feel bad, and the laughing made me feel even worse, but I couldn't stop either from happening. I could have run away from her—she was still in her heels, and I was fast—but it didn't occur to me. Beneath my pants and my underwear, my skin was warming up.

When she finally started hitting me, really hitting me, I suddenly had to pee. Badly. I got scared. What if I peed my pants? I hadn't done that since I was a little kid, practically a baby. I stopped laughing. I panicked. She was propping herself on the bed with her arm, her left hand square beneath my chin. Thinking of Marcus, his eyes, I leaned over her biceps and bit down. When she screamed and tried to push me away, I bit down harder. I wondered if she would bite back.

Instead, her fingers—cold, skinny, a little moist—wrapped around my right arm. She dragged me out of my room and around the counter, into the kitchenette. I fought her, thrashing and kicking, but she didn't let go. I hoped she would hit my face, but she didn't do that, either.

She pushed me down against the counter, pinching my ear between my head and the formica. For the first time, I was in pain. Later, my earlobe would puff up like a pink desert cloud.

She grabbed the plastic bottle of Pūr dish soap off the sink and shoved the tip into my mouth. When she squeezed, bitter air rushed in. The sour bite hit the back of my throat, and I tried to jerk away, but she held my head in place, pressing my neck against the squared edge of the counter. When the soap oozed from my lips, she squeezed the bottle again—more air, more bite—then tossed it away, bringing her hand back to hold my jaw and clamp my nostrils shut between her fingers. Through the wet I caught dim glimpses of her grey blouse, tangled hair, red eyes.

Nose and mouth pinned shut. Couldn't breathe. Lungs worked like a cat in a bag. The excitement was back, making shapes in my chest and belly, in the seat of my pants, as if she was still hitting me there. The longer she held me close, the more excited I got. She was strong.

Just as I was about to pee my pants, I let go, gagging on the air as I swallowed. The soap went down slow, coating my throat like poisoned syrup, turning the warm parts inside me cold. Mom's hands went away. I wasn't excited anymore.

Squatting on the linoleum, coughing and gasping, that weird feeling between my legs leaked down toward my ankles. Just as I was about to catch my breath, I threw up. There's lunch, I thought, looking at the mess, bubbling like a bath.

"Here."

Mom was above me, brushing hair out of her face. She was catching her breath, too. She handed me the tube of paper towels.

As is the case with all true fetishists, Vivi's obsession with homicide was more of a sensibility than a sexual orientation. Based on her feeds, you'd think her closest friends were lifers in San Quentin. She did aspire to an incarcerated pen pal, but she kept getting paired with fathers of four serving seventeen years over a joint or Water Protectors locked up for protesting oil pipelines. Nonhomicidal crimes bored her.

She had a knack for hijacking conversations and turning them into lectures on obscure murderers and their misdeeds. If you let her, she could go on forever about the kind of stuff only *true* true crime nerds care about: the Macdonald triad, interdepartmental cop drama, statutes of limitations, childhood TBIs. Name a tristate area in the continental US, and she could list at least three killers who had operated there over the past century. Give her a specific serial killer, and she could reel off the Christian names of at least three of their victims, her voice dropping into the singsong of rote memory, like a kid reciting the presidents for the class.

I have to admit I thought it was cute at first, but it lost its charm after our second or third date. The reason why I kept seeing her was, as it always is, the sex.

"Do you like it?" Vivi would ask in this sweet, daring voice when I was fucking her. "Do you like killing me?" She sure liked being killed. That really did it for me.

The problem with fetishists is that it's easy for them to get into ruts. Just because only one thing gets them off doesn't mean it doesn't get old after a while, and that goes triple for whoever they're playing with. With Vivi, everything always had to be a certain way. I had to say the same things, touch her in the same places, and the lights always had to be off.

"Doesn't it feel scarier in the dark?" she would ask, reaching for the lamp. I humored her, but I really hated that requirement, which helped, in a way. She liked me more when I was angry. "I'm not scared," I would say. It was exactly what she wanted to hear.

Vivi talked a lot, so I knew she was getting close when she finally shut up. That was the other annoying thing about her fetish: She couldn't finish at all, ever, unless she was pretending to be a fucking corpse. A fucked corpse, her body frozen in rigor mortis, her cunt vibrating like a flip-book. Personally, I prefer it when they struggle. I like to see faces and hear sounds. If a girl faked an orgasm with me, that would be one thing; if she faked a scream, it might break my heart.

Still, the sex was good for a while. But can you blame me for getting bored? Eventually, I got it together enough to ghost her. I haven't seen her since, but she did get me hooked on a true crime podcast that I still listen to. It's hosted by a white woman who was born in Tulsa and a Bengali American woman whose family emigrated to Boston when she was little. The two of them met like a decade ago on a deserted Fort Mason pier at 5:30 in the morning. They had come separately to mark the anniversary of a triple pedicide by a Contra Costa County woman who drowned her children in the Bay. When asked why, the woman maintained that she hadn't done anything, that she had never even had children to begin with.

The hosts have been best friends ever since, bonded by their fascination with the rape, torture, and murder of other people, and by extension the potential rape, torture, and murder of themselves. They open each show listing the ways they've taken their lives into their hands over the past week, describing in microscopic detail lonely jogs during the new moon or creepy late-night rideshares, breathless as teenagers trying to finger-fuck on silent in the back row.

The rest of the podcast is dedicated to the world's most famous murders, solved and unsolved alike. The hosts piece together exposés and news articles for their listeners, sprinkling in jokes and personal anecdotes as they go. Their murder stories feel like fairy tales: We all know how they end, even if we don't know all the details, but we want to keep hearing them anyway.

I listen to the murder podcast when I go for my late-night walks, salt squeaking beneath my boots. In the dark, I'm not a pedestrian or a potential victim. I'm the street silhouette observed—or not—by those inside. I'm the dangerous one. I like that. There's something reassuring about the names of all those serial killers. You could make a rosary of them, the sensible triads, sensual couplets, silly mononyms: Joseph James

DeAngelo, Issei Sagawa, La Bestia. *Beach, bed, lungs.* It used to
help me sleep.

The host's voices are soft and bright and almost identical. It's
like a single person is there in the studio, a beautiful, well-
educated woman telling you a very ugly story. You stop waiting
for the words to happen and start letting them land where they
may. Listening to them talk to each other about murder is sort
of like looking up into a sky spackled with stars: It's too much to
take in every individual pinprick, so you permit yourself to stop
trying. After a few minutes, their voices put me into what feels
like a trance or a really solid body high, like when you take just
a little too much of an edible and you feel really inexplicably
good, right up until the paranoia hits.

Because there's something reassuring about this particular kind
of death. The murder podcast is a reminder of how easily I
could get shoved onto train tracks or sniped in a movie theater,
a grounding exercise for the existentially challenged. Getting
homicided (most likely by someone you know, statistically
speaking, but who knows if you're like me and have a tendency
to walk around alone after dark in my part of Brooklyn) sounds
a lot cozier, more personal, more intimate, more human than
being told to leave—or worse, getting shipped off to wherever.
When I listen to the podcast, I feel nostalgic, reminded of a
time that felt unsafe in a completely obsolete way. It's one of the
only distractions that still works.

Of course, there's always someone trying to bring you back
to reality. "You know, I heard that exporting isn't even real,"
Aisha told me a few weeks ago. Her voice was almost a whisper,

as if that made a difference to the software wiretapping her straight from the phone in her cardigan pocket. Like her on-line shopping habits weren't being shuttled back to seven thousand different government contractors and third parties. Like her pulse, blood pressure, hydration levels, and menstrual cycle weren't for sale to the highest bidder. Like there wasn't a camera in every fucking monitor, corner, outlet, fixture, and interface. "Someone told me it's just another way to get disappeared, only you go into it willingly, thinking you're getting out."

Triskit trembled in her lap. I imagined him with a long white beard and wizardly spectacles. All roads lead to the detention centers, Triskit intoned.

"And the place they send you, it's not like the normal camps, either," Aisha went on. She meant the immigration detention centers, where adults sign paperwork agreeing to sterilization in a language they don't understand, where orphaned children are left outside to raise infants in bedless cages. The continental Gitmos of the high deserts, the urban islands, the Deep South; the places that get more feed coverage than our regular degular prisons. "This one is different. You know how they're doing it in China with all those Muslims? Millions of them? It's like that. Out West somewhere."

One wall good, four walls better. "Spooky," I said, hoping she was done.

"I mean at least *we're* still here," said Aisha. Did she mean in our office? Our city? Our country, provided we weren't in some kind of cage? Unclear. Aisha is straight and no kind of criminal, as far as I can tell, but her family is Syrian. Could her parents get export letters? Could she? "There are a lot of places in the world where it's way worse."

I didn't feel reassured. If anything, knowing that I could die right here and at any time for reasons unrelated to the police state and empire and all that is what's getting me through. And if I exported to another country—Iceland? Swaziland? Thailand?—who's to say I wouldn't end up dead in one of *those* places? When you factor in the John Wayne Gacys with car accidents, suicide, early-onset colon cancer, unsecured suspension points, shower slip-and-falls, and gun nuts, you start to buy into the idea that maybe your odds are as good, or as bad, as anyone else's.

That's why the murder podcast used to put me in such a good mood. After an episode or two over the course of a long, cold walk, my shoulders would loosen and my sternum would sink back down to where it belongs. I'd stop wanting to charge into every man that passed by and trip every foot that entered my bubble, to shank the voices that screamed through my headphones. In a world of certain death, what could I possibly have to fear?

"Take no shit."

That's what Mom used to tell me after I watched men come on to her at the auto shop or the grocery store. "You're too ugly to be staring like that," she would coo, smiling like a dental ad as she walked away. I trailed behind her, wondering if I would be as wanted as she was when I grew up.

This wasn't how she approached dating, although to Mom's credit her boyfriends usually had pretty short shelf lives. She had a high tolerance for their bullshit—usually booze, sometimes drugs, occasionally being broke or married—but you could never anticipate what would put her over the edge, and the switch always happened right around the time when the guy in question started to get comfortable.

There was one who was around so much he might as well have paid rent, though of course he didn't. Kyle ignored me, which was fine. He mostly ignored Mom, too, unless he was doing little things to remind her that he was in charge, like lightly slapping her upside the head like one of the Three Stooges, or pinching the skin around her waist to find the flab.

She never really did anything about it until the day he called her a drunk because she spilled his beer on his lap. *Stupid*, *lazy*, *bitch*, those were one thing. But a *drunk*? She crunched his wraparound sunglasses under her sandal and kicked him out of the apartment. He went without a fight, looking like he pissed his pants. I think he was too wasted to know what was going on.

"I liked him, you know," she told me the next day. She was going through her drawers with a pair of tongs, grabbing his briefs and tossing them inside a cardboard box that would later go in the dumpster behind the building. "He was a realist."

####

"Hey, love," says Camille. "How was it with Venus?"

Door: locked. Bag: dropped. I pluck out my headphones. Camille is sitting on the floor by the coffee table, looking back at me above the cotton frame of her gold-threaded tank top. I can see the top of the port-wine splash, the tattoo that says FLÁVIA.

"It was good," I say. In general, I prefer to play with pros. They're more jaded than almost anyone else, so they have to get creative when they want to have some real fun. They don't try to show off, not if they've been working for a while. Venus certainly didn't. *Weird* doesn't necessarily mean bloodiest or most dangerous or uses the most complicated hardware. It doesn't mean buying the most expensive harness and showing up at the right parties and having the richest clients. *Weird* means gross. It means funny. It means absurd. It means the opposite of boring, which almost everything is. I can make it work with almost any pro, even other tops.

Like one of the first lovers I had in New York was a domme who went by Sable, though with me she was May, or Maybelline. She was a classically trained disciplinarian who struck terror in the hearts of the white men who paid a thousand dollars an hour to be locked in one of her closets, where they could listen to her work over other, richer white men. After a few hours she'd release the closet cases, put them in chastity, and torture their tits to confetti, laughing as it dawned on them that their cock wasn't going to be freed before they were told to leave. They would have to come back, at her convenience, to retrieve their freedom, and maybe, just maybe, an expensive, awestruck nut.

After a long day at the office, May's favorite way to relax was to come over to my apartment, where my bathtub would be filled with rose petals and Epsom salts. I would massage her shoulders before gently holding her under the surface while she struggled, her breasts rising and sinking like feeding koi. In the water, her face was like an angel: shining, many-eyed, misshapen.

"Did you find out anything from Venus?" asks Camille. The real mystery wasn't where X was hiding, but why Camille didn't already know who she was.

I forget how exactly Camille knows Venus—maybe she told me, or maybe she didn't. While I case the cabinets for something to eat, I tell Camille about my night at the dungeon, how it didn't yield much other than confirmation of Venus's acquaintance with X.

"But I think I have another lead," I say, checking my phone for the time. "Wow, you're home early." There's a pot growling on the stove, an open box of vegan gluten-free soy-free nut-free mac 'n' cheese on the counter beside it.

"My reward for being a good girl," Camille says, pointing to the floor under the coffee table. A carpet of bills is fanned out on the hardwood, which she sorts and rubberbands with the grace of a longtime stoner. A pyramid of dingy green rises between her legs.

"Damn." My mood improves slightly. Camille's very generous when she has money, so she might not mind if I'm a little short on my share of the rent this month. Not that it's my fault—there's a delay on our paychecks at work. A few people threatened to quit over it, but then at a staff meeting our manager, Forrest, reminded us of our contractual obligations and alluded to the possibility of employee insurance being reinstated next year. After that, no one talked about quitting anymore. "At least I can still bring Triskit to the office," chirped Aisha.

"It was pretty okay," Camille says, turning again to throw me a wink. She reaches for her joint and takes a hit, then stands up, knees and voice cracking through the smoke. "I'm ovulating, so I feel like shit, but I stink like sex. Hustled like mad so I could come home early."

I get the hot water bottle from above the stove and shake the POMPEII IV to see if it's empty.

"So what's the new lead?" she asks, scratching her hairline with an acrylic as she pads into the kitchen. She squeezes me and the hot water bottle, one of us in each hand. She's wearing the pricey lash extensions, the ones that make her look like Gene Tierney.

I'm suddenly too tired to get into it, exhausted by how much my body hurts. "I'll tell you if it goes anywhere," I mutter.

"So how do you even know she's still here?" she persists. She frees a hand to turn off the burner. The mac 'n' cheese looks like hot glue. "Like in the country?"

Despite my exhaustion, my heart floods. I have wondered that, of course, but hearing someone else say it makes it seem not just possible, but likely. "I don't, exactly."

"What'll you do if she's already gone?"

It feels like a taunt. I shrug, digging my fingers into the rubber. "I don't know." The POMPEII IV is already whispering.

"A lot of people are gone," she remarks. "Or leaving." A smile cracks her lips. Because Camille rarely takes anything seriously, she assumes no one else does either. Most of the time I like that about her. It makes everything seem equally small. But right now, it's irritating.

"I'm aware of that," I snap. 198, says the POMPEII IV. 199. I wonder if I could talk a masochist into letting me dunk them in a bathtub full of boiling water, like an enormous tea bag.

"So then what's so special about her?" asks Camille. "Like why do you care?"

I flip the switch right as the POMPEII IV begins to scream. I've shaved Camille's asshole once or twice, when she's had a last-minute client and couldn't fit in a waxing appointment at the salon. When I had the swine flu a few years ago, she sat with me in the bathroom and told me knock-knock jokes while I shat out everything short of my soul. I like to sleep alone, but every once in a while she wakes me up and drags me into bed with her so someone's around to hold her when she flashes back.

We're close, is what I'm saying. We have been for years, ever since we met. But I don't feel like I could explain everything to her. Camille knows I met someone at that warehouse party we went to, and that that person's name is X, but that's it. For all Camille knows, X and I stayed up all night playing tiddly-winks. Whatever she thinks she knows is fine, as long as it isn't the truth. She can't know about the room with the mattress, the Christmas lights, the metal table and all the tools on top of it. She can't know what my body looks like under my clothes. Is it the pride of a former gold-star top? Or the shame of something unrequited? I don't know, but neither will Camille. I'll make sure of that.

So I don't answer her. Instead, I fill the hot water bottle, screw it closed, and place it in her hands. Silence works.

Camille rolls her eyes all exaggerated. "Okay, bitch," she mutters. She returns to her pile of money and plops down beside it, bladder over bladder, the warm rubber sinking into her belly. "None of my business, I guess."

####

"I like these," Petra said, looking at the mirror. The caning welts, delicate as pâte feuilletée, are laced up the back of her legs from calf to ass. "I look better this way."

I admired my work. The welts, scabbing over broken skin, were spaced evenly as piano keys. Each was exactly the same size and color as the next. It hadn't been easy to do. Sitting on an ice pack afterward, she massaged my hands, leaving kisses on my fingers.

"And I like how fast it is," she said.

"You do?" When I reached out to push on one of the welts, she slapped my hand away. I reached out again, and this time she allowed me to glide my fingers over her calf, cupping its heat.

"Yeah," she said, smiling back at me. I stroked the soft, dark hairs springing indifferently from their follicles. "I like that I can get up in the morning one way and go to bed that night completely different."

I also enjoyed the difference, the way the welts were harder and hotter than the skin around them. But someday soon they would cool and sink again, and her legs would be normal until something else happened to them.

"You know your word," I said when the blood had first pearled on the bamboo.

"Yes, sir," she said. "I know."

But she hadn't used it. I knew it wouldn't be an easy scene for her, especially because I told her beforehand that it would be discipline only—no sex. I loved it when that happened, when I fucked her without fucking her, when the scene ended without the kind of orgasm you can get with a few minutes of simple vibration. I've done plenty of nonsexual scenes over the years, but Petra is the only person I've ever done that with in a romantic way.

I leaned my head against her thigh, stuck out my tongue, and licked one of the welts. She dragged her finger through the saliva and rubbed it into my scalp like pomade.

####

Mom didn't care about god. One of her parents—can't remember which—was Jewish, but she wasn't raised in the faith. She was just fine with this.

"It's too much work around the holidays," she said. "Any holiday. And gifts cost money."

It's not like I never got presents. Like one day, a day that wasn't my birthday, she took me to Walmart and told me I could pick out whichever pair of rollerblades I wanted, no matter how much they cost. I hadn't really thought enough about rollerblades to want them before, so I chose the first pair I saw. They were acid green, with silver lightning bolts. She said I could put them on in the store, and I wore them in the car back to the apartment.

"Nice, right?" said Mom, like she'd glued them together at the factory herself. In the passenger seat, I peeled the cancer warning off one, then the other, and stuck the stickers on my knees.

When we got back to the apartment, I skated up and down the sidewalk while the foster kids watched from the concrete stairs that led to the second floor. I liked their attention more than my new toy. "She gives me whatever I want," I bragged to them.

But I wasn't able to use the rollerblades much. Soon after that, I had to go back to the hospital, and by the time I could skate again, I had outgrown them. Mom told me to give them to one of the smaller foster kids, but I waited until nighttime and threw them in the dumpster.

Sometimes I resented that we didn't eat ham with pineapple halos during the holidays, like they did on TV. But Mom did make special meals, which, like her gifts, occurred without warning.

Every so often, I would get home to find Mom already at the apartment. "Played hooky today," she would announce. That was what she called it when she was so hungover she had to call in sick. She'd always recover by the afternoon, and I'd find her rushing around the kitchenette in her only apron, a green, grease-stained smock that sagged around the waistline, whacking the side of the cast iron with a spatula, flicking on the food processor that overheated at the slightest resistance. Rising up out of the steam like a movie monster, she would command me to set the table. I'd drop my backpack and rush to work.

Until I was a teenager, I had to pull up a chair to reach the cabinet where she kept the nice wineglasses and the white plates with blue and gold trim. "Watch it. That's your dowry," she would joke. I carefully set every slab of porcelain on the table, even the gravy boat. Then I folded paper towels into long darts, like de-constructed airplanes, and laid out as many pieces of silverware as I could find on top, arranging each one by length, like I imagined they did on the *Titanic*. When I finished straightening the chairs, I would stand at the counter to watch her cook.

I liked Mom when she was cooking. She was the same as usual, with the same wineglass and the same fast way of talking, but she moved a little more softly, in curves instead of angles. Her jokes were directed at the men she dated instead of at one of us, and sometimes she even sang to herself in a wiry voice that made me wonder what she would be like when she was old. I wasn't allowed to help.

When the food was done, we would sit down at the table. That was the only time we used it for meals together. I always waited for her to start so I could match my forkfuls with hers. She ate glamorously, her posture perfect yet casual, like a centerfold in *Martha Stewart Living*. Mom didn't usually eat much, so a meal together felt special, almost like a real Thanksgiving, or how I imagined one would feel.

"Here's to you," she would say, knocking her glass of wine against mine. I liked how it tasted, sharp and pointy, like the lights in a grocery display. We stuffed ourselves until our stomachs hurt, but there would always be leftovers, wrapped optimistically in plastic and then stacked in the fridge. They went bad in favor of nukables and handfuls of cereal straight from the box.

Although I wouldn't have known the difference back then, I do think Mom was a good cook. She always said that she taught herself, but she picked up a lot from her boyfriends, who for some reason tended to work in restaurants. When a man was over for dinner, she merely picked at the colors on her plate, slipping her fork through vegetables and jumping up for a new bottle of wine every twenty minutes.

My favorite boyfriend of hers was Mark, who worked at a fancy Italian place downtown. Mark was handsome and funny. When they had sex, Mark was as loud as Mom was. Unlike a lot of her boyfriends, he didn't mind having me around, and even let me help when he was cooking. "What else is there to do around here?" he would ask. When he gestured around the living room, he seemed to mean the whole apartment complex, the whole town.

As he chopped and measured, Mark fed me bits of food like I was a lapdog. "Here you go, baby," he would say, popping halved cherry tomatoes and snowflakes of pecorino into my mouth. "Down the hatch."

I liked that he called me *baby*. No one else did. "Here you go, baby," I would say when I handed him the spatula or a towel, and he would laugh. He called mom *baby*, too. Mom called him *Marco*. Mark sometimes called himself a hedonist, and whenever he did, he would hold up a knife, kissing it against its honing rod and wiggling his eyebrows like a cartoon devil. For years, I thought a hedonist was someone who ate meat, like the opposite of a vegetarian.

Mark wasn't around for too long. When he told her he wanted to have kids someday, Mom stopped answering his calls.

####

Petra was a good girl, but she didn't come that way. When we met, she was still a brat. Inexperienced masochists sometimes are. I hate brattiness, but it didn't take me long to teach her that there's such a thing as bad attention.

One day, a few weeks after we started seeing each other, she tried to manufacture a beating instead of asking for one like a normal person. Eyes on mine, she knocked over the cup of water next to her, intentional as a cat. The glass didn't break, and there was nothing on the table that could have been damaged by the water, but it was the principle of the thing.

"What was that?" I said.

"What?"

"Why did you do that?"

She arched her eyebrows. "Who, me?"

"You're not usually clumsy."

She sniffed and batted her eyes. "Today I am," she said.

I took hold of her shoulder, thumb pressed into the joint like cookie dough.

"Am I in trouble?" she dared me.

She was having fun. It's fun before it starts hurting. I took a piece of her hair in my fingers, rubbed the black bristles across the pads. She wasn't afraid yet.

"I—" she began. The first slap, then the next. Now she was startled. I came in closer, licked my fingers, and touched her hair again. Her cheeks were red, approaching fear. A few more slaps and she'd cry. Petra cried easily in the beginning.

As she got less bratty, our play got subtler but more intense. Sometimes all I needed was a look, or to hear her laughing in a certain way, or to watch her push a fork over to the side of her plate, movements right on the edge of recalcitrant. As our relationship deepened, the hair trigger to violence grew more sensitive. Like one time I broke a wooden ladle over her ass because she shattered a plate, and afterward, when I asked her why she'd done it—it had been so long since she'd done something so *obvious*—all she could do was laugh.

"What?" I kept saying. "What?"

"It really was an accident," she said when she finally caught her breath. She was lying on the ground, and I was propped on my forearm above her. She wiped her eyes. "I really wasn't trying to make you angry."

When she laughed again, the black of her hair convulsed on the carpet. I laughed, too.

####

The morning after I moved my stuff over to Camille's, I woke up horny. I had a few regulars in my rotation I could have called, but you know how it is after a breakup. I needed someone I didn't know.

I quickly found one on an app and met at his place. He took me back to the room where he and his wife slept. There was the bed where the big crocheted pillow sat on top of the comforter in the daytime, and the open closet with sundresses on one side and ironed jeans on the other. There was a friendly mutt that the guy pushed back out into the hallway with his foot before closing the door.

He dropped to his knees, taking my zipper down with him. I let him get to work, staring down at the crown of his head, at the lime-shaped spot of hair just starting to thin. He gagged. The dog scratched. I was just starting to get wet when I felt a sudden wave of nausea.

I tried to ignore it, imagining what I was going to do to this bitch when I got tired of his busted straight-guy BJ, but the nausea got worse. A cold sweat beaded my hairline. *Beach, bed, lungs.* No, not working. I thought about other things instead: razor blades on my forearm, nails under my nails. *Blood, blood, blood.* But not even the old standbys would stick, and the cold sweat got colder, and my head started to spin, and suddenly I was looking up at the married guy from the floor, hypnotized by the drool spilling over his lower lip.

"Are you okay?" he said. He was squatting over me, hardon fat against his jeans. The dog was whining in the hallway.

There's enough space between the short, mossy fur and the collar around it that the woman could slip a finger in there and guide the dog—foxy, graceful, dainty—away from the shit still cooling on the curb.

Instead, the woman jerks on the leash, a lipstick-limned cup of coffee clutched in her other hand. Between her fingers, a vape pen hangs on for dear life. She wears an expensive backpack and expensive glasses and has an expensive, horrible dye job that suggests her stylist is a fag with a grudge.

The dog is very clean. She wears booties that match the woman's backpack. The dog wants to eat the shit, but the woman prevents her from doing what she wants. The dog's body is a single muscle, not a spare bit of meat, not a hair out of place. Every whorl looks like it was painted by Raphael, texture without imperfection. When the dog's tongue unfurls from the black hollow of her mouth, a thicket of colorless hairs tessellate over the healthy pink of wild-caught salmon.

While we wait for the light to change, the dog gazes up at the woman, alert and yet calm. She trusts the woman completely. She's not curious about where they've come from, or anxious about what's next. She's just waiting, with the patience of the faithful.

Lately I've been noticing animals more, which is weird, because I usually don't care about them. I don't mind having them around, except for cats, but I'd never want one of my own. It takes a lot of work to keep even a goldfish happy, not to mention something like a dog. At best, a dog is another roommate that needs to be taken out to piss. Any way you slice it, a pet is another thing that needs my attention, and I don't have the energy. I hardly have any friends anymore, and I still have too many to worry about.

Now, when I see animals in the street or my feeds, I feel drawn to them in a way I haven't since I was a kid. I think about taking a picture of the clean dog, but decide not to. Like what would I do, look at it later? For what? I can google a dog whenever I want.

The light turns green, and the woman lurches into motion, ReflecTec shining, coffee back at her lips. The dog moves gracefully and efficiently, like a modern dancer. Her nipples are tiny, and her cunt has the kind of neat economy that humans pay surgeons big bucks to create. She's a dog that probably inspires people to say, "What a beautiful animal!" without irony or a sense of shame.

The leash is slack. The woman isn't paying attention, but the dog stays close enough that she doesn't have to tug in order to keep her in step. It's as if the dog has trained herself, is naturally obedient in a world where people are so stupid they need that little glowing man to show them it's safe to move.

I would have once looked at this dog and thought, She shits in public and can't eat chocolate without dying. What's to envy? But something has changed. I would never have noticed before that this dog is beautiful and content and will never have to know that the Great Barrier Reef is gone forever. Maybe I'm confusing her dependence with happiness, her quiet with emptiness. But still. A dog wonders, but doesn't question. What a way to live.

It happened in the town Mom grew up in, which is why I notice the headline among the stream of nightmares ticking through my news feed: fascist paramilitaries, state-sanctioned austerity measures, violent coups, forced mass migration, blah blah blah.

BISMARCK COUNTY COUPLE CONVICTED OF MURDERING EIGHT-YEAR-OLD SON.

Click.

After years of viciously abusing their child, a man and a woman took turns clubbing him to death with a metal bar that the man brought home from the dump. The article has many details about the child's appearance and preferred extracurricular activities, and about the parents and their jobs and how very normal this white family seemed to their neighbors and church friends and the lady who rang them up at the supermarket. It describes how the parents would force their child to have sex, and where, and under what kinds of physical and emotional duress. It all seems like information that certain laws are supposed to prevent from being published, but since the child's name is not included I guess it's okay. He's dead, anyway, so what does it matter.

Under the headline is a photo of the family: the dad, the mom, the son. The mom's arm is around the kid's shoulders. Her yellow hair looms. One of the kid's arms is behind his back. His face is blurred out, making it appear, incidentally, not all that dissimilar from what it probably looked like after his parents got through with him.

I read the article twice, then go lie down on the couch and masturbate. Camille is at work, so I have the place to myself. It's just me and the plants.

After I cum, I select a book from my library, which is what I call the stack of paperbacks I keep on the floor next to the couch. The book is a writer's memoir that begins with his childhood in the 1920s. I flip to the beginning, to my favorite part, where the writer tells the story of his first sexual arousal. It happens when he encounters the night-soil man, which is what everyone calls the guy who goes door-to-door collecting the shit from people's chamber pots. It's a filthy job, which means the person who does it is also filthy. The night-soil man is the most beautiful thing the boy has ever seen.

When I cum again, I see the night-soil man, tall and raven-haired, gleaming through shit. The boy sees him, too. I cum a third time.

####

Camille is beautiful, but only from certain angles, like Jeff Buckley. She's smart enough to know this, but she doesn't try to hide it, which proves her intelligence. Her enlightenment, even. When she comes across unflattering photos or videos on Cyte or Instagram, she doesn't take it to heart. "I've succeeded in totally objectifying myself. Feminism is over!" she jokes. I can't stand this talent of hers. It gives me the creeps.

I think Camille's like that because she's younger than me, twenty-five or so. She was born after the first recession that I was old enough to remember. She has no memory of 9/11, not that mine's all that great—just staticky surveillance footage flashing across the TV screen, grainy like a photo of a photo in a book. A man on the car radio talking about window jumpers. Mom holding her finger parallel with the Tune button, as if she was going to change the station. We drove all the way to school like that, her finger hovering like she was halfway through casting the evil eye. The bus had been canceled, and she was pissed about it. "Today would be a good day to start smoking again," she said, but she said that every day she wasn't smoking.

When I told Camille about this memory, she looked bored. Fair enough. She may not remember the attacks, but she was living in New York when it happened. I wasn't.

The internet was basically privatized by the time Camille started using it on her own, which means that, like everyone who's ever turned a trick, she's shadowbanned as all hell. Anyone can post pictures of her, but most of what she uploads herself gets disappeared. As a result, she rarely posts selfies. When she does, it's just as likely to be a good photo as a bad one. The pic might be from an angle where her power pout bursts from poreless skin, with that cheek muscle that can't decide whether or not it's a dimple gathering the light like a cut-glass saucer. Or it might catch her chin and neck at the wrong distance from the lens, the light now the villain, creating bags and emphasizing improper bones.

Camille's ID confirms that she's thin with brown hair and brown eyes. It's her good side in the laminated photo. She's dazzling.

"Lucky you," I said when I saw it for the first time.

Camille shrugged and plucked it back from me. "It's a fake," she said.

####

I think that married guy wanted me to stick around, but I left as soon as I could, kicking his dog aside on the way out. Nothing like that had ever happened to me before. But I hadn't been eating well over the past few weeks, I reminded myself. Bad sleep. Drinking a lot. Just a weird fluke, I decided.

A week later, I went to play with a bottom I occasionally hit up when no one else is free. I figured a scene with someone I already knew how to play with would take some of the pressure off. This pazrticular bottom was a masochist who went hard but tended to be too stoic about pain for my taste. Not that he was a total bore. Even post-phallo, he liked to be humiliated for his tiny cock. Humiliation relaxes me, and sometimes you need an easy scene. Self-care, etc.

When I got to his apartment, he answered the door with a whip in his hand. "Good boy," I said as he kissed my cheek.

With every lash, I felt better and better. See, I was fine. Fuck that married guy! And fuck Petra! She didn't even like getting whipped (Too loud! she complained). My bottom moved in rhythm with the lashes, balancing like a sunning lizard against my force on his shoulders. I couldn't see what his face was doing, but I knew it wasn't much. Every twenty lashes or so, he would roll his head all the way around and shrug his shoulders up to his ears, like he was warming up for a boxing match. He didn't speak. His silence made me feel like I was watching him be alone. Sometimes that spooks me and sometimes it bores me, but just then it was pleasant. When the blood came, I got excited. I decided I was going to break him, make him red, which I'd never done before.

But when he made the first noise—a whimper that melted into a moan—I almost dropped the whip. Something was wrong again. My head pulsed, my stomach tingled. *Beach, bed, lungs.*

I wasn't going to let it get to me this time. I decided to slow down—maybe I was just moving too fast. The bottom was stripped down to his jockstrap, muscles tight under his skin. He and I had never fucked, but it occurred to me that a little rape might take the edge off. My body responded to the idea. I decided I'd hit him a few more times, then take a break for some renegotiation and, if all went well, romance. Regaining confidence, I threw the whip.

A mistake. His moan hurt my ears. The cold sweat was back. Angry, I threw it again, harder than I should have, and this time he screamed, just like I wanted, but the bad feeling stayed, hurting my head, cracking me open. I knelt, and the pain knelt with me, sinking into my chest, then my guts. My head pounded. My body roiled. If I shit myself, as I was suddenly afraid I would, I couldn't just leave him and go home. He was tied to the hooks by his bed, naked and helpless and dripping with blood. If I shit myself, I would have to set him free with my pants wet and reeking. I thought he was still moaning, but my whip was on the floor. It was me making the noise.

Somehow I kept it together and set him loose, but it was obvious that something was wrong. He texted while I was getting on the train, asking if I was okay. I blocked him.

It kept happening, the fainting, the panicking, the migraines. Once, I puked. No matter who I was with, it always ended the same: I had to leave before the scene or hookup was over. After the first two attempts, I wondered if maybe the problem was that I had been with men. I mixed things up with a high-femme pillow princess who could take whole limbs up her asshole, a cross-dressing stockbroker I found playing in some public urinals, a butch bimbo I used to breed when I was new to the city. None of them worked.

After a while, I gave up. After Petra, my body didn't want to work for me anymore.

####

Camille is late to everything except for parties, for which she always shows up at exactly the right time. It's like a sixth sense.

True to form, we arrived at the warehouse just as things were getting going.

For raid-proof queer events, warehouses have never been more popular. The one we went to that night was big, with grimy, two-story windows. A crowd milled over and around the standard artpunk warehouse stuff: raw pipes, painted sheets, extension cords. A corner sectioned off with tarp and plywood was guarded by a burner-type with a pastel-blue beard on a stool, making sure no one stumbled into anyone's private living space. A bird with long white feathers and a cruel beak clung to a hook above their head.

We bought drinks from the bar, a crepe-strewn door someone had stacked on two barrels near the wall, then wandered over toward the stage. Camille handed me her cup so she could get the pinky-size jar she keeps in the front pocket of her tiny plastic backpack.

"Want one?" she asked. She was wearing a latex dress that I'd never seen outside of her apartment. A lover had made it for her, but they'd had a falling-out not long after it was finished, and it had been languishing in her closet since that fateful text fight. I wondered why Camille felt like she could wear it now, at this party of all parties. It wasn't anything special, as far as I knew—I'd already forgotten what the flyer said. The fresh layer of silicone shimmered across her flanks like cum.

"Thanks," I said. I put the pill in my mouth, hoping it would cut the boredom. If I was lucky, it would kill me before a Narcan-wielding punk could save the day.

Camille and I stood around with our drinks while we waited for things to kick in. As usual, I didn't feel like talking, but also as usual, Camille was happy to fill the silence. The topic was the high drama of an ostensibly vanilla boy-dyke/girl-dyke couple she'd been courting.

"They got their first place together a few months ago, so they're just about ready to kill each other," crowed Camille. "They're either going to have a terrible breakup or dig in and find a fag to knock them up. They're desperate. Now's the perfect time to try out something new." She grinned, her hands making a batter-up shape, her latexed ass out and waggling. "They met on one of those lez softball teams. Sporty and horny. I really feel like I could make my baseball fantasy happen. Finally. The American dream."

Camille has a big US flag in her bedroom that she painted with blood and blue drugstore eyeshadow. Across the middle of the flag is a big brown smear that she always has a different explanation for. Shit is never mentioned, but you wonder. I think that's part of the whole thing—the mystery of the brown smear. I didn't know what her baseball fantasy was, exactly, but I suspected the flag was involved.

"We're BE CRIME," someone yelled. A band appeared onstage and started to play.

"That's Syd's band," Camille said, putting her hand on my forearm. I rolled my eyes, and she laughed. She knew I couldn't stand that idiot, though she herself was Syd-neutral; Switzerland always proved to be the best position for receiving the most delicious gossip. She frowned and squinted. "I don't see them."

I didn't, either. There was the bass player, a muscle-bound femme with long braids. I recognized the drummer, this horrible bitch I knew from a job I had at a Williamsburg bakery years ago. She tried to get me fired for I can't even remember what bullshit reason, and even though I managed to keep my job, I still wanted her dead. The lead screamer was a they/them with a bowl cut and a drawn-on unibrow that I recognized, but they were a new addition to the band. They had replaced another screamer, someone who had exported during the first wave. A Jewish doll with relatives in Spain. She saw her chance and took it.

As they played, Camille and I monitored the growing crowd, noticing people we knew as well as people who should have been there but weren't. I thought about how we used to come to shows without assuming that someone's absence meant that they had died or exported. I guess that's part of growing up.

"I want another drink," hollered Camille.

"Already?"

We shoved each other for a minute, but eventually I gave in and rejoined the crowd swarming the makeshift bar. The bartender glanced at me, then ignored me. Someone elbowed past to order. Rather than get mad, I turned around and walked away. *Beach, bed, lungs.*

I should just go home, I thought. The night was already turning to shit. I could tell I was bumming out Camille—she sent me for a drink so she could get a break from me. I might feel bad for leaving, but how could I feel any worse than I already did? Camille couldn't stop me. If she tried, that just meant she wanted me to suffer, and a real friend wouldn't want that, right? I could make up a headache and beg off, but then again, why lie? I deserved to leave. Fuck Camille if she had a problem with it.

I watched the bartender with their carefully averted gaze and the crowd of already drunk gays, watched Camille leaning to giggle over someone's phone, the mélange of faces I either recognized and hated or didn't know and didn't want to know. It wasn't like anyone would miss me. What would people think if I exported? Would they care?

I slowly started backing away, not wanting to start for the door until I was sure that Camille wouldn't notice me go. That's when I saw X.

####

When Mom came home with a carton of orange juice, that meant it was time to go to the doctor again. It would come out of the paper bag and slide into the fridge alongside the Diet Coke and the white wine. I knew a glass of it would be waiting for me on the kitchen counter the next morning. I knew it would taste good except for the pocket of bitterness at the bottom. Mom always bought pulp-free.

By the time we got to the doctor's office, I would already be sleepy and a little confused. Some days I drank two glasses, so I would already be gone, if not exactly asleep, by the time we arrived.

The only part of those visits I can remember is being back at home afterward. It was usually a workday, so I would be alone by the time things started coming together, sitting on the barstool with my head on the counter where I had my orange juice a few hours before. Eventually I would make my way to the couch and lie down to watch TV. *Zouzou*, *Red Dust*, *Grand Hotel*, screwballs like my favorite, *The Awful Truth*. I loved the dog, Mr. Smith, and the way his rich, happy owners fought over who got to keep him.

Eventually I would make my way to Mom's bed. Sinking into the spongy mattress, I would feel my eyes swell and then constrict, slippery and unfocusable. With the white noise machine roaring around my head, I would search the room for something to distract me—an object to examine, a pattern to explore.

I don't know why I always went to her room and not mine. Mine had my framed pictures of Cary Grant and Toshiro Mifune, my melted G.I. Joes and a few mutilated lesbian Barbies. There was a quilt on my bed, red, my favorite color. Mom's room was a blank. She didn't like knickknacks and didn't frame photos. Her comforter was blue, her empty walls bivalve grey. Her clothes went into neat stacks in her drawers while they were still warm from the downstairs dryer, or else were hung in the closet, arranged by shades of white, behind the sliding door that always came off its tracks.

Exhausted as I was, I was rarely able to fall asleep. Most of the time I stayed awake until Mom got home from work, when she would come find me and tickle me until I cried.

####

I think about exporting all the time. Everyone does, or everyone I know, at least. We didn't even know how good we had it back when it was merely skyrocketing unemployment and crumbling civil rights. It's all fun and games until your failed state asks you to leave.

The first wave happened fast, right after midterms consolidated the slightly more fascist party's power. They rolled out the export program, at which point the slightly less fascist party made a middling outcry, one that, as to be expected, was used as leverage to fundraise for the upcoming presidential election and not much else. After the slightly less fascist party's presidential win, a celebratory new front was opened on the Middle Eastern land war, which led to an economic upturn and a lull in the letters. Big feed headlines promised that the program was on its last legs because all the criminal elements had either left or been safely locked away from the regular citizenry.

Didn't last, of course. Shortly after the election, a few well-timed massacres by white Christoterrorists got Congress off their asses. Now more than ever, we needed the export program to offset the [insert nonwhite minority] insurrection threatening us from the inside. Thoughts and prayers just weren't cutting it anymore.

The second wave has been different from the first: slower but harder. Now there are more export letters than ever before, their language more vague and aggressive. You're told to leave the country, but given little information as to why, how, by when, with what means, and to where. You have to read in between the lines to find out which alterations to civil, criminal, and citizenship law have got you cornered. There are some incentives, like a one-time cash payout, or so they say. But the message is unmistakable: *Don't let the door hit you on the way out.*

And the letters are just the beginning. I've heard of people getting calls at all hours from the feds trying to hook them up with a social worker to do their "exit counseling." Or it's their bill collectors calling, warning them that existing debt is now past due but can be permanently expunged in exchange for their passport. I've heard about people's bank accounts magically springing a leak, their credit scores inexplicably plummeting, or their family in prison suddenly having their sentences extended by years, decades even, because of their relationships with "known national security threats who have yet to decamp under federal recommendation." The export letter isn't just a letter—it's a formal notice equivalent to two strikes on your permanent record. Civil and criminal fines get bigger, cops get more interested in you, insurance gets more expensive, jobs get harder to find. Get the letter, and they double down until you leave or die anyway.

According to a few NGO studies, the whiter you are, the straighter you are, the richer you are, the healthier you are, the less likely you are to get a letter. But you can never be too sure. During the first wave, they went out to the usual suspects:

nonwhite immigrants, those on the no-fly list, known commies and antifa, Jews and Muslims, black and brown leftist organizers. The second wave was that but much more: unbuyable journalists, anyone who's ever taken BLM into the streets, anyone with a felony for being criminal or crazy or selling ass. Drug users, sex changers, and lots and lots of poor people.

It stands to reason then that if you're in one or more of these groups, you might start trying to leave before you even get a letter. The problem, of course, is that most of us aren't wanted elsewhere. Like I wouldn't even know where to start looking. I certainly don't have an ancestral claim in another country. Mom's parents were born here, and their parents before them. That's about as much as I know. Family wasn't something we discussed much.

"My mother," Mom would hiss, slicing the air in front of her face with her hand, flat as a straight razor, whiteknobbed knuckles crowned with blue from all those years of drinking. I would wait for her to go on, and she just never would. My grandma was named either Betty Lou or Betty Lee, and that's all I know about her.

It would be easy enough to find out more. I could use one of those sites where you enter your SSN and pay a flat fee for an email telling you just how long your family has been in this country; where your ancestors came from, if you happen to be of settler or kidnapped stock; and if those homelands have some kind of system in place for people like you. And I've got some things going for me: I'm still fairly young and fairly strong and more or less healthy. In some places, I even pass as a man sometimes, though I can't think of a bureaucratic process flexible enough to confirm my gender. That ship has sailed—just ask my surgeons, or Camille, the only person I'll let sissify me, but only when she's really in a funk. ("I need cheering," she'll roar, and then and only then will I submit to Mistress Camille, MUA and faggot tech.) I've got a lot more going for me than a Yemeni, or a Rohingya, or a Somalian.

But even if I were only a generation or two removed from some Western European country, I doubt it would have a visa for people of my type (monolingual), my profession (nonessential data monkey), and my kind (white and yet, for reasons of lifestyle, undesirable for procreation). America's not the only jawn with gender-fraud legislation. Would it actually be of any help to have fourth cousins in Maastricht? Where would that get me?

At any rate, escape is relative. Though a few of my exported friends were able to move thanks to relatives or a dual passport or a generous daddy, most had to find other ways to latch— working under the table or having babies or doing the whole sham-heterosexual-marriage thing to lock themselves in like ticks under the epidermis, in the global backwaters that aren't yet underwater, like Uzbekistan, Uganda, Uruguay. If I got a letter, I tell myself, I could do that. People all over the world leave their home countries, or attempt to, all the time. Sometimes they make it.

And sometimes they don't. Every day I watch the drowned bodies of Guatemalans, Hondurans, Salvadorans floating between selfies, Cyte's recaptured surveillance footage, and censor-safe influencers grinning like memento mori. I watch the Syrians swimming wintry Macedonian rivers under copfire just to be caged like Tyson chickens at the German border. For everyone who exports successfully (whatever that means), how many fail? How many get disappeared within this country, or imprisoned in the next? The big question is this: Is the export letter your last warning, or is it a sign that it's too late?

I guess I'll find out. I figure my letter's not long in coming, but I still don't know what I'll do. I could stay here and keep trying to fly under the radar, I guess. I don't need a FOIA to know that the government has everything it needs to detain or export me in some minuscule corner of its back end, if it cared to scratch just a little. My medical and criminal records are all right there. Maybe the law will change back again before it happens to me, if this city doesn't get sucked into the ocean first.

"I'll probably go to Mexico before I get a letter," Camille says. "But I'm gonna wait it out for a while. I'm keeping my ear to the ground."

But she's not keeping her ear to the ground. After everything with Flávia, she's just too scared to get on a plane, which means she'll probably stay until it's too late. If I had family in Guadalajara, I would have sucked it up and exported ages ago. There are still trains and automobiles.

Not that it's much, if any, better there. But at least it's somewhere else.

####

Three years ago, Camille's wife, Flávia, got a deportation notice for no reason any of the pigs involved would tell us. What
had she done? What had changed? Could it have possibly been
related to the export program? No one could say, and every
time Flávia resubmitted her paperwork to USCIS for verifi-
cation, it disappeared. Legally speaking, everything was in
order—Camille could be very competent when she had to be,
and Flávia was a Virgo, after all—but that didn't matter. It disappeared anyway.

Camille had a lawyer friend who worked in immigration justice. He said not to panic, which was easier said than done, what
with the websites that wouldn't load, the phone calls that got
dropped, the typos and misprints and requests for further ver-
ification, not to mention broken printers, a disconnected scan-
ner, weird deadlines, irregular office hours, and endless requests
for ten-page documents with fields for multiple ten-digit codes
that needed to be filled in with the same tedious information.
At least Kafka's labyrinths were analog.

For weeks, Flávia was a wreck, and Camille wasn't doing so
hot, either, but they kept it together with speed, weed, and an
expensive juicer that a client had given Camille for Hanukkah.
It took that lawyer friend and around-the-clock phone calls to
finally figure out that Flávia's file had been flagged for *inconsis-
tencies potentially indicating fraudulent identity*, even though she'd
changed her gender marker and legal name back in Brazil, long
before she'd ever been to America. She'd been outed, though it
was unclear when or how or by whom.

"Don't you have any idea?" I asked.

The usually sunny Flávia glared at me. "What difference would it make if I did?" she snapped. Camille wrapped her arm around her shoulders, pulling her head to her chest, and gave me a Look. "Sometimes I think you like making people sad because you don't know how to make them happy," Camille said later that night when we were fucked up.

When it became clear that deportation was inevitable, Camille and Flávia made a plan: Flávia would go to Manaus right away, and Camille would join her as soon as she found a sublet for the apartment. They would hire a lawyer, and Flávia would work on getting her documents fixed while Camille saw Brazilian clients. They would consider themselves <pinky out> on vacation until things cooled off. Once life was fixed, they'd come back to the States, and everything would be peachy.

"See?" said Camille, pointing to her own smiling mouth, as if Flávia were a child scared by thunder. I was driving them to the airport in Ahmed's car, watching them in the rearview. Flávia was crying again. "See, I'm not worried! Don't worry, baby, everything is going to work out just fine."

I was at their old apartment helping Camille pack when Flávia called. She didn't sound good. She'd gotten an infection in the processing facility she'd been in before they put her on the plane.

"Okay, baby," Camille said. "Totally. Okay."

From across the room, I had her at a bad angle. Camille's face was almost unrecognizable, except for her eyes, brown as usual but rimmed with gross crimson.

That was the last time Camille heard from Flávia. We weren't informed that she had been detained on arrival in Manaus. All we knew was that her phone went to voice mail, and her emails went unanswered. Camille was frantic. Flávia's Brazilian friends were doing everything they could, but we couldn't find her. It was like she'd dropped off the face of the Earth.

It was the wife of a cousin, one of the only family members Flávia was still on speaking terms with, who finally emailed Camille; blood relatives were kept abreast from the beginning, it seemed, and Flávia's friends had put her in touch. It had been sudden, the relative reported. Flávia had already been sick when she landed. "Foi o que nos disseram, de qualquer maneira," went the email. I read it on Camille's phone, which she handed to me on her way back to bed, under the American flag with the brown smear.

A few days later, the relative emailed again to tell Camille when and where the funeral was happening, in case she wanted to attend. I read it first; she was terrified of more bad news, although I couldn't think of what could possibly have been worse. Would she go, I asked her, petting her hair.

Her answer surprised me. "I don't think I can get on the plane." Camille wasn't afraid that the plane would crash, but that she would die just stepping onto it. It was illogical, she knew, but there it was. The girl who grew up taking the commuter between DC and DF was now terrified to fly. She wouldn't go, she said. She couldn't.

"It'll pass," I insisted. I was trying to be gentle. "Don't you think you'll regret it if you aren't there?" Her bags were already packed and everything.

She shook her head as she took her phone back. "I just can't do it," she said. Light flooded her face as she read the email for herself. She was beautiful again in a synthetic kind of way, like a sex robot. Her eyes were still rimmed in red.

The night before the funeral, we stayed out until the sun came up. There's something about bad hangovers that I actually enjoy—they make suicide seem reasonable. I remember sitting outside the bathroom the next morning, waiting for Camille to finish puking so I could have my turn. It was probably for the best that she hadn't gone, I thought. They buried Flávia as someone who didn't exist.

check this out.

My friend Nino, who moved to Jacksonville last year to study the Florida shrink for his climatology postdoc, sent me an article from one of the state's remaining regional papers.

big fat tw, his next text cautioned. Nino's tender like that.

The bus had left Tallahassee for Hattiesburg at 6:55 a.m. According to the article, it was almost to the Mississippi border when the man started to scream. Until then, he had been quietly sitting in a twelfth-row aisle seat with his headphones in.

In the linked video taken by someone seated farther back on the bus, you can see him screaming, wordlessly and at a surprisingly high pitch, his face pointed dead ahead. At first, I thought that the bus was about to crash into something, and that the man was reacting, too much and too soon, to a death he knew was only seconds away. Then the video ends.

By the time the cops got there, the screaming man—identified as "the suspect"—had already killed six people. The survivors somehow managed to evacuate the bus while finding a way to trap him on it. This was the only reason more weren't dead. "A pretty good hustle," one of the cops is quoted as saying.

Just above the footer was another video showing fifteen or twenty passengers standing around on the side of the highway. There is a crying toddler and a crying kid, both of whom are yanked from the camera's line of sight by a twisted wrist. There are a few white people among them; I don't know why none of them had a gun, or if they did, why they didn't stand their ground and blast the screaming man a new asshole. They were coming from Florida, after all. After the other passengers barricaded him inside the bus, the screaming man climbed through the porthole onto the roof and sat there with his legs folded, Indian-style, as Mom would make a point of saying. He didn't move much, except to pull his hat up to protect his bald head from the sun.

It was almost noon before the cops got him down. The weapon—a big, fancy steak knife, the kind most people are too cheap to buy for their own kitchens—clattered onto the asphalt.

The comments were divided between people who wanted him to die like his victims and people who wanted him to live a long, healthy life in the belly of the prison industrial complex. "export this scum!!!!!" was the most-liked comment.

that's crazy, I texted Nino. *even for now. weird i didn't see it anywhere.*

i didn't either. my friend sent me the link. could be a deepfake but if it is its a super good one.

That's the last text I have from Nino. Petra and I broke up not long after, and even though I tried to get in touch a few times, Nino never responded.

####

I met Camille through my friend Kitana, who I went on a blind date with when I was like twenty-two. Kitana and I had chemistry, but it turned out we were both stone tops, and neither of us would budge on it. None of that top4top stuff for us. It's probably why she and I got along so well.

Kitana used to get her business cards from this Greenpoint indie press run by an anarchist named Leslie and her polycule of acrobats and drug dealers. Kitana came up with the design herself. On the front was a line drawing of her face, the lock of hair that skimmed her forehead intertwining with the cat-o'-nine bordering the card. On the other side was the address at the encrypted email server where she could be contacted. I thought it was pretty good. Leslie gave Kitana a discount on the cards because the two of them used to live in the same co-op, back when Leslie was flying solo.

The first wave kicked off not long after that, and we soon found out that Leslie was planning to export. *If you have the means,* her letter read, *relocation is strongly encouraged. This will save you and your family the time and resources that will otherwise likely be dedicated to being in compliance with next fiscal year's rollout of enhanced security procedures.* No financial incentive was mentioned, though there was a link to a website that Leslie said didn't exist. She called the 800 number and ended up waiting an hour to talk to a robot caseworker that could only take messages.

The letter was watermarked with a new subdepartment of ICE called FLEC. We recognized the acronym from other letters, some federal emails, and a little feed coverage, though sometimes it was listed as FLECC or FLECT. No one knows exactly what it stands for, and it's never spelled out in chyrons or op-eds.

"But they don't tell you exactly why you have to leave?" I asked.

"All it says is that I'm *at risk* and a *security challenge.* Maybe they didn't have enough room on the paper," Leslie laughed. She had more than one felony, including one for "incitement" (garden-variety anarchist rabble-rousing—she may have worshipped her, but Leslie was no Emma Goldman), and north of 300k in medical and student debt, which she had proudly defaulted on years ago. Leslie said she wouldn't think of leaving if it weren't for her family in Vietnam, one of the countries that offered qualified exporters a leg up in the naturalization process in exchange for robust American subsidies. She was going to move in with her grandparents, who owned a cellphone shop in Đà Nẵng.

"They're getting up there," Leslie said. "I won't have another chance to be with them like this. It just makes more sense to go than to stay."

The week before Leslie exported, Kitana, Camille, and I went to Greenpoint and printed as many hooker business cards as we could carry, all free of charge. Camille hands them out with an almost terrifying disregard for discretion—I once watched her slide one into a cop's baseball cap while blowing a key-lime gum bubble—but the day she does anything discreetly is the day she gets a job in an office or an Amazon warehouse.

"What will you do for cards, once Leslie's gone?" I asked Kitana, fanning out a handful like a royal flush. Things aren't like they were even ten years ago, when you could advertise online with a website or paid ads. These days, explaining Backpage to baby escorts is like walking Zoomers through the concept of dial-up internet. Now it's almost impossible to advertise online, even with a personal account, so the girls and gays have had to get creative. Word of mouth only gets you so far, and regulars get bored or go broke or try to rape you or go silent, as regulars do. I guess some of them export, too, though more often they're probably just dying in their houses with their wives and their health insurance.

Kitana shrugged. She's beautiful and fat, with long, black, Elvira-esque hair. She branded herself *Goth Girlfriend*, and there's a certain kind of trick—middle-aged, former hipster, fancies himself too cool to buy sex—that loves everything about her. "Guess I'll just cross that bridge when I get to it," she said. "Maybe I'll start learning Vietnamese in case I ever visit Leslie. Parents love me. I'm sure grandparents do, too."

I don't know if Kitana has visited yet. One of her clients got her a coveted Belgian visa, and she's been in Brussels since last year.

can't wait for you to visit, she texted a while ago. I'm sure I'll never see her again.

I saw her boots first. They climbed up over her legs like PVC pipe, big and black and slick.

Stalking in from stage right, X bent smoothly over a speaker to twist a knob with her fingers, a cord pulled taut down her side. If her interference had any effect on the noise BE CRIME was making, I didn't notice. All I could hear was the blood in my eardrums. When she turned to the audience, white neon blaring through a skylight washed her eyes like Garbo. Hand to heart, it was just like a movie. For the longest five seconds of my life, I just looked.

There was something about her that was familiar, the way she held and moved her body, a visual aroma twisting against itself, a dynamic tension—as if the Helmut Newton photos of Grace

Jones and Sigourney Weaver had locked eyes in the midst of an orgy, recognizing each other from a previous life. I didn't know her, but I instantly knew something important about her, which was that I had never seen anyone like her before.

I hated her. I found Camille, latex wiggling like an oil stain, her body now curled around an unsuspecting masc with a buffalo-nickel-size gold medallion and a baseball cap decorated with Looney Tunes decals. I was sure Camille would know who the person on the stage was and why my instinctive loathing was completely justified. No one was clean, and Camille always had the receipts. I had to tap her shoulder a few times to get her attention. The masc, higher than a kite, didn't notice me.

"What?" murmured Camille.

"Who is that?" I said.

"Who?" Camille was gazing at the masc, fingering their chain. The masc giggled.

"Them." I poked her again, then pointed at X. The boots were stepping down from the stage, sidestepping some scaffolding, electrical cords thick as snakes. Their right arm and leg were visible for just a moment longer than the rest of their body, but then they, too, disappeared into the depths of the warehouse.

"I didn't see," said Camille. Her voice sounded weird. When I turned back to her, she wasn't even looking toward where I'd pointed. Her pupils, big as bugs, swam in the overhead light.

How had she come up so quickly? I felt the same as I had when we left the house, only angrier.

"You really didn't see her?" I asked. "Tall with a buzz cut? Big, black boots?"

When she turned to me, her mouth was turned down, scooping into her chin. Eyes almost closed, teeth white as snow. She looked like the Nanny pulling a face when she did that. "Lots of those around here," she said. The masc giggled again. "Hey, where's my drink?"

"Why don't you have your boyfriend get it for you?"

She rolled her eyes and went back to whatever she was doing with her masc. BE CRIME was dragging its stuff offstage while a new band set up. The new band—I missed its name. Something *slit* or *spit*—began testing right away, and their feedback was even louder than BE CRIME's. Then the bassist launched a throb and they were off, halfway through a song before we even knew what was happening. The lights went out.

Drink forgiven and forgotten, Camille started to move, swaying into me, throwing her arm around my shoulder. Everyone in the suddenly packed warehouse was moving. All the bodies pressed together, soft warm curlicues trembling at the behest of the noise. Camille's elbow slid down to my ribs, that masc's hand was on my back, an unknown wrist was pushing against mine. "Hey, babe," in my ear, and I turned to see Ahmed's bleached curls and golden tooth, with his boyfriend Prinz only just behind him. Friends had finally arrived. But I didn't want to see them.

"I need air." I yelled it directly into Camille's ear, but she didn't seem to hear me. Evading Ahmed and Prinz, I shoved off, dividing the throng of people with my hands pressed together like a shark fin.

I like crowds. I can throw an elbow or sink my weight down into a foot and then just keep going, from back to front to back again. It's one of the best ways to pick a fight, if you're in the mood for one, or dish anonymous violence without any repercussions, if that's where your head's at. But I wanted outside so bad that I couldn't enjoy the crush. The noise from the new band was deafening, the jewelry and ReflecTec and teeth of the crowd all too bright for my eyes. And then there was the smell. The tidal wave of colognes and perfumes and swishers and smoke and SPF 100 and armpit and groin and fried oil and punk dog was making me nauseous.

When I pushed my way through the front door, I was surprised and disappointed to see that there was no one outside. I wanted to bum a real cigarette. The mica of parties past—glitter in the gutter, emptied Double Scorpios—twinkled around my shoes. The false spring had given us a warm night, but instead of offering relief from the hot muffle of recycled carbon dioxide, the temperature dragged my bones closer to the surface of my skin. I felt like I'd just snorted a line of speed but left all the good parts on the mirror, which reminded me that I still hadn't come up yet. Maybe Camille had given me a dud.

If I couldn't smoke, I could at least stretch my legs. Home was only a few miles away. I could just walk back, back to my couch and my pilly blanket and a cold beer to ferry me to sleep, if I was lucky. Maybe I'd even sleep all night. Camille wouldn't know what became of me until she crawled back up the stairs tomorrow morning, and by then I would be up and flipping pancakes from an allergen-free mix that she paid for, ready to coddle her through the hangover with genetically modified bacon fat and a new lease on life. I was still trying to decide what to do when something in the corner of my eye, something shiny, caught my attention.

I turned. Between the warehouse I had just exited and the warehouse next door was an alley guarded by a chain-link fence. I took a few steps closer for a better look, my hands in my pockets, squinting into the dim. There was no one and nothing there, except for a door at the far end of the alley.

I was dying to know where the door went. I pulled my hands out of my pockets, put them on the gritty chain-link, and gave it a tug. The diamonds felt good, cold and hard. My body felt young and strong, and the fence seemed shorter than it should have. There wasn't even any razor wire along the top. It was almost too easy to jump. The door at the end of the alley was locked but not deadbolted. It was almost too easy to kick open. Inside was a narrow, trash-littered hallway. I entered, feeling like I was supposed to be there, like I'd played this game before.

More doorways dotted the stretching darkness. The correct one looked identical to the others, but its correctness couldn't have been more obvious if it had been outlined in gold or shrieking my name. I had no choice. When I tried the handle, it was unlocked, just as I knew it would be.

The door opened into a room full of boxes and lumpy, tarp-covered shapes. White Christmas lights were strung up along the top of the four walls, where crown molding might have been if there had been a ceiling for it to connect to. Beyond, the band played on to the crowd I had just escaped. Affixed to the wall across from me was a spectrum of rubber, leather, metal, plastic, vinyl, and nylon artifacts: every torture device known to dyke.

I had plenty of time to memorize those details later. But when I walked in the door, I didn't notice any of it. She was there, waiting for me.

####

Petra was a good girl. She was so good she didn't need irony to pull off Irish lace and Mary Janes. She was so good that sometimes I almost felt bad about bruising her pretty face. It was pretty because she always looked like she was about to do something bad, even when she was flinching, and especially when she was crying. Even when she was bad, she was good, and she was usually bad.

But it wasn't just looking good that made her good—not even I'm that shallow. It was this sense of anticipation vibrating around her, a featherweight aura of something that felt like menace. It was the way she moved, like she was so happy to be alive that she just couldn't wait to get on to the next thing. When the next thing was me, it was intoxicating. When she jumped out of bed to plug in her dead phone and I realized that the next thing really was just any old thing, it was devastating.

It didn't matter. Being around her transformed me into that horny cartoon wolf that pounds the table when he sees the sexy cartoon showgirl, the one with the Lucille Ball hairdo and the Lucille LeSueur slouch. The first time I made her bleed, she turned her head around and laughed in my face. Petra made me want to burst out of my own chest and holler, "WHAT A WOMAN!"

We met at the Met, where she was wandering around the first floor in a miniskirt, charcoal tights, and an enormous marigold faux-fur jacket. She obviously had plans for later that evening. I had noticed her jacket at the ticket booth, its fringe shaking like a flapper skirt, and when I came across her again not long after, I stopped behind a statue of Athena to watch.

She was studying one of the display cases, her right arm crooked behind her back, a contemplative left-hand finger tapping her chin. She looked like she was seconds away from reaching through the glass to cop a bold feel of the busty bust inside it. Her hair was thick and black and hideously styled, gelled into Tsukamoto-esque spikes and waves.

Suddenly, she spun around to face me. The voyeur behind the grey-eyed goddess caught red-handed. Me in my black sweatshirt, black hat, fucked-up sneakers—all the things a person wears when a lonesome trip to the museum is their only plan for the evening because they got banned from the monthly dyke play party, *again*, for the same stupid reason (drinking blood), and there's nary an interesting new bottom in the metropolitan area to be found.

I later found out that she had recently moved back to Brooklyn after a few years in Chicago, but everything I needed to know at that exact moment was right in front of me. I could feel my vision becoming superhuman. I could see the mouth desperate for chapstick and the green vein arcing in her chest like faulty wiring. I could imagine what it would look like if I pinned her down to watch the shape of my hand against the vein, to blot it out then allow it to reappear, like a lightning-struck skyline in negative.

Our eyes slopped all over each other like molasses. As if she knew what I was thinking, she stuck out her tongue.

####

I ran into Margot again not long before I met X. I was at a bar minding my business when she walked in, drunk as a skunk and all by herself. If I hadn't been just as drunk and twice as lonely, I probably would have left, but she marched right up and asked me to buy her a shot. Her finger in my belt loop, all was forgiven.

When a sadist and a masochist have chemistry, it's easy to forget breakups and bad experiences. I was at that bar to black out, not to meet anybody. But Margot had this charming way of looking like she was full of blood. The telltale signs were everywhere: the easy blush, the drinker's flush, the pulse that moved on beat with the pop music blasting above us. Maybe this time I won't get sick, I thought. Maybe this one is the one that breaks the spell. Margot stuck her ass out to lean over the bar and pay for our shots with my money. "Tequila makes me so crazy sometimes I think I'd even fuck a man," she laughed, skinny legs twisting. All I could think about was pussy, tits, and tears. If I couldn't rearrange this bimbo's guts without fainting, it was a sign from god to just kill myself. Salut. Down the hatch.

I told her I was staying at Camille's, but that she was gone for the night. Once a few drinks had us feeling good and violent, I took her back to my couch.

Everything was going as it should. No dizziness, no nausea, just a little crying on her part, bite marks, both of us wet as rain. But somewhere during the choking, Margot's eyes closed, and then they stayed that way. When she woke up one too many seconds later, she said she was fine. It was just the drugs, she insisted, and a touch of exhaustion ("exhaustion"). She hadn't said anything about drugs back at the bar.

"Why didn't you tell me?" I demanded, though I knew the answer. If she had told me she was on something weirder than liquor, I wouldn't have played my little breathing game. Everyone who knows me knows I have rules. "What the fuck were you thinking?" My life was playing on a loop behind my eyelids—I'm too pretty for men's prison.

But Margot wouldn't give me a straight answer. She walked to the kitchen and back, as if to prove that everything was fine.

"See?" she said, pinching her cheeks and fluffing her hair, like that meant something. She had the balls to ask if we could keep going. I refused, of course. I'm not insane. I was too angry to play safely, anyway. I wanted to choke her to death for real this time.

"Please," Margot whined. "Please, please, please."

Beach, bed, lungs. I slid a cigarette from the box on the coffee table and walked to the window. It was raining, the drops going *pep* on the glass. I glared through the water down into the street. There was something dead in the gutter, fur shining like petroleum.

"Come on," Margot said. "It's not a big deal. Come back over here."

I heard her hand thumping the couch cushion. For a minute or two, she talked about how horny she was, then she lost the thread. She was still high. She sounded like a voice-over in a diamond commercial: slow, incurious, vaguely mid-Atlantic, droning on about a back piece she wanted to get when she saved up enough. A squid, something stupid like that. When I glanced behind me, she was lying on her side, talking into the back of the couch.

I turned back to the window, focusing on the first flicker of nicotine. I thought I'd tuned her out, but then something in her voice changed.

"So," she said, "did you hear about Petra?"

Somehow, I kept looking straight ahead. I'd done such a good job of removing Petra from my life and eliminating everything that reminded me of her—I stayed out of our old neighborhood, blocked most of our mutual friends—that I had no idea what she was implying. Not that Margot actually wanted an answer. She wasn't gathering information. She was sending me a message: I know something that would hurt you to know. The cigarette was going cold in my fingers.

When I didn't reply, Margot repeated herself like the sociopath she had proven herself to be. I steadied my hands and relit the cigarette. *Beach, bed, lungs.* I took the world's longest drag, letting the silence gain weight before I answered.

"I don't know what you're talking about," I said. I studied my face, pearly in the glass, and relaxed a little. Amanda Lepore couldn't have looked more unbothered.

"Oh," said Margot. She had asked if she could smoke a real cigarette when we got to Camille's, and at the time I saw it as a hospitable concession. And anyway, she *was* putting out. A good host doesn't raid their guest's box of analogs, but etiquette's out the window when the breathplay's gone too far. "Someone told me . . ." she began.

When I whipped around, she stopped talking. She was sitting up again, slumped over, mouth slack and shoulders twisted. She looked stupid. She looked like an inanimate object I should be able to just unplug and put away. I took a step forward, zeroing in on her fat-pupiled eyes, and even she, in her state, had the sense to flinch. How had I not noticed how fucked up she was before? I must have been drunker than I thought. The me inside of me wanted to spit in her face, but neither of us wanted to give her the satisfaction. It was what Margot wanted, and she wasn't going to get any more of that with me. Trust a masochist to be too freaked out by intimacy to not fuck up a perfectly nice date.

But I would be merciful. As she watched me, I ashed on the windowsill, knowing she wished I would use her face. "Get out," I said. I liked how steady my voice sounded. I felt like Jesus. "Get out of my house." As if it was a house, or mine. (Somewhere in my skull, like a ghost: *I am the concierge chez-moi, honey.*) Now that I was more sober, I couldn't believe I'd invited her over.

"Fuck you," spat Margot, but she hunted down her panties and gathered her things, mincing by me and out the door in a breeze of sage perfume, clopping down the walk-up like a baby deer. Once the first-floor door slammed below me, I snatched my phone and blocked her, then lit another one of her cigarettes. *Beach, bed, lungs.*

It's easy to get paranoid with pain sluts. A lot of them—most of them, let's be real—are just looking for someone to get mad at. They'll tolerate almost anything, so long as they can earn an excuse to hate somebody other than themselves.

With Margot, I hadn't even given her that much. I had refused to hurt her like she wanted, but she was determined to get the pain out of me, one way or another. Nothing was too despicable, including the mention of that fucking bitch, Petra. Petra. Who gave a shit what she was up to.

I sucked down the cigarette, yanked up the window, tossed the butt through the frame, and immediately regretted it. It's funny. It doesn't matter what the doomsday clock says—I still feel guilty when I litter.

The little grey cylinder disappeared into the darkness, but Margot's white leather glowed all the way across the street.

Mom only took me to church one time, when I was twelve. She didn't get along with most of her coworkers, she told me, but she had liked Jackson just fine. Mom said that black people always liked her because she wasn't racist.

"I'm overdue for a funeral, anyway," Mom said. "Plus, the air conditioning will be nice." Ours was out, and the super had been ignoring her calls. It was supposed to be one hundred degrees by 10:00 a.m.

We sat in the parking lot while she put on eyeliner in the rearview. The hatchback's AC had broken the summer before, so she sat with her lotioned leg, already slick with sweat, sticking out of the open driver's-side door. I got the impression that I wasn't supposed to ask how Jackson died. Probably a horrible accident, I concluded, watching her blink down over the wand. Or something embarrassing, like a heart attack on the toilet.

Outside the church, it was a hot, cloudless summer day. We stepped through the foyer to discover it was even hotter indoors. "Shit," Mom muttered.

At the end of the aisle, where brides and grooms are supposed to stand when they say "I do," was a big picture of Jackson on an art easel. I hadn't met him before he died—only Mom's boyfriends visited our apartment—but I was pleasantly surprised to see how sexy he had been. I liked his muscles and his big, thick mustache. I knew he was around Mom's age, so it was obvious that the photo was old. Judging by the colors of his shirt and the cut of his jeans, I decided he had definitely been a fag. I tried to curl my lip like he had his, wishing that he had been an uncle instead of Mom's coworker.

The chairs on the left side of the church were mostly filled with white people, and on the right side, mostly black people. Mom led us to two empty seats on the left side. As if he'd been waiting for us, the priest got things started immediately after we sat. On the wall behind him, Jesus was hung up like a door knocker, his body stretched out from the tips of his fingers all the way down to his bleeding feet (American size 9, maybe), each middle toe just slightly longer than the hallux. I fanned myself with one of the home-printed programs, wishing I could be almost naked, too. Surrounding the priest were a bunch of boys around my age wearing smaller, brighter versions of his raiment. Their eyes were fixed on him, their pink-and-blue lids flicking in the sunlight that cooked the stained glass.

We stood and then sat again, then stood, and then music started playing. Mom didn't sing. I wanted to fit in, so I moved my lips without making any noise. The women on both sides of the aisle wore blouses and skirts. Their hair was tucked back neatly behind their ears, flat ironed or hot combed, instead of covered in veils or the little hats you stick to your head with bobby pins that I had seen on TCM. The men, indelicately scratching themselves and staring at the skylights, wore polos and slacks. Unlike most of the black people in attendance, who wore mourning charcoal, the other white people wore beige and brown. I was the one exception, wearing a blue dress Mom picked out for me, because it was the only one I had with sleeves and without a pattern. She was wearing a slightly wrinkled white linen shirt and capris. Everyone was sweaty and fidgety, edgy.

The only white woman wearing black was sitting ahead of us, in the first row. She was crying into a kleenex, instead of a more cinematic cloth hanky, her shoulders shaking dramatically. She was old, much older than Mom. No one else cried; everyone else's faces were neutral, rather than grim or resigned. They didn't appear to be particularly affected by Jackson's death. Mom kept swatting her neck. A fly buzzed somewhere behind my right ear. Everyone was shifting in their seats, the pews undercutting the music with abrupt, eerie creaks. It was almost noon, and with only the pair of sluggish ceiling fans above us, we oozed like meat in a broken fridge. I could smell every hole in the room. The priest was dripping. He crossed his hands over his crotch, his big arms straining, the white square on his pink throat as sharp as a razor.

When we were done singing, the pallbearers took Jackson down the aisle and put him into the hearse. It drove deep into the cemetery, and we followed on foot, everyone fanning their faces. By the time we got to the grave, Jackson had been lowered down inside. We surrounded him, sniffing that hot-lawn smell, suffocating and clean, and watched as people got up behind a podium.

"Jesus," Mom muttered. "More talking?"

As the speakers droned, I noticed a small group of people standing off to the side of the crowd, almost behind a hedge. They hadn't been with us in the church. I would have noticed the men wearing women's clothes and women wearing men's clothes, the colorful makeup and crazy hair. Unlike everyone in the church, all of them, white and black and brown, were in mourning. They were crying just as hard as the crying lady, who kept her face turned away from the hedge when she took her place behind the podium. She had been Jackson's mother, she said, wiping her face with a fresh kleenex.

Mother. It sounded so weird. Under her arms, parabolic pit stains bloomed against the black. I bet she smelled bad. *Mother* was a word for Disney movies and adenoidal rich kids and royalty, not for someone who hadn't been able to stop her kid from dying of AIDS or whatever. I was craning my head to look at the weird people again when Mom poked my shoulder.

I thought I was in trouble for staring, but she leaned in close to me, so close we could have kissed. "I have a lash," she muttered, peeling back a lid, eyeball big as the moon. "Do you see it?"

"Jackson," said Jackson's mom, like it was a complete sentence.

I was hurting my girlfriends long before I even knew what *sadist* meant. We were just doing things because we wanted to, without knowing how to do them the right way. There weren't classes or parties or clubs or things like that where we lived. I didn't know where the leatherdykes hung out, or if there were any. We just figured stuff out on our own.

My first serious girlfriend and I were so basic. We liked to get fucked up and choke each other, put cigarettes out on each other, stuff like that. She didn't like needles, which was too bad. I thought I was hot shit because I knew how to stab myself without getting an infection. It was exciting, but even we knew how low the stakes were.

Maybe that's why we got careless. One night, we were drinking and tying each other up with some rope we got at Ace Hardware. When it was my turn to tie, I left her on the bed for a quick cigarette, and when I came back, she wasn't breathing.

The rope was tight around her bluing skin, and her eyes were closed. I didn't know what to do. If my roommate hadn't been home, and if she hadn't been smart—unlike me, a total fucking idiot—who knows what would have happened to that tied-up girlfriend? Rosemary. I think that was Rosemary. We were so young, all three of us, like nineteen. My roommate might have been twenty. I didn't feel anything except confusion until maybe-Rosemary came to and started to talk again.

I didn't figure out what happened until later. Her body had shifted, and her weight had pulled her down so that the rope caught her neck in just the right way to cut off her airflow, and the more she squirmed, the more it choked. "Thank god you came and got me," said my roommate. I got so angry I had to go back outside by myself.

I didn't meet May, or Maybelline, until a few years after that, right after I moved to Brooklyn. She taught me a lot. She came up in one of the old Parisian houses, a manse built on bone-strewn catacombs, where she had been dubbed the unimaginative Ébène by an ancient white domina. She spent her nights in marble lavatories and leather-upholstered bedchambers, unless she and her fellow initiates were on summer sabbaticals to Château de Lacoste for gimp-chaperoned field trips through fields of sunbaked lavender. Her education was flowers and flagellation and fornication, like an opium dream from the guillotine age. I eventually broke up with May, but she was one of my best relationships. She taught me everything I know, and made me feel like I could do anything I wanted to a body, including keep it alive. That part was important.

"You wouldn't want to get a bad reputation," May said. "We hurt, not harm."

That part was sort of a joke, because May absolutely didn't mind harming people. She was a sadist, after all. But she was right. Going too far was a bad look.

"Then you'd have to start taking your victims by force. And that's a lot more work. And really"—that was back when she was affecting a slender gold cigarette holder, which she flourished like a rich bitch—"who has the time?"

At first glance, I thought it was an albino cockatiel because the tubes were splayed on top like a watery pompadour. A closer look revealed that it was a disembodied and drained human heart. A silky, harmless sac.

I zoomed in and out over the picture, studying the empty ventricles, the way the superior vena cava drooped like pasta al dente. Like all organs, the heart looked satisfying to squeeze, but also too fragile to withstand more than one good contraction.

I used to have a membership to one of those sites where you can find everything bad on the internet. I paid for access to a curated dump of ISIL beheadings, FBI black site footage, grisly accidents, snuff. It made me feel tough, like it proved I was too strong for bad things to bother me: I was the kind of person who could get ready for bed while watching a man be forced to eat his own fingers. (This was years before I started listening to my murder podcast. A nursery rhyme in comparison.)

I let my subscription lapse a long time ago, but every once in a while I feel the urge to log back on for a walk down memory lane. My litmus test is a video of a woman struggling in bondage while someone off-camera pushes thumbtacks into her meat. The model is very pretty, with a girl-next-door smile. Her name is Monique, and her screams sound authentic. She's one of my favorites.

Usually the video turns me on so much I can't wait to cum, but occasionally Monique will leave me cold, even at the end, when her body sparkles like a bloodied Leigh Bowery costume. It's not enough that she wants it, that she giggles between the screams. It's too much, actually. There are just some nights that consensual sadism can't cut it.

That's when I end up tracking down the site, or one just like it—they're all the same, really—and get lost for hours. I wake up the next morning feeling like a million bucks. Sometimes I don't even remember that I was on the site until the following afternoon or evening, when it starts coming back to me in little pieces, like the fragments of a blackout.

Tonight might be one of those nights. It's the worst it's been since the warehouse. I'll get close to dozing off, dropping into that gauzy place where everything feels slow as mud, my head sinking down so low that it feels as if my legs are up in the air again, my head below my hips, moving slowly, dreamily back until I feel that movement down there, hear her voice—and then I'll jerk awake, heart racing, skin prickling.

What will I do if she exports before I see her again? My hands shake. I feel sick. Fuck her. I'll go jump off the Brooklyn Bridge.

I don't know what I would say to X if I saw her again. I haven't planned that far.

What kills me isn't the fear that I won't see her before she goes. It's knowing that she doesn't think about me, not even enough to hate me. I don't know how I know that, but I do. It feels like the only thing I know for sure.

Why couldn't the night at the warehouse have gone differently? I could have kept walking, instead of jumping that fucking fence. I could have followed Camille and her boytoy around the party until we went home and took turns peeing on them or had a wrestling match or got high. I could have never gone out at all, just stayed right here on this couch and jerked myself off to sleep. Or I could have died. Like there we were, in a squat failing every imaginable fire code, and it could have burned down with all of us inside, snuffed us out before we had the chance to realize how wrong the heat was, to wonder where the smoke was coming from, like Ghost Ship on another coast.

But it didn't. Everything that happened, happened. X happened. Now I can't think about anything else.

I open my phone, scroll for thirty seconds, close it, stare at the ceiling for ten seconds, then open my phone again. Again. Again. Again. I know it doesn't help, but I can't stop scouring the apps—crisscrossing the concentric circles of friends, acquaintances, strangers, networks. It's like hunting for a needle in a million haystacks, but I keep looking anyway, convinced that sooner or later I'm going to stumble across the connection that's connected to the connection that has a photo of her that leads to her number that leads to her that leads to I don't know what.

I click through images of tall women in black leather. One of them bears a passing resemblance to X—similar stature, buzzed head. I think about my fist and her face, the give of cheekbones, her lips smeared like jelly. I put down my phone, close my eyes, and stick my hand in my underwear. I move my fingers and think about choking her to death on her table, her life suddenly gone forever, like an orgasm, but when I cum her hand is in my mouth.

While I wait out my refractory period, I pull up the site. Little has changed since the last time I was here. Its design is a time capsule of bad UX, but just as I suspected, the content is as fresh as a daisy. I often wonder who maintains sites like this one, and at what depths they're operating, emotionally speaking, that they can look at shit like this on a daily basis and not off themselves, or somebody else. But who says they don't?

The thumbnails bubble up under my little arrow like time-collapsed toadstools. I take my time deciding where to go first. Corpse in the wood chipper? Daniel Pearl's final moments, or perhaps Dick Cheney's? I think I've already seen those ones. A while ago, someone made a CG "dramatization" of Kissinger's death, advertised as more violent than the real thing, but I don't care how good it is. I'm not interested. Knowing that he actually went in his sleep is torture enough. I squint and move my face a little closer to the screen. A lot of the thumbnails have descriptions in languages I don't know and images I can't quite parse.

I choose one at random. Click. The video eats the screen, and the black fades onto what looks like a residential street. The camera pans over a bunch of dead kids lined up on the asphalt like railroad ties. Snore.

I go back to the main screen to do more hovering. Here's an interesting one, and it's in English: VITAMIX DICK. I almost click, but the time stamp suggests it's too short to be worth it. Nothing more than a glorified gore GIF. But there's such a thing as too much coherence, too. There's nothing worse than storytelling when what you're really looking for is content.

I hover over another. Okay, I think, I have to stay with this one for at least a minute. If I'm bored after sixty seconds, I can find another one. Click.

It's dark. Flashlights. A vapor of voices through which one man's cries slice. Fear or pain. Can't tell if we're indoors or out—is this a Matthew Shepard or an Abner Louima? Air whips against the camera as it moves. The voices blend with the pop of bone, but his screams are as precise as puncture wounds. I can't see clearly, and I don't understand the language being spoken, but the minute passes and I don't click away.

Inside me, it starts slowly. My heart picks up speed. Instead of leaving my brain behind, I fill it in. My body—the ache of a bruise as I shift, my clenched hand, the tightness of my jaw—fades away. It's just me and the black screen and the sounds from the video and the sound of my heart. It's like when I'm in a scene and the adrenaline kicks in and my eyes feel like they're rolling back into my head, like Jaws going in for the kill, and I feel good for like the first time in my life, like I've never been sad or tired before, and never will be again. The screaming is real and nothing else is, least of all this victim, the stupid fuck who really thought he was going to escape the greatest pain of his life.

I feel it in my eyelid and my shoulders and my gut and my cunt, everything all coming together.

"I can't do it if you're wearing clothes," X said.

She was sprawled on the mattress in the middle of the floor, leaning on a forearm over her laptop, her boots caking mud on the filthy fitted sheet. The floor was filthy, too, spotted with balls of hair and bits of trash, and there was a puddle in a corner, but the room's contents—the boxes, the tarped shapes—were clean and neatly organized by size. Next to the mattress was a well-preserved black duffel bag and the kind of backpack that people bring with them to escape the grid: dun-colored, sewn with a million pockets, riddled with carabiners.

"Do what?" It was all I could think to say. The toys hanging from the wall were arranged with the same care as the boxes, equally spaced in ascending order. Closest to me was a scarlet quirt, its miniature braids shiny as challah. On the far end, right above X's head, a bullwhip was coiled like a nautilus. Behind the wall, the music blared. The feeling that I was meant to be here was like a low frequency.

"You heard me," X said.

She sat up and shifted onto her palms. She wasn't smiling, but I could tell she was happy. Her expression was calm, just like her voice. She moved slowly and with ease, as if she were getting up from a beach towel. People aren't really like that anymore, except for children. Like kids still laugh on the train and yell in the street, when they're young, anyway. But it doesn't take long for all of that to go dull. That lost happiness radiated from X. It felt aggressive. Dangerous.

"Okay," I said. The silliness of it all washed over me, and I laughed. So *this* was what we were doing. I liked her confidence, even if it was a little embarrassing. Liked it enough to play along, anyway. I laughed again and closed the door behind me. "Whatever you say, boss." I started to undress.

But I took my time. I slowly removed my shoes, my sweatshirt and the shirt beneath it, and my pants, dropping each on the floor as I went. My briefs and my socks stayed on. When I was done, I folded my arms and waited, eyeing her. I assessed the length of her arms and the muscles in her legs, trying to guess how long it would take to pin her down.

Not even her eyes moved. "You heard me," she said again.

I laughed some more. "Well, excuse *me*," I said, but she didn't laugh with me. She surveyed me as I took off my socks, rolling them down into little buns, and then my underwear. It reminded me of my first trip to the doctor's office, or the first one I could remember, anyway. I was twenty-one or twenty-two, and was asked to take my clothes off for no reason that I could discern. Bemused, I had complied, charmed by the novelty of being naked in front of a new kind of stranger.

I kicked the pile of fabric off to the side with a bare foot. For the first time, X smiled. She was still on the mattress, but now her legs were pointing straight ahead of her, her arms propping her up from behind. One of her feet twisted in a lazy circle, over and over, like she was trying to crack a joint. Her smile turned into laughter.

"What?" I said. But she just kept laughing. "What?" I demanded again. My voice surprised me. It came out sharp, a little high.

The laughter stopped, but slowly, as if it had run its course, as if it had nothing to do with me at all. She nodded. "That's better." She threw out her palm, cocked her head, and squinted, as if presenting me to herself. Her eyebrow arched like a spider. I thought she was going to start laughing again, but with a decisive shake of her head, her hand gestured at one of the tarp-covered lumps along the wall. "Now go take that off."

I had a brat on my hands, that much was obvious. I strolled over to the lump, taking care to move as if no one was watching me. When I turned, her eyes were hovering around my ass. I crossed my arms and waited for her to look at my face again. They did, briefly, then returned to my body. Moving slowly to match her nonchalance, I reached for the tarp.

I had pictured myself pulling it off in one quick movement, like a magician yanking the tablecloth out from under a stack of cups, but it took three tries, each one resulting in a hollow woof as the tarp shuddered and crackled against itself. Behind me, X laughed some more. Pretending as if I didn't hear her, I dropped the tarp and turned toward her. I waited for her to say something, but she didn't.

"Now what?" I didn't try to hide my irritation, but my voice surprised me again. I sounded like a person requesting something from a person with the authority to refuse.

Eyebrow still arched, mouth screwed up, she looked as if I hadn't spoken at all. It was possible that she actually hadn't heard me—interspersed with pauses between songs, the music was still loud, voices and guitars and feedback roaring like an approaching army. But when she laughed, I could hear *her* just fine.

I prompted her again, keeping my voice calm. "Well?"

X looked at me, and then at the table I had just uncovered, and then back at me. She was drawing a pattern with her eyes. It was obvious what I was expected to do.

The table was upholstered in puckered black vinyl. Two metal stirrups stuck out from one end, and from the other protruded a padded headrest. It looked like a massage table, aside from the stirrups, which reminded me of a medical porno. Even as an adult, I'd only been inside a few doctor's offices, mostly for appointments related to my surgery. I no more remembered the examining rooms of my childhood than I did the rules for undressing in them, only the waiting rooms and lobbies that came first, or perhaps an elevator or, once or twice, a creaky flight of stairs, Mom following a little behind, her hand on my shoulder holding my upper body still while my legs moved slowly, agreeably forward.

I found myself putting my hands down on the vinyl and then, after a glance back at X, quickly lifting one leg, then the other. Despite myself, I clambered awkwardly up, the softness of my skin sticking to the table's hide. Its base stayed steady beneath me, bearing my weight without a sound or a shudder. I wondered how much something so well-made could have cost, and had a few guesses as to how someone living in a punk commune could afford it.

I looked back, half expecting X to be on her laptop again, but she was standing. It was weird to see her like that. Her posture was resigned, as if she were waiting for a bus that always ran late. When I had seen her the first time, out on the stage, she hadn't looked particularly imposing, not physically, anyway. Up close, I saw that she had at least two inches on me, maybe more.

"What?" I said.

"No," said X.

"What do you mean *no*?"

"Get on your back." She smiled as she said it. "Please."

I rolled over slowly, a little afraid of tipping the table. I could feel my muscles and my fat shifting as I moved. I thought about what my skin looked like as it pulled over the soft parts and the bony parts and the gristly in-between parts.

I settled my spine. The only thing I could see without turning my head was the ceiling. It was bumpy with slime-green stickers that once glowed in the shape of the Milky Way, and pocked with craters ranging in circumference from BB to bowling ball. When X's face slid into view above me, I became aware of the way the air in the room had become more dense.

That's when she touched my shoulder. I couldn't see it happening, but I wish I could have, just to remember it better: her eyes getting harder and harder, and then the sensation, somewhere below, smooth and cool. Her touch was light, if not gentle, but it left an impression. Aldrin's prints in the moon, or Cook's in the sand, rhythmically filling with the blood of their maker. Even if it's dangerous, or results in death, the first time is always special. I remembered her hand on the speaker back on the stage, her long fingers. Now two or three of them were touching me, concentrating a great weight in the tiny fraction of skin that melted into mine. She was closer to me than ever before. Her smell—strong, like healthy blood—was layered into the room's odors of dust and metal, and of its climate, manifested in a kind of dirty moisture. When she smiled down at me, I almost smiled back.

"You're tense," X said.

I'm always tense. Her room was cold, despite its humidity, but I could feel waves of heat flooding my body, as if the two of us were suspended in the firmament of a volcano. The music over the wall had gotten a little quieter, but something had changed; in the back of my mind, I registered that a new band was playing. The beat was like a hammer on a felt-coated anvil.

But nothing could relax me, no extreme of temperature, no vicissitude of volume. The more I thought about my tension, the more I could feel my muscles tighten, like a clock being wound by hand.

"I guess I am," I said. My heart was beginning to accelerate, which reminded me to breathe.

"Don't talk anymore," X said. "I'll let you know when it's time to speak."

Beach, bed, lungs. The acceleration slowed a little. The waves of heat receded.

She circled around the table, putting my eyes level with her hips. They looked good. I thought about what it would be like to touch them, to reach out and pull her down on top of the table, then pull us both to the ground, where our heads would burst like melons on the concrete floor. Thought about X lifting herself up above me like a gymnast, opening her legs, and then lowering them down onto my head. About being slowly rolled back into unconsciousness beneath the full weight of her body pressing spineward down into her sacrum, splitting it over the bridge of my nose, each half of my face crushed by—

The pain appeared at the top of my thighs, red and wet on the skin. I made a noise, instinctively jerking my head to look, but there was nothing down there but the narrow mark of retreated blood banding across the skin between my hips and my knees, a burning bisection of a birthmark. Whatever she had used to do it, something long and thin and hard, was now parallel with her right leg and concealed from me by her body.

"Stop thinking," X said.

She still sounded calm, but the temperature of her voice had plummeted. It was positively bureaucratic: authoritative, yet disinterested.

"I—"

"And what did I say about talking?"

I caught myself before I spoke again. Instead, I turned my head back toward the ceiling. I listened to my heart in my ears, the breath in my nose. *Beach, bed, lungs.* Her boots scraped the ground.

"Tense," X repeated herself. Another sensation of something moving across my skin. "And a little sweaty."

Her hands landed on my shoulders again, light as birds, before sliding up the hollows on the sides of my neck. How much pressure would she have to apply to really loosen me up? How much more pressure would it take to kill me?

Her hands stayed where they were, reminding me that my throat was nothing more than veins and arteries, taut little tendons, bruisable muscle, the thinnest of skin. Her hands were huge in relation to her wrists and arms. Sweat pooled under her fingers. With hands like hers, she could squeeze my throat until it popped open and everything inside spilled across my chest. I wanted a cigarette again.

"I don't know why that would be," said X. Her hands lifted, and the skin she left behind cooled under the sweat. Through the corner of my eye I saw her head dip and her phone glow. "Sixty-one degrees Fahrenheit in here, and you're naked. And yet you're warm. Maybe," her voice rose in register, to the pitch of playful dismay, "maybe you're running a fever!"

"I feel fine," I said, and the pain happened again, starting cold at my ears and springing hot down my chest and groin and ass, back to that same place on the front of my thighs. I didn't make any noise, but only because I was too shocked.

Her face came close. "That's the last warning," said X. "The next time you speak without being asked to, you will be punished."

The music behind the wall was slowing down. Now the beat plodded and churned, pumping ugly muscle inside me. A finger slid across my thigh, tracing the shape of the whole, wide welt.

"You can never know for sure if you have a fever, you know," said X. "At least at the beginning. You don't know when your body is heating up because you have no point of reference—until it's too late. Like a frog in a pot."

She disappeared. Whipping over the music came the sound of another tarp being moved, this one willowy as a tree branch. I followed the sounds inside my head, then turned to see X uncovering a smaller second table.

It was made of stainless steel, and laid out like servingware were metal implements, glimmering under the Christmas lights: scissors, scalpels, tweezers, needle drivers, tissue forceps, white plastic pods of color-coded sterilized needles. There were a lot of them—even I didn't recognize everything. Some were argent and some were coppery, some were naked and others were tipped in rubber or shrink-wrapped to a sheen. Surrounding the tools were unmarked bottles with twist caps, stacks of gauze, skeins of plastic thread. I spotted a white medical stapler, like a slender-headed xenomorph. I noticed the dildos, three of varying sizes, all cast from stainless steel.

There was something about the lighting in X's room—low, moted—and the noise behind the wall that made everything on the cart seem harmless, almost unreal. Like it was made for children. A memory, another from a doctor's office: There was a play set designed to look like a dentist's chair with two other kids, the three of us kneeling in a triangle around it. We were playing Doctor, of course, because we were in the doctor's office together, and all of us had spent lots of time with doctors. It's a memory I have every so often, one I'm always surprised by, because it's so vague and from so long ago. I realized that I was high, and had been for a long time. When had I come up? I didn't know.

"Excuse me," said X. Her voice commanded my full attention. "This is none of your business."

She had known before I did that I was watching her body as she leaned over the metal table. She was doing something with her hands that I couldn't see. I looked away, back up to the ceiling. The ceiling looked the same as it had before. Experimentally, I drummed my fingers on my thighs. They made silent but very phosphorescent waves that zoomed across the room. It appeared I was getting visuals.

I don't usually do a lot of drugs. They make me feel young, too young. But after Petra, I started doing them more than I ever had. It wasn't even that I had started enjoying them. I just couldn't stop myself when they were offered, which had never been difficult before. I would watch my hand go out and take whatever pill or tab or straw, and then I'd get high and think about what I was feeling and why it was bad. Another memory: steaming a medical cabinet with my breath, a long stroke through it with my finger, examining my shadow under the condensation. In my reflection, I'm naked. I don't remember why.

"What?"

X had reappeared above me. Now she was wearing an apron. Sexy black rubber. I looked at her, or at her chin, rather, then took my eyes back to the ceiling, drilling holes into its holes. I said nothing.

"It's okay," she said, touching my shoulder. "You can tell me."

Still nothing.

"I'm giving you permission to speak. What's wrong?"

I glanced at her from the corner of my eye. "It's fine," I said.

X laughed, gold glimmering near the back of her throat. Her tongue was wet in her mouth. She looked like a music video I liked when I was a kid. It had models playing unplugged electric guitars. Their mouths were lined with black and red, and they would periodically throw their heads back to laugh, silently offbeat.

"This whole thing goes both ways, you know." She leaned an elbow on the table, fingers stroking my arm again. They felt good and clean, like mouthwash. "You are silent until I say otherwise, and you speak when spoken to. Tell me, what's wrong?"

I swallowed. "It's fine."

"You're blushing now!" she accused. "Is it that fever? Or maybe," she lifted her finger and enunciated slowly, as if she was addressing a five-year-old, "you're thinking about something you shouldn't be thinking about?"

"No," I said, but against my will—always, always against my will—appeared Petra, trussed up like a turkey, my boot on her neck.

When it comes to play, I'm used to thinking about what the other person wants. If you run the fuck, that's your job. Mere pain or mere orgasm are easy—anyone can land a blow or hold a vibe. Topping means getting inside their head, knowing them. I'm used to that knowing. But in there, with X, I didn't know anything at all. My body hardened on the vinyl. My shoulders climbed closer to my ears.

"No," I said again.

"I'm not sure I believe you."

I was beginning to resent the effort it took to speak back. Every time I began to relax, there she was again, prompting, prodding, refusing to let me disappear.

"I'm not thinking," I insisted. My empty mouth felt full. My brain went slow. "Like you told me to."

"You're uncomfortable," she countered. She leaned her face so close I could feel her breath on my throat. She rested her elbow on my chest, digging it into my pecs, letting it slide down into my ribcage. Her fingers played in my hair.

"I'm fine," I said, gritting my teeth. The noise from over the wall was inside my head, getting louder and louder, which I only noticed because it stopped for a moment, long enough for me to turn my head away from her and toward it, but then I felt her hand on my chin. She pulled my face back to hers.

"Open your mouth," she said. I fought, but she held firm. "Open it," she cajoled, soft as a kiss.

I opened, wondering, with a stab of panic, what my breath smelled like. I couldn't remember the last thing I ate. The concept of food felt as far away as Camille, as Dubai, as the sun. Watching X's eyes move, merciless, fast as a rattler's tip, I could feel my body segmenting beneath hers, the pieces floating apart like loosed balloons. She smiled big and wide, and then in an instant, her face was empty. It retreated and then came close again, her hand still deep in my hair, the other propping her up on the table, so close to my hip I could feel the negative space between us.

Her proximity so momentous. Thought I was gonna laugh. Her skin hard, bones harder under her skin. Everything moved with perfect precision—her hips, her mouth, her hand when it touched me. Her tank top tight, low-cut. I looked there because the alternative was her eyes, and I couldn't handle that.

"Oh dear," X said.

Oh dear. That bolt of fury you feel when the name-tagged person behind the desk informs you that something is Wrong. Suddenly even more self-conscious than before. A molar chipped? Blisters in my throat? My head twitched against her hand, and there it was, the pain again, this time so close to my cunt that a fresh cascade of sweat shivered beneath my hairline, nausea bellied up my throat.

She didn't say anything, and neither did I, but only because I didn't have the chance—the noise beyond the wall started up again. Her hands left me. When I lifted my head to see why, she was locking the door. She walked past me to the smaller metal table, where she took two sterile gloves from a cardboard box. The gloves were dusted and matte, not shiny like her boots. I'm not allergic to latex, but she didn't ask either way.

"There is something wrong, even if you won't tell me what," X said. She pulled on the gloves. "So I'm going to give you a little examination. Just to make sure."

I laid my head down so she was no longer in my field of vision. Just the slime stars, the horizon of over-the-wall. Beyond it, people stomped and whistled, but the music dimmed.

There she was. In her gloved hand was a thermometer, a slender purple rectangle with a rounded metal probe at the end. Exam tables, white paper sheets. Mom's bed. Lights in my eyes. I felt myself tightening again, my asshole clenching. I didn't realize my body had lifted until she took my jaw in her hand, gently, and pushed me back down onto the vinyl. Most of the time it feels like my brain is in an airplane above the clouds, radioing directions to a robot a few miles below. I felt like this with X, but different, too. Though unpleasantly blurry, the body below me taking orders was in fact tethered to my senses. It felt good and bad.

"Open," X ordered, and with relief, I obeyed—it was an oral thermometer, thank god. Her lips parted in a porny smile, and under my tongue it went, settling into the convex softness beneath the muscle, dimpled as the surface of the table. The smell of blood intensified. I could feel mine moving around inside me, bubbling between my ears, whispering through my femoral vein. A few seconds later: *meep.* X pulled the rectangle out of my mouth and shook her head as she examined its little face. "Just as I suspected," she said.

Had I truly been about to speak, or was my intake of breath—rapid, gulping—a blameless, intentionless bodily function? It didn't matter. The pain came back, the wetness squishing between my legs. The blood smell changed. It was my blood, but in a way I'd never encountered it before, like the difference between coffee cherry on the branch and a cup of espresso. More memories clicked past: crashing a bike into the curb and flying over the handlebars. Crashing in the rollerblades, too, tearing up my knee because Mom didn't spring for a helmet or pads. Learning how to use needles by practicing on my thighs because I wanted to be good at it when I finally found a girl that would let me do it to her. Fistfights with exes and the boyfriends of exes and men who talked to my exes and, once, a client of Camille's who went from zero to sixty on PCP while I was doing security for their session. Whipping my boy, and other boys, strangers at parties who lined up wet for my kiss, people I didn't know and never will. And my period, of course, too much of a continuum to constitute a memory, crusting hard as a penny between my legs, straight women staring at me in the tampon aisle like I'm some kind of criminal.

I'm not usually interested in my own blood, but just then the scent was wonderful, lovely, erotic. I would never have imagined that it could have been so beautiful, so bright, so pleasant to observe and smell and, in a distant way, taste. My blood suddenly had the ability to interest me in the same way that a lover's would. Was it the drugs?

The slender pressure of the thermometer was replaced by something thicker and warmer. It was her finger, a latexed index, pushing through my lips and between my teeth. I gagged, but she kept going, drawing circles on my tongue. My tongue explored the finger, at first unconsciously, then tentatively, and then, as she didn't say anything or stop me, it moved with more confidence, pressing back against the sharpness of her nails, the hardness of her joints. But then more fingers joined it. Her hand was in my mouth, moving down my throat. The fullness ballooned. I gagged, my lips splitting at the seams. She pushed back and down, and I felt my eyes going with her, lifting, crossing, bulging.

Just when I thought my head was going to crack open, the hand would pause, wiggling a little, like a cat gearing up to pounce, and then try again, forward and retreat and return, a wise animal that knew when I needed to breathe, and when I didn't. I couldn't smell anymore, but I could now taste the bite of the latex, the salt of my skin. I was wet, I realized.

"If you bite down," X cautioned. "You will regret it."

I registered what she meant soon enough to resist the urge to chomp when the pain came back again, then again, and again, shooting up and down my thighs, steady and hard as hail. The air whistled around the implement, the apron creaking against her arm. The pain softened and intensified as it moved in me. When the implement slammed across my pubic bone, it overwhelmed the slithering sensation that came with it. I thought I heard X say something—*Still wet*, perhaps, but how could she know? She kept going, my body jerking on the table, my jaw on fire.

Relief came when the implement finally, briefly, moved to hammer on the thickest part of my thighs. The pain was so much less than when she hit my public bone that it almost felt good. The bile began to pool around her fingers. That felt good, too.

Suddenly, everything stopped. "Good," X said. The hand retreated from my throat and back into my mouth, then rested there, like a pearl inside a clam.

No urge to respond. Jaw blown out, eyes wet—if blood had been coming out of them, I wouldn't have been surprised. The tops of my thighs were somewhere else. I could have held her hand like that forever.

"Now I'm giving you another chance to tell me," X said. "What do you think is wrong with you?"

I only hesitated for a moment, but it was still too long. The pain came back. It was not what I had wanted—a fact that made me realize I was, to my surprise, wanting things. (There it was again: hum in a white room, lying on my back, gentling between sleep and awake.)

"Come on," she wheedled.

The hand in my mouth didn't move, as if daring me to harm it. It was in the internationally recognized fisting shape, with all the fingers together, meeting at the nails. When I tried to speak past it, I gargled like a broken drain. I didn't know what I was trying to say.

X giggled. Slobber slid down my neck, pooling on the black vinyl under my ears. It was humiliating, what she was doing to me, but I couldn't feel the humiliation. I wanted to feel it. My bleeding lips peeled apart to smile around her hand. I tried again, moaning, eager for her laughter.

She gave it to me, laughing and laughing, throwing her head back, Gilda-style, throat sharp as the prow of a ship, like, *Sure, I'm decent.*

"I can't understand you, little one!" she taunted.

This time, the pain came across my chest. Muscles I didn't even know I had hardened and cried out. Then the pain moved down, one inch at a time, over my nipples, my rib cage. I thought of my navel, the softness beneath it, and tensed more. When the pain crossed over there, too, I thought I really was going to puke.

"Excuse me."

The laughter had left her voice. I'd tightened my jaw—an infinitesimal amount, but enough to have disobeyed. The hand quickly slid away, the other pressing on my forehead to hold it in place. My mouth chased after it, my tongue sticking out hungrily, the suck of her leaving. From somewhere deep inside me, *come back* bubbled up, almost escaped.

"How can I examine you if you won't cooperate?" The gloved finger was tapping on my chest in a tempo of disappointment.

The tone of her voice had taken another step away. "I can't help you if you insist on fighting me."

I almost apologized. I shook my head instead, and felt the pain on my thighs. I wondered what it looked like down there. It felt like being waist-deep in swamp water: warm, slimy, mysterious.

"I really didn't want to do this," said X. "I really didn't."

Despair broke out over my skin. Above me, the Milky Way raged. Was she going to leave me?

I heard fabric running against itself, the clink of metal, and I felt things, light, like a bird's footsteps, crossing my torso. Straps. They tightened around my chest and my waist, tensing—for a moment, too much—but then the table shuddered, and they loosened again slightly. My body had tightened along with them, but when nothing landed on my throat, or below my hips, a little tremor of relief eased through me.

She leaned to adjust something beneath the table, and for an instant, her face was close to mine again. She smiled, maybe at me. I inhaled her scent. *Beach, bed, lungs.* I found I could move my legs if I wanted. I shifted them, twisting against the restraints, testing my limits as she pulled away and continued to adjust the straps. Though the table was as sturdy as ever, I felt like I was in a boat that was going somewhere. When she pulled out the stirrups from beneath the table, the tang of metal was light and true. I heard ropes creaking, sails snapping against the wind.

"Lift," X commanded.

Her voice was closer again. Her fingers were under my right Achilles, and following their pressure, I lifted it, bringing the other foot along. My legs went higher than I could hold them on my own, and then the stirrups lowered, settled, locked into place. I looked down. My heels were hooked into the stirrups, a few inches above my torso.

"Now relax," she said.

A command that closed with her name, the consonant shattering in my head. I felt the narrow pain sinking into the inside of my elbow again. Mom squatting in front of me, hands on her knees, looking into my eyes. "Relax," Mom said, frowning. "It wouldn't hurt if you would just relax." She reached out as if to touch me, but didn't.

"There you go," murmured X.

I heard a metallic crunch, and with a jerk, the stirrups lifted. The crunch came again—a crank, the ripple of gears—and again, and again, and my legs continued to ascend, pulling apart a few centimeters with every shudder. Beneath her blood scent, I could smell myself.

I had my first and last pelvic exam a few years ago, and I didn't remember the stirrups ever going that high, and yet they kept going, up and up. I found myself resisting. It wasn't a choice.

It was my body, not me, that refused. But there was that pain again, this time on the underside of my thighs.

"I'm sorry," I gasped. Wet. Wetter.

She didn't say anything, but the pain came again. Not punitive, but acknowledging. As the air cooled on what felt like newly opened parts—fresh flesh, new meat—the warmth inside shifted. *Noted*, the pain seemed to say.

Even though I was straining against the wraps over my chest, even though, if I had been free, I might have run away from her, the spill, an ooze, moved up into my core, climbed out from my cunt, evaporated in the cold air.

"There you go," X soothed, and I felt the glove alight on my thigh. Petra coiled into my throat, under my head, soft as a dove, as my legs ratcheted up yet again. Sweat streamed from my forehead, armpits, elsewhere, down beneath me, spilling off the vinyl. What if she kept going, all the way vertical, a full inversion? My heart. My heart. I can't breathe.

The cranking stopped. My legs were lifted, but not so high that it hurt. Her hand was gone again. I couldn't see her. I craned my head. Where was she? I missed her. I wished she would touch me again, my face, my hair. Wanted to lick and kiss and bite her hand. Maybe even bite it off and then drink the blood.

Her face again. Now it was above me, shaking from side to side.

"This is unfortunate," X said. Her once-happy eyes were full of sorrow.

"What?"

The sorrow trembled like anime. "You're sick, little one," she whispered, pupils shining. "Very sick."

Mom and I driving to a hospital far away from our apartment. Mom leaving me to sleep there. *I'll be here in the morning.* Wished that X would come just a little closer and touch me again, and then she did. For the first time, her fingers on my arm lengthened into a stroke, a pet. The hair on my skin stood on end. Wanted more hair. Wanted more skin.

"I need to do a more thorough examination," said X. She went away again.

Of course I cried. I knew what she was going to do, but I wasn't angry. When I was a kid and I was bored, I would sometimes think about all the kids I hated, like Marcus, so I could make myself angry, to distract myself. But this wasn't like that.

Noises and movement down by my legs. Two clicks in such close succession that they were almost a single sound. A glow from below. X had a flashlight. The clank of metal on the metal table.

I wanted my anger, but I couldn't find it. My body moved, fighting against the straps and the metal—every surface and edge, pulling me closed like a dead bug—and I looked down

on it, watching it, wondering when it would give in. I waited
for the anger, but it didn't come.

Red. I thought. *Red Red Red Red.*

But I didn't say it. Would she have honored it? I don't know. I
don't care.

When Jacq exported, we threw them a big party. We did stuff
like that during the first wave, partied like when we were baby
gays raising money for our friends' new pussies and chests and
chins. Jacq's party was supposed to be cheeky like that. Laugh
so you can't cry, etc.

"It's not forever," we kept saying, aware that this might not be
true. JACQ'S MOVING, said the invite post, like they were pulling
up stakes for Philly instead of a different continent.

We may have been lying to ourselves about what exporting really meant, but everyone loved Jacq. For them, we would have
gone all out anyway. Petra and I spent the day before the party
baking a funfetti sheet cake and decorating Mads's brownstone
with streamers and signs and pictures of Jacq from over the
years. Jacq at the dyke bar, a gibraltar glass in each hand. Jacq
licking hot sauce off a drag queen's tits. Jacq running on an
Oregonian beach behind their collie, Billy Bob, may he rest in
peace.

The next day, we had everyone over to Mads's, a bunch of people I don't see anymore because they've either died or exported.

Or because of Petra. Instead of cutting the cake into tidy slices, we all lunged to scoop handfuls and throw them at Jacq. We pushed them around for hugs, smearing the buttercream on everyone in arm's reach. When the cake was nothing more than a pile of grey sugar, we picked Jacq up and carried them out into the backyard, crowd-surfing them in the sunshine behind the brownstone. We didn't want to, but we cried, all of us— Petra, Camille, Maxine, Nino, Mads, Prinz and Ahmed, Leslie and her polycule. Jacq laughed and cried, their face brightening with every person they greeted, spoke to, remembered with.

We partied until it was time to take Jacq to the airport for their 6:50 a.m. flight. Clutching the carrier case for their cat, Diamanda, wild-haired Jacq got into Nino's truck, and we all followed in a caravan of cars and vans and a couple motorcycles driven by the twelve-steppers among us, sober-smacked on Red Bulls and cake frosting. Honking like maniacs as Jacq and Nino went on to the terminal, our caravan pulled into the park and ride, where we waited for their plane to take off. There was no way to know for sure which one was Jacq's, so we screamed and waved our hankies, repurposed for farewell instead of flagging, at every single plane until almost 8:00 a.m.

As we shared the dregs of an energy drink on the hood of her car, Petra slid her arm around me and pressed her face into my shoulder. She didn't like crying in front of other people; it was one of the reasons why her tears were so precious.

"It's not fair," she said.

It wasn't fair, but then again, it was more fair than we could have ever hoped. The state wanted unwanteds out, and not everyone got to decide how they were removed. But in the way that these mechanisms tend to work against their own ostensible ends, the unwanteds were the people who had the hardest time finding a way to leave. None of us would have thought Jacq, a brown poz punk, would pull it off—not legally, anyway. But they had. A Kiwi LGBT nonprofit created an artist residency for Americans, a sort of refugee launchpad to naturalization through the humanities, and they were the inaugural pick. Jacq was talented, but Jacq was also lucky. They knew it. We all knew it.

"Well," Petra said. Her face reappeared, swollen, wet with tears. She whisked below her eyelids with her fingers. "We'll visit."

I don't mind a convenient lie here and there, but something about this one pissed me off. I looked around us, at our friends sitting on their own hoods, at their big clowny grins waning in the dawn. We were never going to visit Jacq—with what money and what papers?—and they were never coming home, not for a very long time, anyway. Remembering that fact turned our hanky-waving stupid, our smiles haggard. I had never liked Jacq's art (kaleidoscopic murals about "identity" in color profiles that seemed designed to trigger migraine), but it had turned out to be the difference between escape and whatever was going to happen to the rest of us. It wasn't the first time I kicked myself for not learning how to do cunt sculpture or something.

I looked at Petra. Her face was wet, but she was smiling. I could see where her wrinkles would someday deepen, which reminded me of the ones that were already curving along my mouth, propping up my nose like a Roman arch. God, she could be stupid.

####

The first time Petra and I broke up, we'd been together for almost two years. I can't remember what we were fighting about. The argument has a domestic feel in my brain, like maybe I got mad because she left dishes in the sink again. But it also feels like it could have been my fault. Maybe I said something mean when I was drunk. Or maybe it was my fault in the sense that Petra did something and then blamed me for reacting to her. I wasn't the only one who got mean when I was drinking.

The thing about Petra and me is that we never fought well. It's just how it was. When things were good, she could always come up with an astrological explanation for it—moon this, retrograde that—but when they weren't good, she had her standard accusations at the ready. I was cold, she said. I was emotionally unavailable. I was withholding. I shared more of my feelings with the strangers I had sex with than I did with her. With Petra, it was always my fault.

Whatever started it, that particular fight was one of the bad ones where you end up toe to toe in the living room, pulling away from each other only when you need to take something off a shelf and throw it against the wall.

"You can't be in control all the time!" yelled Petra. "I'm a fucking human being. I get to have a say, too."

She threatened to leave me. That's when I felt everything inside my head get cold. The colder I got, the less I could hear.

"Won't you please just talk to me?"

I read her lips. I thought about putting my fist in the wall.

"Please?"

More screaming. When she tried to touch my arm, I walked out. If I put a fist through Petra, I couldn't drywall her.

I went to Camille's. *we're done*, I texted her on the way. *fucking done*. It wasn't the first time I had slept over because of Petra. Camille had recently inherited the couch when a friend exported to Bishkek, of all places, during the first wave. I called in sick the next day, so Camille and I could smoke and drink our coffee together once she woke up for lunch.

"Thank god Sasha left," I said. "I was sick of sleeping on that pile of rocks." Sasha was nice enough, but not so nice that I'd rather have him in New York than get a good night's sleep.

Camille wanted to get to the point. "So," she said, with serious eyebrows. "Are we gonna talk about all this or what?"

I would have rather eaten glass. "No."

She didn't push me on it, but I could feel her thoughts as she got up to turn on the POMPEII IV for another round. She popped open the can of coffee b'ns—CHIC-O-YEET—as she assessed the kettle, face impassive except for the telltale curls at the corners of her mouth, like Bergman biting back on righteous Allied fury. In silence, she refilled it.

I always ended up at Camille's after one of our dumb fucking fights. She wouldn't say it, but I knew that she had wanted me and Petra to break up. Camille thought I was incapable of having a normal relationship, even with someone as fucked up as I am, and that I should just get used to being alone. I could tell by way she was sipping her drink, running her acrylics down the spine of her French braid, eyeing me, with suspicious focus, from across the table. She didn't have to come out and say it. She didn't need to.

Well, she would fucking know, I thought. Camille was the only person who was worse at dating than I was. "If they can't beat me, I don't join 'em" was one of the annoying sad girl jokes that came out when she was super wasted.

"You know, honey," Camille said, her voice quieter than I was used to hearing it. "I can't ignore all of this forever."

I didn't ask what she meant by that, and she didn't elaborate. The POMPEII IV went off, and she stood up to retrieve the water. When her back was turned, I ashed in her cup.

I left not long after. If I'd stayed, we might have talked more, and then I probably would've put a hole through *her* wall, only she would have wanted to fight over it, and my money was on her stiletto nails. Camille didn't mind standing up to me; she only lost her ability to defend herself with the people she fucked. I called Ahmed to see if his couch was available, but Prinz had been hit by a delivery truck (LONG PIG UPCYCLED

MEATS | 10% PROTEIN, 0% CRUELTY) while he was delivering takeout on his bike.

"There was like an insurance loophole, so they're not covering any of it. You know we'd have you in a heartbeat, but we had to rent out the dining room," he said. I could hear Prinz yelling something about the wifi in the background. "Sorry, babe."

There was nowhere to go, unless I wanted to spend the night outside, so I went home to Petra. I slept on the couch, and when I woke up at ten the next morning, we started talking. We talked until the sun went down. It was excruciating, as processing always is. That's why dykes like it so much.

That night, there was supposed to be an astrologically significant meteor shower. Something to do with Venus. This was a good thing, Petra explained, because our Venus signs were complementary, and that mattered, especially because our sun signs were mortal enemies.

A little after twelve, we went up on the roof. We wrapped ourselves in a blanket and looked up for a long time, passing a beer back and forth. The light pollution wasn't too bad, but we didn't see anything out of the ordinary. It was nice, though. When was the last time we did this, we asked each other. We should do this more often.

It's funny. After everything, I don't even remember what Petra's sign is. I still don't know Camille's.

####

Camille wants me to come to the Three Seasons with her. "Please? Pretty please?" Her hands pray.

When Camille asks me to do something I don't want to do, I think about Ariana. Ariana was this preppy little top that Camille fell in love with after everything with Flávia. Things were fine with them for a few months, but one day, when Camille was out of town with a sugar daddy, Ariana invited me over to hang out, and I ended up proving she was a switch on the kitchen table. It wouldn't have been a big deal if things had been good between her and Camille, but they were going through a rough patch because Ariana had never dated a hooker before, and she was having the standard annoying feelings about it.

I knew I should have told Camille what happened, but I didn't. I didn't care if it hurt her, at least not in the moment, with Ariana's face smooshed up against the varnish, her right arm twisted behind her back. Ariana dumped Camille not long after her trip, no explanation. Camille always blamed herself, but I knew it was my fault.

I never did tell her. I will someday. Just not today. Until then, I figure I sort of owe her.

We take a car to the hotel. "Don't worry. It'll be fun," Camille says. "I'd rather do this than fuck him in the butt any day." She hates fucking him in the butt.

The regular is waiting for us in the room he rented, seated on the bed, his hands folded on his slacks. His shoes are off, and his coat is hanging neatly off the back of a chair. The lamp by the bed casts shadows on the rash-colored wallpaper. After briskly confirming the contents of the envelope on the credenza (he always brings an envelope sealed with a Batman sticker), Camille snaps into character.

"You don't mind if my friend joins us, do you?" she purrs, taking my hand. The regular has been pestering her about getting cucked for a long time now. She'd always ignored his requests until it occurred to her that I could help her play a little trick on her trick.

"Oh, I don't know about that," he says mildly. He calls himself Hector. He has thick, curly grey hair around the sides of his head and a very straight mustache. "I refuse to share my wife with another man." His voice is flat, like a court stenographer reading back his notes. Hector is a terrible actor.

I lean against the wall and watch, gnawing on a hangnail, while they build the scene together. Camille is Hector's horny trophy wife who can't be satisfied with a tiny-dicked beta soy boy bitch like him. Hector is furious that she's brought a massive-cocked stranger to their marital bed. Coiled next to Hector on the comforter are a few bundles of white cotton rope, their sexual deus ex machina. While Hector protests ("No. How dare you," he says without raising his voice), Camille begins tying his arms to his torso. She leads him to the chair, tosses his coat on the floor, and, taking more rope, completes her capture.

Hector is smitten with Camille. Every time she gets close to him, he leans his head to shorten the distance, and every time, she gracefully pulls away. It reminds me of this cat Petra had, Godiva. Godiva adored Petra. She followed Petra around the apartment, and laid on her chest when she was in bed, licking her throat. Godiva hated me. Maybe she could tell the feeling was mutual. But as soon as I had her kibble bag in hand—or even better, a can of Fancy Feast—she was all over me, meowing like I was the last sucker on Earth.

Even though I'm the star of this show, Hector hardly seems to be aware of me in the corner. Tired of waiting for my cue, I reach for the digital clock on the night table as if to check the time, and he takes the bait. When Hector notes the size and shape of my hands—a little too small, a little too slender—he does a double take, the second one long and hard. The smile drops from his face. His back stiffens, and he scoots his feet against the carpet.

"Oh," he says to Camille. "I thought you meant—"

"This is my friend," purrs Camille. "I like my friend a lot. I was hoping you could be friends, too."

"I don't think—"

"Don't you want to make me happy, Hector?" Camille is tracing finger shapes on his skull, rolling her eyes at me over his head.

It takes a little convincing, but in the end Hector does want to make Camille happy, and nothing makes her happier than being in charge. She likes it even more than money, but I guess it's sort of the same thing. He walked into this room expecting to see Camille get fucked by a big, veiny dick, and now he's happily suckling a piece of silicone, gazing up at me like a boy at his daddy, a fresh pump of tears streaming down his cheeks every time he gags. Camille's clothes stay on. It took her forever to get into the complicated lingerie under her strappy streetwear.

"Aw," says Camille, playing with one of the curls on the back of Hector's head. "Does it make you sad to know that this fake cock is bigger and better than your real cock?" She laughs and pulls the curl out straight, pulling his head back with it. "This one stays hard, too."

Hector's eyes flutter. His head wobbles back and forth, but he keeps sucking. If my cock was actually attached it would hurt. Thank god it isn't. Stunt cocking is so easy, sometimes I think I was born to do it.

I can't see Hector's dick, but his pants are tight enough that I should be able to know if he's hard. He stays soft, even when Camille gets down from the bed to rub her ass or her tits in his face. She sees me looking.

"It's like this all the time," she says, letting her hand flop into Hector's lap. He flinches, squirming against the ropes. His eyes look like they're going to pop out of his head, but he keeps sucking. She assumes a pout. "It's useless. I do my best to look pretty for him, and yet it's never enough."

Hector is shaking his head now, cock going *gurg gurg gurg* in his throat. Camille cackles. The whole thing cheers me up enough to smile. His eyes strain as she moves behind him and out of sight again. She pushes the back of his head, and I worry for a second that he's going to puke all over me. "Keep sucking, hole," she snips, using her acrylics to delicately tweeze something—maybe a piece of lint—from his curls.

Hector has been Camille's client for years, even longer than I've been around. The worse the laws get, the shittier the johns, but Camille says that Hector always pays her rates without complaining, books every month without fail, even tips sometimes. Not that he's a hero for not being a rapist, but considering how bad things have gotten, it sort of endears him to me. Plus, I appreciate his enthusiasm. It's a little hot, actually.

Camille turns to adjust her hair in the mirror, then makes a face at me in the glass, like, Does this look okay? I shove Hector's head down a little more—*gurg*—and nod. Perfect, I mouth. When we're done here, she has a date with that boy-dyke/girl-dyke couple she's been talking about, and she wants to look cute.

####

When I woke up from surgery, I was back in Mom's bed.

To my left, the white noise machine was going. Above my head, the window gaped. I felt stiff and sore and a little constrained, like I was bundled in bubble wrap. My body was a long shape tucked under the blue comforter. I could move my arms just enough to raise it so I could see beneath.

I was naked. It was bad. Instead of taking away my tits, they had taken away my whole body and put me back in a different one, a kid's body. They had given me the wrong surgery. I was back at the beginning and would have to repeat my childhood. I dropped the comforter.

I was in the body of the child I had once been, the child that had lived in this apartment and slept in this room when Mom wasn't home. They were all in on it together, I realized: the hospital, the government, the social workers and psychologists who had reluctantly approved the surgery. And Mom, too. They had all conspired to put me back in here, back with this blue bed and black window and grey wall, where I would have to do the hellish thing all over again.

I woke up again, but now I was in a hospital bed in a room full of hospital beds. Whoever I was dating at the time—I can't remember their name anymore—was standing beside me. They were reaching for my hand and speaking in a high, far-away voice, like they'd just sucked the helium out of a birthday balloon.

Then they were wheeling me out of the hospital. Now that weird voice was coming from behind me, bouncing back and

forth like a metronome. Their long brown hair tickled my eyebrows when they leaned over me. Then they were helping me
out of the passenger side of their Nissan and into our apartment,
a completely different one from Mom's. Our apartment was on
the third floor, not the first; we went up the cold stairwell, their
arm around my waist. And of course Mom wasn't there, just as
she hadn't been in her bedroom when I woke up before. When
my girlfriend opened the front door, a cat bounced down from
the windowsill, yellow with early spring, and embroidered itself
around their legs, in and out and around. No one else was there.

My girlfriend helped me into our room, and I laid down on
my own bed, my hands resting on the bandages on my chest. I
couldn't believe it was flat, just like I had wanted for all those
years.

It went so good, said my girlfriend. They were wearing a sun-
dress. It's finally all over.

But I didn't feel good. My girlfriend brought me a cup with a
metal straw, and as I drank the water, I listened to the noises
inside me and outside me. Bubbling, breathing. A car honking,
a siren, birds, kids on the tennis court across the street. The
static of being alive.

Everything was as it should have been, but I couldn't believe
that my girlfriend was my girlfriend, or that I was where I was
supposed to be. Was my chest flat because of the surgery or was
it flat because I was a little girl again? It was true that I was an
adult and that everything was different than I had dreamed, but

it also wasn't true, and I knew this because the ceiling in our apartment was the same one from Mom's room.

Where's Mom, I asked my girlfriend.

They frowned. You told me your mom was dead, they said.

For a few moments, I didn't do anything. I just lay there, sensing things, only certain that I wasn't dead because I was awake. My head felt like it was stretched tight over a drum. I could smell leather, poppers, mildew, rubbing alcohol. From where I was, lying down on the mattress, I could see that the table and the cart had been covered with their tarps, returned to their original lumpiness, and pushed back to their places along the wall. I shifted slightly, and my skin screamed. I froze again.

The light that had been reaching over the wall from the main area of the warehouse was now off, but I could still see with the glow of the Christmas lights. X's laptop, duffel, and backpack were gone. X was gone, too.

Maybe I could catch her, I thought frantically, if I ran outside right now. Maybe I woke up because she had only just left, and something—the door closing, her keys jingling—had shaken me from sleep. Oh god, how could I possibly have fallen asleep?

Every movement burning, I got up and dressed as fast as I could. It wasn't just my legs, stomach, and chest that hurt. My back did, too, and I wasn't sure why. I was grateful there wasn't a mirror in her room. I didn't want to see any of it.

As I was shutting the door behind me, I heard footsteps. Someone was coming down the hallway, but the light was too dim for me to make out any details. I waved, but its pace didn't change, the head stayed pointed forward. I stepped in front of it, and slowly, almost grudgingly, it cruised to a stop.

"Whose room is this?" I pointed at the door behind me.

Coke-bottle glasses rippled, St. Sebastian pendant gleamed. In their hand was a mason jar filled to the brim with something dark and viscous. Mouth slightly agape, as if they were shocked or still high from last night, the person just looked at me.

"Do you live here?" I asked.

Mason Jar rubbed the bridge of their nose. A green rattail snaked around their throat. They wore an unbuttoned aloha shirt, periwinkle blue with white palm trees, that was three sizes too big. Beneath it was a black T-shirt that said BE CRIME.

BE CRIME. Camille and the crowd and all the rest of it felt like it had been years ago.

"No," Mason Jar said. "Volunteered for the show."

"But you know the people who live here?"

Mason Jar just looked at me. How could they have volunteered for the show if they didn't, the look suggested.

"Do you know X?" I asked.

"Ex?" Never had a single syllable been uttered so slowly.

"X! You know—" I began. But all I could think of to describe her was that she smelled like blood. "Tall. Uh . . . short hair. Buzz cut. They were working the show for a while."

"Oh. X. Her."

"Yes!" I cried. She was a her, then. Mason Jar's chipped black fingernails disappeared against the blackness in the glass. Their green eyeshadow was smudged, but their eyebrows were too neat for that to have been an accident. "Where is she? Is she still here?"

Mason Jar shook their head. "She's gone now."

"Gone?" The hallway shrank like a hot coal.

"Yeah," said Mason Jar. "Exporting. If they don't find someone to replace her by next week, I get her room."

"Exporting? Today?"

"No. Next month."

The relief reminded me that it hurt to breathe. The fear of never seeing her again outweighed the question of whether I should go to urgent care.

"Where is she now?" I asked. "Is she still here?"

Mason Jar leaned forward and shoved the door to X's room. It creaked open in that interminable way that shitty doors do. "Doesn't look like it," they said, peering into the fuzzy darkness. They were quiet for a moment. "Dibs on the mattress."

I left the warehouse as I had entered it, though much more slowly this time. I trudged down the alley and heaved my body up and over the fence, the second leg dragging behind the first. It didn't occur to me that I could have asked Mason Jar for an easier way out until I was on the other side.

I was too exhausted to care. Staring down at the rideshare app on my phone, I could already feel the sweet headache of an electronic air freshener clipped to the dashboard. I closed the app.

The longer I walked, the more I hurt. Bruises felt like they were spilling open, and every muscle ached, exhausted from flinching, clenching, tightening, brightening along my torso, through my back, between my thighs. The pain warmed as my muscles did, differentiating themselves from one another a little at a time. Soon I could identify where each pain came from, as might a studied butterfly its pins, were it alive to know. When I woke up on the mattress, my body had been a single slab of sensation. Now I could feel the length and breadth of bruises or cuts or whatever was happening on my shoulders, back, ass, thighs, legs. It made me think of a pencil sketch Petra put on the wall above our bed, of a naked woman tied to a stake surrounded by men with knives of every shape and size. The cursive script beneath her read: LA MORT PAR MILLE COUPURES.

I didn't allow myself to think about what it would feel like to sit again, let alone lie down. For my skin to bend over the openings, against the bone, and over the ripples of inflammation

The stairs to Camille's apartment took longer than they ever had before. I stopped to rest on the second landing. For the first time since I moved in, I was happy that my bed was only a few steps from the front door. Keys: dropped. Coat: dropped.

"You're here," said Camille. Still in her latex, she was at the stove, poking at something in a pot with a spatula. Her face was pretty and long-suffering, like Olivia de Havilland when she's been done wrong by a weak-willed man.

"I'm here," I agreed. I sat down and slumped backward, too tired to remove my shoes, or to care if she was mad that I disappeared without even a text.

"Where'd you end up last night?" Her voice didn't sound curious. It didn't sound like anything at all. Her eyes were red as lollipops.

"I don't know," I said. I couldn't think of anything else to say. "What happened to you?"

She took the tongs off the magnetic strip on the wall and plunged them into the pot, withdrawing a girthy aubergine dildo. "Nothing of consequence," she said. Boiling water dripped on the linoleum. Steam curled through her hair, misted the latex.

"Oh." I slumped back onto the couch and closed my eyes.

####

The Hudson River looks like lava strewn with garbage. I wouldn't have noticed, but a man slammed his shoulder into mine, spinning me around so I was suddenly face-to-face with New Jersey. I curled my fist, ready to crank and return it right into his fucking face, but when I spun back around, he was gone.

I turned, and turned, and turned again. Nobody around, except a guy pushing a shopping cart all the way on the other side of West Street. I pulled my baseball cap lower on my face, bumped up the audio on my murder podcast until my ears hurt, and kept going.

Instead of heading home after work, I took advantage of the weather and went on a long walk. It was warmer and wetter than it used to be at this time of year, but what else is new? Camille's usually not home until late, so I spend a lot of time at her apartment alone. After living with Petra for a few years, I thought I would enjoy a little solitude, but I have to admit it got old fast. Sometimes, when I'm sitting there on the couch, I look up from my phone thinking I've heard something in the apartment, only to realize that all I've heard is silence. It wasn't long before I started to catch myself waiting for Camille to get home. It was worse when the power was out, which of course only seemed to happen when I was alone.

It's weird to miss someone. Camille is one of the few people I feel relaxed around. I never got there with Petra, and we lived together. Maybe we were close at the beginning, but it didn't take long for us to start grating on each other. She wanted to get closer. I got jealous of my alone time.

The water keeps pace with my steps. I feel like getting in a fight. I wish that guy would come back and hit me again. I spin fast to see if anyone's behind me, but no one is. *Beach, bed, lungs.*

"God," says one of the podcast hosts. "Andrea Yates."

"It's just such a horrifying story," says the other host.

"Truly horrifying. Five children. You know, the baby was only six months old."

The sun is low, burns my eye. I click back through past relationships, Petra and all the ones before her. Which partner did I have comfortable silences with, if not with her?

X slinks into mind, and I am forced to consider her, as if she could even be included in this retrospective of lovers and playmates. I try to calculate the number of words exchanged between us. There couldn't have been many. A couple hundred, maybe? Most of them were hers, anyway. Screams don't count as speech. The podcast sounds tinny in my ear.

"That's why it's so tragic," says the first host. "She thought she was saving her kids. Like what do we even do in that kind of scenario? How do we stop someone who wants to do something awful for what they are convinced is a good reason?"

"You always hurt the ones you love," the other host replies. The reference is a deep cut for regular listeners. She's quoting another serial killer, a Canadian who offed his wife and kids before scratching out the eyeballs in every family photo in their two-story, four-bedroom home. He said it to one of the cops who apprehended him. His affect was so strange, the cop reported later, he couldn't tell if the killer was mocking him or being serious.

As the wind picks up, the streets empty. It's a relief, and not just because I hate people. I've started seeing X. I mean, it's not really her. But I still see her, or think I do—on my walks, during my commute, once when I went downstairs to the bodega for a midnight loosie.

The first time I thought I saw her, it was a few days after the warehouse. I only have a few white undershirts, and I was worried about staining them with blood and ooze, so I went to the pharmacy for some bandages. Fulton was crowded with rush-hour foot traffic—moms with strollers and Dunkins, dads pooling to gossip outside the masjid—but I saw her, leaning against the brick of a corner building. When I rubbed my fists in my eyes like Ebenezer Scrooge and looked again, she had melted into the lens of the surveillance camera above her head. I could have sworn I saw her shoulders disappear into the crowd, but it turns out that everybody has a pair.

You would think that these visions would fade along with the bruises she left, and yet my head still whips around and my heart still grinds to a halt at each stark figure rounding a corner and every boot that shines in a headlight. All manner of gross things begin happening in my body and mind, though both know that my chances of seeing her again decrease with every passing day. The end of the month is only a few weeks off. Even with a generous, liberal interpretation of what Mason Jar told me, the very last day I could reasonably hope to see her is the thirty-first. And then what?

I look behind me. A black coat becomes a shadow. There's a boot, but it's canvas, not leather, and it's abandoned, footless, by an overturned shopping cart. When the ghost of X ends up ghosting me, my unwanted hope squishes under its own weight, like the cherry of a cigarette put out before its time. But I still keep my eyes peeled. I still look.

I wish I'd never met her. I wish she didn't exist. People who don't exist can't export, after all.

The Tuesday after I met X, I went to work, as usual. The train was late, as usual. As usual, there was a smear of human shit on the second flight of steps coming out from underground, and the same orange pile of fried rice on the pavement outside my office. The coffee from the break room was burnt, as usual. I was using a thumbnail to scratch something white and gluey off my shirt when I realized it was the same one I'd worn the

Friday before, when I had met her. It was as if the intervening days hadn't happened.

Work had slowed almost to a standstill. Instead of taking this as the gift it was, Aisha was all stressed out about productivity. Triskit bobbling like an infant in her arms and anxious wisps of hair clouding her ponytail, she went to talk to Forrest in his glass box of an office. I watched their lips move for like five minutes, Forrest looking resolutely at his monitor, before she came back.

"Will you hold him for a second?" Aisha asked, dropping Triskit in my lap. She was going up to Forrest's supervisor on the next floor. Perhaps *she* knew what was going on.

Triskit and I stared at each other. This neck pillow with a face was what fifteen thousand years of domestication and a couple hundred of inbreeding had wrought. If Triskit could be descended from wolves, maybe there was hope for our human bodies in this hellscape yet. Maybe some hardy New Yorkers would survive long enough to evolve, to learn to thrive on their own piss. It would be *Dune*, but naturally, without those crazy suits. Or Sting.

"What an ugly little guy you are," I whispered. Triskit wagged his Slim Jim tail. When I looked up, I caught my reflection looking back at me from the black computer screen. Bagged eyes. Hadn't had a haircut in months. Underfed. I don't think I'd ever looked worse in my life, and I couldn't even see the carnage under my clothes. I laughed so hard Triskit flipped out of my lap and trundled under Aisha's desk.

It wasn't long before she was back. "They said they're hard at work on it." Aisha smiled as she reached for her ponytail, split it in two, peeled it apart to tighten it against her skull. "Something on the back end."

She called for Triskit and picked him up, then settled into her chair to wait. If there was a god, Aisha would squeeze her hair so tight she'd pop an aneurysm, and we could all go home for the day. I checked the time. I was late for my hourly break.

The hallway was empty except for a woman walking a few yards ahead of me. I didn't recognize her, so I figured she was from another office. Her pants were black and a little baggy, but I could tell she had an incredible ass. I followed her into the bathroom.

We peed for almost the same length of time. We washed our hands next to each other, but she finished first. She held the door open for me, smiling. Normally, I wouldn't have given her a second thought, even with that ass, because most women are straight and who cares. But she was queer. I could tell.

Encountering another homo in the wild still feels like seeing a celebrity. They're easy to spot when they look like me, but I can clock them even when they don't. Femmes notice me (not because I'm gorgeous, although I am), and straight women don't, unless they're looking for something to fuck or fear. And even though I looked like hell warmed over, she saw me. I saw her right back. I wanted to see more.

As she was leaving the bathroom, she dropped her phone on the ground. I went for it. We got to talking. She played with her hair. I played with my keys. I gave back her phone, and she gave me her number, and then I watched her walk away down the hall.

The next day, I went to her bleach-smelling Bushwick apartment after work. I don't know why. I hadn't made an effort to get laid in months—I'd given up. I didn't know what was different, except that something was, and it had to do with X. I brought my favorite cock with me for good luck.

The windows were small and draped. Her couch was red corduroy, a good sign that she was insane, but I took my shoes off anyway. On top of the coffee table were tarot cards, spread out like a bunch of big coasters. Great.

"Have a seat," she said. A flicker of panic—did I really think it was going to be better this time around? When I lowered myself onto the couch, I remembered my body. It had only been a few days since the warehouse, and the bruises were livid purple, the scabs still soft to the touch. Not that it mattered. She was never going to see them. That made me feel better.

She brought me a glass of water and we chatted, running through the standard getting-to-know-you virtue signaling to weed out weirdos, trust fundies, neolibs. Prison abolition? What's the most censored social platform? Coke or Pepsi? She didn't work in my office building, but had been there meeting a friend for coffee. She told me about her job as a barber. I imagined a straight razor against her neck. What would happen if she flinched? How far would the blade have to slip to take her from human to something else?

Even though it wasn't yet on my body, I could feel my cock getting hard. I interrupted her to ask if I could tie her up. She said I could. I stripped her, then told her to go lie on the bed, facedown. I got my ropes out of my bag and tied her in place. Wrists and ankles, nothing fancy. I was surprised by how relaxed I was, how easy it all felt.

For a long time, I didn't do anything except look. I hadn't seen a naked woman in months, aside from Camille, of course. Her ass was big and wide. It was firmer than I like it, but the skin was soft. I stroked it, then gently slapped it, listening to hear what sound it would make. I knelt down and examined the little hairs, the way they darkened around the inner thighs. I looked beneath for more hair. There it was. I wanted to grip it in my fingers and pull hard, but I restrained myself.

More spanking, playful to start. I touched the rest of her, too. I wanted to soften her, ease her into it, until there was no more resistance, no tensed muscles, no ticklish jerks, nothing.

Quietly, I got the rubber cane out of my bag. She wasn't expecting the first hit. Her thighs gave perfectly, but she didn't make a sound. I hit her again, and then again. No noise. Interesting. I got into a rhythm. Her shoulders shook, but she didn't struggle against the ropes or speak, let alone ask me to stop.

I was glad I couldn't see her face. It's better that way, especially if it's someone I don't know very well and they can handle a lot of pain. But as I kept going, breathing faster and faster, I started to get a bad feeling. It wasn't like the sickness I had been feeling since the breakup, the nausea every time I tried to get my dick wet. It was more psychological. With her face down, I felt like she was hiding from me. I started to get angry.

"Hey," I said. Her ass was beginning to resemble her red corduroy couch. "Hey."

She didn't reply. I prodded her shoulder with the cane. I really felt like I needed to see her face. "I'm going to turn you over now," I warned her.

The head shook a little. A deep breath. "Okay."

Her voice was too quiet. I untied her as fast as I could. When she rolled over, her face looked normal, exactly the same as it had when we were talking about the weather. It was a smart face, both pretty and sad, but something about it disgusted me so much that I thought, for a moment, that I was dreaming.

"Are you okay?" she asked.

No. I forgot about her ass. I forgot about my cock. I wanted to hit her soft belly. I wanted to break her teeth.

"Hey," she said. She lifted herself up onto her shoulder. I thought about shoving the rubber cane up inside her, and my chest tingled. Finally I got wet. I felt the rubber in my hand. I thought about it some more. She made noises. Then she pulled it out and pushed me away.

She forced a hug on me before I left, but that was the worst of it. No aftercare, thank god. I pulled my coat on in the hallway and put my shoes on standing up. When I lifted each leg, the pain on the front of my thighs met the pain shooting down my shoulders and into my lower back, cobwebbing in red darts that sliced every time my meat twisted. I took my time going down the stairs.

It was late, and outside it was dark and quiet. The brownstones were neat as chocolate bars, the black-painted gates shut tight before them. The cold air filtered through my clothes to land on the newly cracked scabs. My body hurt. I wondered what it would be like to see X and go through all of it again, but over these bruises instead of virgin skin. It would be even more painful, even more terrifying. And I knew I would do it. In a heartbeat, if someone gave me the choice.

That's when I knew I needed to see her again.

A few years ago, I had this pup that loved getting scruffed like a real dog. Since humans don't have that baggy sack of skin behind our necks, my pup had to settle for being squeezed, hard, beneath her hair. She told me that she wanted it—she begged for it, in fact—but it always made her cry.

"Stupid bitch," I'd say. She'd hump my boot and I'd kick her, and she'd cry even more.

I didn't understand the point of rewarding an animal that resisted correction, but after we hung out a few times, she told me she didn't actually like pain all that much. She wanted to know if she could just be my puppy instead, the kind you pet and feed and train and let sleep curled around your feet at the bottom of the bed. I blocked her.

####

I didn't know where to start. Mason Jar said that X had moved out of the warehouse, so that was a dead end. But maybe there were other people living there who knew where she was staying until she exported. I decided to go back. I had three weeks until the end of the month.

When I went down into the train station, the sun was setting. When I came back up again, it was gone. The warehouse was a few blocks away. I put in my headphones and queued up the latest murder podcast episode. The hosts sounded even more like each other than they usually did.

"I just think awareness is such an important part of safety, overall," said one.

"It's a safety issue," agreed the other, or maybe it was the same voice.

"A safety issue for everyone, and women in particular. Now, you and I, we don't victim blame people if something bad happens to them. But if even just one more woman took a self-defense class or called the police when she wasn't sure, instead of just passing it off as an anxiety, then I'll have done my job, we'll have done our job, because—"

The murder podcast hosts used phrases like *victim blame* and *slut shame* and *bad apples*. They were talking about a recent news item: a woman on a London train had called the police because another passenger gave her what she described as a "very bad feeling." According to the police, three bombs were found in the other passenger's backpack.

"Who knows what would have happened," said one of the hosts, "if she didn't trust her instincts that day?"

"Absolutely," said the other.

"Now, no one is arguing that we can tell who is dangerous and who isn't just by looking at them. I would never suggest that—"

"We would never—"

"—But we have to stand up for ourselves, and for each other. And part of that is educating ourselves. When we look at other people, at strangers, what are the warning signs? We have to learn how to protect ourselves. We have to learn how to trust our guts."

"Our gut instincts."

"And I can see how some people might think we're being paranoid, but honestly, I think it's just realistic."

"I feel the same way. I say, if you see something, you should say something."

When X exported, I wondered, how would she do it? Would she take a train? Would she drive? As I rounded the corner on the warehouse, I imagined her getting on a big boat, a cruise ship like Marilyn and Jane, sliding through the Atlantic like a spoon through soup. To my right was the chain-link fence. I stopped in front of it and squeezed the diamonds again, squinting through the darkness and into the alleyway. I lifted a leg and felt the stiffness in my haunch. Some of the cuts—hashtagging my skin like the char on grilled ham—reopened if I moved too much. I decided to explore my other options before I tried to jump the fence again.

The front door was boarded shut and covered with SOLD signs, just like in an old movie. I couldn't believe it. Less than a week since I had been here and the warehouse was already kaput. Fuck. So much for Mason Jar's dibs.

Underneath the SOLD signs were even older pieces of paper. One of them, the flyer from the show, was still clean and glossy. Among the graffiti-esque scribbles, BE CRIME beamed. I made a mental note to text Syd. I didn't know if they knew X, but it was worth a shot.

I went back to the chain-link and saw what I hadn't noticed before—razor wire had been installed sometime since Saturday morning. I thought about climbing it, I really did. I even put a hand up, then a leg, but the pain stopped me from going any further. I wouldn't have made it over the razor wire anyway, not on my best day, and I hadn't had one of those in a long time.

The block was deserted. Wind stirred the empty lot across the street, and bits of trash flinched like startled women. A streetlamp slowly pulsed; I felt as if I was watching it through water. I wanted to go home, but all I had was a couch in Camille's apartment, and she wasn't even there. She had told me not to expect her back that night.

As I walked back to the train, I thought about X on her ship. I imagined her falling over the side and drowning. I imagined holding her underwater. I felt her fist in my mouth again, smooth and hard, tasteless at first, then giving me back my own taste.

Camille is smiling like the purple demon emoji. "Margot Kuhl?" she echoes, arching an eyebrow.

"Oh my god. What do you know?"

"Margot Kuhl . . ." She settles deeper into the easy chair. On the table beside her, the one that doubles as my nightstand, tonight's second highball idles, gathering condensation like a storm cloud. Camille refers to all alcoholic beverages as *highballs*.

"What?" I demand. "Tell me!"

She chews on one of the giraffe-shaped swizzle sticks she buys in bulk to spice up her drinks. "I don't kiss and tell," she says, brandishing the giraffe at me.

Bullshit. Camille the Gossip Queen and Margot go way back. Before they were friends, they were lovers, which isn't surprising in the sense that all these gays end up sleeping together but is surprising in the sense that Camille is a switch who prefers to bottom. "I can top in an emergency," she likes to say, but it always sounds like a joke. What on earth she and Margot, Miss Bottom Supreme, got up to, I'll never know.

"I don't need gossip," I say. "I just need to find her."

One of the things I love about Camille is she rarely asks why, and she doesn't now. I wouldn't mind telling her more about the Margot and Syd situation, per se, but all roads lead back to X, and I still don't want to go there with her. Not her or anyone. I don't know why. That straight therapist I used to go to probably would have called it *toxic masculinity*.

Camille furrows her brow, opens her phone, and pops her thumb through some apps. The lamps flicker, then go out. "Perfect timing," she says, rolling her eyes.

"There wasn't supposed to be one tonight," I grouse.

"Can you check and see how long it's going to last?"

I look at the app. Energy savers are supposed to be shorter on weeknights, but the twenty-four-hour digital clock that tells you when the outage ends says 00:00.

While I light the candles, Camille goes to her room, returning a few minutes later with a little black book. "My hard drive," she jokes, flicking it open bottom to top, like Hildy with her writing pad. Long excommunicated from most major platforms for social media, banking, messaging, and advertising, Camille uses this book to keep in touch with people. She pages through it, the candlelight illuminating the translucent yellow paper. A moment later, she turns the book around and points at a phone number. "Try this," she says.

I take a picture. "So when was the last time you talked to her?" I ask.

Camille makes a great show of thinking, squinting and propping her chin on her free fist. "I can't remember," she says, setting the book down and picking up her highball. "But I doubt she can, either. Whenever it was, I'm sure she was more fucked up than me."

"Sounds like Margot," I say, sighing. So what if Camille can't remember the details? A phone number isn't nothing; when

I unblocked the one Margot used to use, it had been disconnected. A new one might be the lead I'm looking for. "Thanks,
baby."

Camille twists the giraffe between her teeth. "XOXO, Gossip
Girl," she says, pursing her lips.

####

saw be crime play last weekend.

I stopped and deleted the text. I tried again.

missed you at the show on friday.

No.

I was at work, on the sixth morning after X—fifth, techni-
cally, since I didn't meet her until after midnight—and a few
of the smaller bruises were just starting to yellow, the hema-
tomas encircling blank space like the chalk outline of a bunch
of murdered bodies. They itched, and as I scrolled through
my phone looking for Syd's number, I scratched them through
my jeans.

do you know X?

I almost sent that one. Like maybe straightforward was the way
to go, given the situation. But then I thought about what I

knew of Syd and realized it would probably just scare them away. I had already lost six days.

I can't remember what I eventually texted, but whatever it was, it was obviously the wrong thing, if there was even a right thing. Syd didn't respond.

####

Before my surgery could be approved, I had to convince a bunch of doctors that I really, truly, sincerely wanted to ruin my body. Like everyone else, I was sent to a therapist I couldn't afford.

At the time, I bitched about it to my friends, figuring, like everyone else, that surgery would be semilegal forever. For six months, I sat in an overstuffed chair once a week so some heterosexual could feel smart for confirming that I am, in fact, a disgusting, fucked-up person. I didn't know how lucky I was to have the opportunity to go so deeply into debt to be cut open.

As usual for someone so well educated, the therapist had nothing interesting to say. At first, I talked just to talk, making stuff up to pass the hour, but she was so credulous I shifted to honesty after the first few sessions, telling her about my life and Petra and the people I slept with and my shitty, boring job. Turned out it was kind of nice to have a place where I could talk through things. This was back before I would have worried about something like the notes she took on her legal pad. I would get going, and she would just melt into the background, a silent presence that would occasionally murmur, "Can you tell me more about that?"

I don't remember the therapist's name, or even what she looked like (do straight women look like anything at all?), but I do remember that she had impeccable taste in shoes and never wore the same pair twice, moving through a rainbow of chic flats, sleek mules, textured animal prints. At least my money was going toward something worthwhile, I thought. I mostly looked at her feet, which I judged were a size 7, maybe a 7½ (long toes), during our sessions.

Not that she was totally worthless as a therapist. She taught me about deep breathing and meditation and all that. She would occasionally share her theories about why I am the way I am, which I didn't mind. Doesn't everyone like to be talked about like their life is a story instead of a series of accidents? I imagined her back at her expensive therapist school clicking through a PowerPoint full of pictures of yours truly, a walking case study, with bullet points next to my body that said things like AVOIDANT ATTACHMENT STYLE and DISSOCIATION. The idea of it was flattering, in its own way.

When my six months was up, the therapist gave me my surgery letter and told me that she would love to continue growing with me.

"Absolutely," I said. I blocked her.

####

The hosts of the murder podcast disagree about why people murder. That's the million-dollar question, isn't it: Are murderers born, or are they made? Same debate people have about perverts and queers. No comment.

"I think it's what we call the devil," says one of the hosts. "Some people just have it. Maybe it's their wiring, and maybe it's their soul. I don't know."

"But that's . . . I know it sounds stupid, but that's just not fair," says the other host. "Like maybe we're all born with the capacity for evil, but I have to believe that something happens. Some kind of brain trauma or abuse or something, and a switch is flipped. Like if I didn't think we all have some choice then I wouldn't be able to sleep at night."

Of course, people only ask this question—*Why are you the way you are?*—because the answer is also a solution. If there is a way to turn people into murderers, then there must also be a way to turn them back. To fix people, whether it's by hacking their genes or raising them in safety helmets. Personally, I can't decide who's worse: the people who think circumstance is the whole story or the people who think *born this way* actually means something. Like how many times did Richard Ramirez get hit on the head? How many times did a man rape Aileen Wuornos? What's the magic number? As if there were an answer and as if, the way everything's going, individual acts of violence are our biggest problem.

Not that I'm blaming them, the women who host the podcast, or the millions who listen to it, or all the people who'd rather

not think about how bad everything is. Better to distract ourselves with crimes of passion (homicide) rather than crimes of
calculation (Prison. Pipeline. SpaceX). It's nice to think that the
problem could be bad apples instead of a bad barrel, or a deadly
apple allergy. Because I'm no different from them. I listen every
week. I never miss an episode.

It's probably bad—in some queer theory–type way—to wonder
why I'm a sadist, but I do. Like with Petra. Despite everything,
I was in love with her, and I knew it from the moment I started
to plan how I'd style her for her funeral viewing. I know that
wanting to see your lover dead and beautiful isn't normal, but
it's always felt normal to me.

I would lay Petra out like a doll still in its original box, with
a transparent veil draped over the top. Her coffin (white and
lined with satin, à la Norma Desmond) would be surrounded
by vases crammed with red roses and baby's breath. Gold can-
delabras above, gold brocade below. I would dress her in a
black velvet dress with a Peter Pan collar and wrist-length
sleeves. The skirt would skim the tops of her knees. She would
have bangs and patent-leather shoes and lace-frilled socks.
Her makeup would be light, almost unnoticeable. Nude lip.
French manicure. A single beauty mark tailing her left eye,
like Sherilyn Fenn.

The image came to me after I drew her blood for the first time,
almost a month after we met. (Who says dykes move too fast?) I
didn't tell her about it until we celebrated our first year together,
when I made her a vision board, with pictures of Leontyne
Price, JonBenét Ramsey, Traci Lords (*Cry-Baby*) and Tracy

Lord (*The Philadelphia Story*), all glued to vinyl trimmed with lace. She loved it. She cried. Then I used a scalpel to spell my initials into her skin. That made me cry. It was very romantic.

It's too bad, the way blood works. You have to drain it from the body when you're preparing it for burial. But Petra always had the most beautiful blood. You could feel its liveliness just by being around her, and when she was in the act of bleeding, her blood stayed alive, sparking and dangerous, ready to change course, betray itself at the lightest touch. Her blood was not inert, even when it was separated from her vitality. I knew it wanted me. It had to come out. It had to be released.

What kind of sicko wants that from their lover? The same kind of sicko that wants to give that to their lover, I guess. Whatever it is that made me like this made Petra the very same way. Whatever kind of person I am, so was Petra.

I wonder how X became the person she is.

####

A man and a woman are flirting with each other on the train. They're standing in front of me, sharing a pole, her tote squeezed between her boots on the floor. We're packed in so tight I can't get away. I can't even turn around. But even if I could, I'd probably still watch them. It's like a car crash.

Of course, the woman is beautiful and the man is ugly. She is round and colorfully dressed, even though it's wintertime, and her lips broaden every time he speaks; his coat is too small across his shoulders, and his lips accumulate more moisture with every word he speaks about his "political entertainment" podcast. How could he, or any straight man, really, believe that a woman could find him attractive? The man laughs and the woman mirrors him. He's not much taller than she is, but he hovers overhead like a broken umbrella.

What I'd give to be able to delude myself like him. Then I could take shelter in the fantasy that X might be thinking about me, even though we only met once, briefly and anonymously. Even though she left the warehouse without saying anything, or even asking my name. If this man can believe that this woman would even deign to be aware of him, then I should be able to do the same. It's only fair. Gay rights.

####

I dream of X, then wake up alone in the dark.

The couch is too narrow for a normal pillow, so I sleep with a cushion under my head. Both the cushion and the blanket I'm wrapped in are Camille's. The only things in this apartment that belong to me are my phone, my library, my backpack, a duffel with some clothes and toiletries and toys and a few pairs of shoes, and whatever I put in the refrigerator that hasn't yet expired. I guess the expired things still belong to me.

3:57 a.m. Is X awake, too? We're now twenty-four hours closer to her export, which is roughly (maybe) two weeks from now. Where would someone like her go? Europe, I bet. Or like Hong Kong. Auckland. Buenos Aires. Kuala Lumpur.

Does X have family or friends or clients wherever she's headed, or is she going to have to start all over again? Based on what Mason Jar said, she seems to be taking her time with exporting. A lot of second wavers do. Rumor has it they get a bigger payout from the feds, too, but who knows for sure?

The government does grease the wheels for second wavers when they're getting ready to leave. It's not just parties with friends anymore. It's Events, branded for maximum engagement with personalized hashtags, yard sales, and State Department–sponsored ads about why it's so great to export. All of this still doesn't cover the costs, of course, which is why a lot of people still have to crowdfund—which, like the quotidian medical, housing, and unemployment fundraisers, has become normal—because who knows what they might encounter on the other side? Those of us who are staying pony up because that's what we do, and because we know that we could be the ones exporting in a year, six months, two weeks.

I wonder if X actually received a letter, or if she's preempting it, as some people do. I wonder where she is. Maybe she left the city and is using her last month in the States on FMTY clients, drumming up some cash before she has to convert it all into crypto. Or maybe she's traveling just because. America the beautiful. If I were exporting next month, maybe I'd want to visit all the places I haven't seen, and say goodbye to the places I love, although at the moment I can't think of where that would be. On the lam, like Humbert and Lo. Because that's what it is, isn't it? In the FAQ section that comes with every letter from FLEC or FLECC or FLECT, it says: All United States citizens who choose to voluntarily export under the aforementioned terms in so doing relinquish their American citizenship and all rights, privileges, and responsibilities with which it is associated. Once you export, you can't come back as an American, which more or less means you can't come back.

It doesn't matter where she is or what she's doing. She could be in Kenya or next door in 2C. The distance is irrelevant because she's not with me.

And it's not just that she's not here. It's that she doesn't even know I exist. When I think about her never thinking about me again, about her going to her postapocalyptic grave without even once considering that night I spent with her, I feel like I'm going to explode. Her thoughts a universe, but empty of me. Her brain's grooves full of memories and feelings and loves and hatreds, hungers and thirsts and desires, and yet lacking *me*. Why me? Why not me? What is wrong with me?

I feel like I'm spinning inside a microwave. I feel like killing something.

This is it, I think. I take a hit from Camille's bong and examine the phone number she sent me this morning.

margot? I texted back.

you know it baby, texted Camille.

I send the number a short, direct message. I don't know what I'll say if Margot agrees to meet with me, but I'll cross that bridge when I get to it. I also don't know what I'll do if she doesn't respond. Maybe I'll show up at her place, if it's still her place, and just start pounding on the door. Break in if I have to. Scour her house for clues. Steal her phone and find someone to hack it for me. It's a good way to get my ass kicked, or arrested, but I can't think of any alternatives. I mean, who knows. Maybe it's not even her number at all.

Margot texts back almost right away, as if she's been waiting for the opportunity. *u miss me?* the text purrs.

Fucking pain sluts, man.

I have a few friends who aren't into leather, or I did, before Petra took them away. I met Maxine long before Petra, at a straight bar where I was cruising her friend, another straight girl. I was still new to the city and still young enough to feel more comfortable around heterosexuals than around normal people, which was why I was there in the first place. Straight girls are easy.

Though the object of my affection looked afraid of me—the little flirt—Maxine narrowed her eyes at my jokes and rolled them when I asked her friend if I could buy her a drink. Whatever bathroom or bed that tryst ended up in, it wasn't long before I blocked the straight girl, but I kept Maxine's number. She wasn't scared of me at all, and it turned out we loved the same deep house DJ. We got to know each other over nights spent dancing in dark clubs, on long walks home while the sun was coming up.

Straight as she is, Maxine's art is good. She does these hyper-realistic self-portraits that are slightly out of sync with reality. Her first series consisted of five paintings of herself seated on a chair in an empty room. She wore different clothes in each one, tank tops and roomy linen pants you'd recognize if you knew her, but instead of coffee-brown curls running down her shoulders, she was bald as an egg. Her arms and legs, normally lustrous with that same shade of hair, were utterly smooth, like a coke mirror after a good windexing.

If not for these strange subtractions, the paintings would have looked like a collection of Polaroids. Everything was perfect, her brushstrokes invisible, down to the smallest details: the lightning-thin lines around her eyes, the plummy cups of skin above her cheeks, the soft flesh welling over the top of her jeans. Maxine was a magnificent technician.

Each passing series had a few more weird changes. The crown of her head began to widen, but it happened so gradually, so subtly, that it was almost undetectable. As her head grew, her body diminished, and her cheeks sank into her skull. Over the years, she started to resemble a Roswell alien, and as the alien features became more pronounced, her eyes got bigger, more glassy, and her pupils began to fade.

Maxine eventually started getting a lot of attention, once the weirdness became unavoidable. In the final series, her fingers, set to rest on her knees, were twice as long as her hands. Her skin had become metallic. The critics loved the cumulative effect of her work and accounted for it as predictably as you might expect.

For female creatives, the art world is a war of attrition . . .

As general access to higher education plummets, artists seem to be interrogating, more aggressively than ever, the purpose of formalized schooling . . .

Etc.

"So what *is* it all about, anyway?" I asked her. We were in her studio. I was stroking my cheek with a clean paintbrush, soft as eyelashes. "Is it like a commentary on beauty or something? Or on like last capitalism?" She had artist's statements, but when I tried to read them I got bored.

"Not exactly," Maxine said, taking the brush from me. She didn't like to talk about her paintings, not with me, anyway.

"Don't be crabby," I said, making pincers out of my hands. June baby Maxine was sensitive about her shit.

"If I wanted to explain it with words, I would have written a book." As far as I knew, Maxine never dated, but the way she withheld herself was so sexual. I think that's what drew me to her. I wanted to know more about her life, her art, her thoughts, and all she wanted to do was dance.

It wasn't long after that that she got the diagnosis. The "Cancer with cancer" jokes got old fast. Still, the timing couldn't have been better. She had recently been hired by a fancy private university with excellent insurance. Aware of her luck, she felt as if it would have been in poor taste to talk about her pain in the interviews she was suddenly being hounded for. Her reticence was read as cunning mysteriousness. As much as she tried to avoid the subject, it made her even more popular, her fans even more fascinated.

"This is nothing," I said. "After you get better, the publicity will be insane. Just wait."

Maxine would smile like I was an idiot, but I knew that if I caught her in the right mood, talking like that would make her feel tough. Sometimes that helped.

Six months after her diagnosis, she was doing chemo treatments while prepping for her big solo show. Everyone was talking about it, including the RN who was always at her appointments. "It's a retrospective," Maxine explained to her. "You know, like I'm already dead. But don't take it personally—I'm sure you'll keep me alive." The RN laughed.

I went to the show the day it opened. I inched through all three rooms, looking at each of the paintings in the order they were created. That was when it hit me how much Maxine looked like her new pictures, the weirdest, most alien-like ones, the outstretched fingers with the too-big joints and the odd wrinkles around the tips, like she'd been pruning in the tub for hours. Bald as an egg, wrinkled as a nug, eyes deep in her face, the portraits looked back at me like I was Maxine and they were a bunch of mirrors. It was like she knew, years ago, that this was going to happen to her.

#####

Keys: hooked. Purse: dropped. Coat: draped over chair. She has a fresh highball ready in under a minute. Only then does she swap her shoes for the turquoise kitten heels that never go outside, mincing her way to the easy chair like a kid in Daddy's slippers.

I'm lying on the couch, looking at my phone. What started as idle Cyte scrolling has turned into another search session for X. "How was work?" I ask, turning my screen away from her. She's picking up shifts at a straight club where her friend tends bar.

Camille puts an invisible Glock to her head and squeezes, the plosive followed by a couplet of hard consonants so I know it's real. "Take this job and shove it," she says, her voice flat as a gluten-free pancake. It won't be back to normal until the highball is gone. Sometimes it takes more than one.

"You won't have to be there long." Either escorting work picks up again and she can quit, or she gets fired for inevitably being herself. She's already toeing the line. The club is supposed to be classy, high-end. Blue eyeshadow is against the dress code, but there it is, a weird, beautiful disease hugging the curve of her eye socket. Camille's makeup always looks really good, like a drag queen. Her first legal job was at that mondo beauty supply chain, but she got busted for not busting anyone for stealing, so it didn't last. It was a matter of conscience, she told me. These days she has too much debt for conviction. "You'll find another job," I reassure her.

"If you'd pay your rent on time, I wouldn't need to," she snaps. She starts in on the highball.

I pause (*beach, bed, lungs*) because I don't actually want to say what comes to mind, which would definitely start a fight. I wait a few breaths before I let anything out. "I'll get it to you this week."

Camille nods, looks away from me. She knows I'm just saying that. I might get paid this week and I might not.

Since the bathroom is the only place in this apartment where I can have some fucking privacy, I get in the tub fully clothed and turn up the volume on the murder podcast while I search archived femdom sites, scrutinizing faces and boots. Camille is still out in the living room, sitting on the couch even though it's my bed, even though I pay rent here, or usually do, anyway. She knows just as well as I do that she would need another job whether or not I was paying to sleep on her shitty fucking couch.

####

Margot and I agreed to meet at a bar by her new place in the LES, but at the last minute she texts me asking if I can pick her up at her apartment. *i need to drop my bag*, she explains.

I wait in front of her building, checking my phone every thirty seconds. If I'd known she was going to be late, I would have stopped for coffee first. I haven't slept in almost three days.

When I settled into the couch a few nights ago, I had that buzzy feeling, that restlessness that feels so out of place when you don't have any drugs to blame it on. Then there was that false start where I fell asleep only to be woken up by an unplaceable noise. Sleep was out of the question after that. Everything was too loud—the sirens, the radiator, the rats. Earplugs didn't work. Headphones didn't, either. So I lay there in the darkness, awake with the city around me, grinding my teeth and sweating through my blanket. Right when I was finally about to fall asleep for real, I realized it was too quiet. At some point in the night the sirens mostly stop and the screams are too familiar. I got the quiet that I wanted, but it turned out I didn't want that, either.

The next night was just as bad. By 3:00 a.m. I gave up and pulled out my copy of *Frisk*, touching myself as I read. After a few hours, I got out of couch and got ready for work. For breakfast, I stole some iffy takeout mapo tofu Camille had in the fridge, hoping she wouldn't notice.

I don't remember Margot being the type of person who shows up late. Maybe she's punishing me, trying to make me wonder if she's going to ghost. Though I don't know how she could. I'm at her place, after all. Melted snow drips from the black-cloaked scaffolding above my head.

Just as I'm about to actually *call* her, I feel a tap on my shoulder. There's Margot behind me, tote in the crook of her elbow, hair thrown up in a chignon.

"Hey, babe," she says. She gives me a gay cheek kiss, Judas style. "You look good."

Jesus, has it come to that? I don't tell her how she looks, which is good, actually. She already knows. It's part of her whole thing.

I follow her up the stairs to the third floor. Her apartment door screams open after she unlocks like twelve different bolts. A little dog with an underbite (not a chihuahua) stands before us, wagging its tail.

"Pepper!" Margot exclaims, shrugging off the tote and kicking off her shoes. She gives the dog a pet, then rushes to the kitchen and throws open a cabinet. "Want something to drink?" she asks, rummaging inside. Pepper is racing in circles around her. "Did you take her on a walk?"

I think the question is for me, but a voice rises up from the couch. "Not yet," it drawls.

The couch pillows shift to reveal some undercutted fuckboy in lavender overalls. They're blinking all shiny, their mouth hanging open above their phone.

"I thought we were going out," I say to Margot. I don't want any interruptions.

"Drinks are on the house here, though," Margot says, holding a glass in each hand. Pepper runs up her leg, falls back down to the linoleum, tries again and again.

"I have something kind of serious to talk about."

"And you want to talk about it at a bar?"

I sigh. "It's about Syd."

"Oh." Margot softshoes away from Pepper as she sets the cups down next to a huddle of velas—Juliana de Norwich, Sor Juana Inés de la Cruz, Pauli Murray. It's obvious she doesn't want the fuckboy to hear that name.

The fuckboy slaps their feet down on the floor. Their pen glows blue, then red. The window above their head opens onto a wet brick wall. Margot grabs her keys and rejoins me in the doorway, watching them all the time.

"Be back later," she says, raising her eyebrows.

The fuckboy doesn't reply. They radiate irritation, and I can't say I blame them. I don't know why Margot acted surprised when I mentioned Syd. Why else would I want to talk to her? We haven't seen each other since I kicked her out of my place, and now, not long after she and Syd have this explosive breakup, I just hit her up out of the blue. Is she so narcissistic as to think I'm here just to get some? Is she so stupid that she doesn't recognize the timing?

At least I won't have to come up with a tricky way to get what I want. The fact that she's still agreeing to get a drink means she's at least a little curious about Syd. Maybe she's been waiting for her chance to get back in touch with them, and I'm bringing it to her like room service. All I have to do now is ask the right way.

There's a sleepy dive a few blocks from hers with dim lights and cheap drinks. I order us both doubles. Under the influence of the neon and alcohol, we're soon having a real conversation about what we've both been up to since we last saw each other. As if I didn't kick her ass out in the middle of the night, she giggles, touches my leg, making not-so-subtle references to being in pain. She tells me about cutting herself while slicing an apple last week. "The blood ruined my Pink Lady," she says, winking grotesquely.

I change the subject. It's fairly easy to get her to talk about Syd. The hard part is keeping her on topic.

"Oh. Them." When she hears Syd's name, she drops the flirt and rolls her eyes. "I'm sure they gave you a whole story, didn't they?"

"I mean," I say.

The flirt flickers. She touches my leg again. "Syd is a liar. Everybody knows that."

"They said you'd say that."

"Then they were being honest, for once. Probably because they wanted something."

I'm impressed with her insight, but before I can ask more, a straight appears, standing just a little too close to us. Margot notices me notice. She and I make brief eye contact, and then I go on. "Syd told me you stole some of their stuff."

"Stole?" She snorts. "I bought that guitar. I let them borrow it for shows. It belonged to me."

"And the drugs?"

"Flushed them. Syd was acting crazy. I was scared they were going to hurt themself."

"And what about you?" I ask. "Did they hurt you?"

I don't know why it matters. Maybe I'm just trying to soften Margot up, acting like I care so she'll help me find X. But I'm a little curious, too. The success or failure of her relationship with Syd means nothing to me, but I'm still invested, like with the reality show where people exchange organs for debt repayment. Or the one where men fight to the death for the chance to take the virginity of a C-list former child pop star.

Before Margot can answer, the lurking straight says something to her. Its finger dances on her shoulder.

"Fuck off," advises Margot.

It does not fuck off. Instead, it sinks its hand into her hair. It's lucky Margot doesn't have a knife handy, but a half-empty beer bottle does plenty of damage on its own. We run out of the bar before we get bounced or worse.

"Fist isn't far," Margot points out. In a few minutes we see the line in front, full of homos talking shit and smoking Juuls and analogs.

"Oh my god!"

It's Peach. She's working the door tonight, as I hoped she would be. I shove my way to the front of the line and throw an arm around her shoulder. "Hey, love." I kiss her cheek.

She's surprised to see me. "I guess I didn't think—" she begins, but then Margot is beside me, hand in my pocket, wanting to know if I have an analog to spare.

You'd think TS Princess Peach and I would have dated at some point. She's one of those switches who's willing to do anything, and I mean *anything*, twisting the line between curséd sadism and doe-eyed masochism. A true champ, really. She's certainly my type—beautiful, bitchy, brassy, brave—but I'm not hers. We had a romantic moment at the gang bang where we met and she let me solo ride for a week or so before she ghosted for like six months. She couldn't have been more clear if she'd rented a plane and skywritten JUST FRIENDS in the blue above Riis.

My loss. The last time we played together, I put 150 needles (big gauge, which is how you know I was feeling tender) in a chain from her shoulders down to her groin. She yanked out the whole thing herself, screaming like a demon from hell. Child's play compared to what she'll do when she's actually in love, which I've had the bittersweet pleasure to witness. I've watched her put out a few cigarettes short of a pack on trade. I've seen her carve FUCK ME into her own ass. I held a torch for Peach for way too long, but over the years, we've reached this thing that's sort of brother/sister, though not in the sexy way.

"I'm girl crazy. It's in my genes. You were a moment of weakness, I guess," said Peach. "But if you ever decide to detrans . . ." She slid a nail down my sternum. For her, I'd consider it.

Peach runs DYKE ADJACENT, Fist's monthly leathergirl party, which I had completely forgotten about until just now. Fist used to be my favorite leather bar, but I don't know if I can honestly call it that anymore. I haven't been since Petra and I ended things. I'm not sure if Peach knows about the breakup, and I don't mention it as we make the requisite chitchat, Margot lighting up my last cigarette behind me.

"Can we . . . ?" I say. Peach always lets me cut the line.

"Yeah." Peach glances over at the bouncer, that big butch, Mary, who's arguing with someone on her phone. "Yeah. I'll be in soon," says Peach. She squeezes my arm and nods us through before dropping back into her element—bombing group selfies, batting her eyelashes at every high femme in line—like a goldfish into a brand-new bowl.

Margot and I duck through the low door and stand for a minute as our eyes adjust to the neon-lit darkness. Same old Fist, though over the past few years some superficial changes have been made. Behind the bar are the same dykes with Stevie Nicks hair and the same fags with skinny mustaches, but now there's always at least one cissexual on shift, in case of a raid. When I first came to Fist, the walls were papered in old posters for fisting parties with names like Rubin Sandwich illustrated with Crisco cans and Tom of Finland daddies and G. B. Jones girls squeezing Harleys between massive, greased-up thighs. Those have disappeared. There's still a velvet-draped photo booth in the corner and a coat check staffed by walking mullets and go-go boys. People still swishily recline in the recessed couches between dances, but the energy is different, more reserved. *I used to beat him with a turquoise chain, yeah* blares from the speakers.

Post-X, I've learned that every new location is a lesson in disappointment. I understand that she's not here before I even realize I'm looking for her. It never stops being surprising. All of a sudden, I want to go home and curl up in bed, but then I remember I only have the couch, which I'm too tall to curl up on without my knees tipping over the edge. When Margot touches my shoulder, I almost swat her hand away. I close my eyes. Breathe. *Beach, bed, lungs.* Another drink will help.

I take Margot's hand and pull her toward the bar. She plays with her hair as we wait for our order, batting her eyes as I scan the room. Now we're safe, surrounded by purple and black hankies peering over pockets and curling around foreheads. More colors—hunter green, baby blue, fuchsia—dance over acrylics and enamel. Two dykes are arguing in a corner, and their body language suggests that, with any luck, they're not far from throwing punches. It's warm, and Margot sheds her jacket, hanging it on a hook beneath the bar, and I remember Petra and the black skirt she wore the last time we came here together. Thank god our drinks come quickly.

"Listen," I say to Margot. "I need you to do something for me."

"Really?" Margot gnaws her straw like a rat. She's picking up right where she left off, still trying to be seductive. I can't wait to disappoint her.

"I need you to talk to Syd."

She snorts, wrenches her eyes away.

"Please," I say. My least favorite word to say. "Will you do it as a favor to me?" Many women have told me that I can be charming when I want to be.

"A favor." From the look on her face, you'd think I just asked for her good kidney. I may not have grounds to ask a favor, but at least I didn't behave like a giant child the last time we saw each other. If she has any long-term memory left, she should at least consider that before she denies me anything.

But I stay charming. "It's important," I say. I pretend to hesitate, then put my hand on her thigh, half on her skirt, half on her skin. Same skinny legs. They feel good, vulnerable, which is irritating. "Syd knows someone that I need to find."

She pretends to ignore my hand, slurps up the drops clinging to the ice cubes in her cup. Unprompted, the bartender refreshes our drinks, catching my eye as he does. He looks familiar. He's probably blown me before.

Margot's cheeks go concave and more booze disappears down her throat. She breaks the seal with a snap. "Who?" she finally asks, pouting a little bit.

"Her name is X."

"What was that?" Margot leans in, palm cupped behind her ear. The bar is loud.

"X!" I shout. It comes out too loud this time, right as the song ends and the roar drops.

"Did you say 'X'?" There's a hand on my shoulder. It's Peach, fluffing her hair with her free fingers.

"You know X?" I demand.

"Her?" chirps Peach. "Yeah, she's here. Didn't you know?"

She's speaking to me, but she's looking over my head, admiring herself in the mirrored wall above the bar. She should. She looks good. Her eye catches Margot's in the glass and a flicker of tongue escapes her mouth. Margot blushes.

####

A man on the train is singing "What's Love Got to Do with It." A shredded hospital wristband hangs under the cuff of his suede jacket. Everyone leans away from him, not because he smells bad, or because nothing he says makes sense—although both these things are true—but because he reeks with the desire to speak to other people. His singing voice is nice, and his speaking voice is beautiful, but nobody on the train wants to hear either. *Makes my pulse reAAAct,* he sings.

Mom went to an outpatient program a few times when I was a teenager. Rehab was a waste of time and money—sometimes she got sober, but she never stayed that way. But the worst part about her "working on herself," as she put it, was that she talked about it constantly. I hated it.

Things were different when she was drinking. We just lived. I would watch TV on the couch while she cleaned and drank and wrote in her notebook. She would go out with her boyfriends or bring them back home, and sometimes one of them would sit on the couch with me while she cleaned and drank and wrote. Like yeah sometimes things were bad and she screamed at me, or at one of them, or she didn't talk at all, but sometimes things were fun, or funny, or at least normal.

When Mom was working on herself, things stopped being normal. Sometimes she would want to talk about things that had happened a long time ago, back when I was a little kid, so I would put my fingers in my ears and sing songs to drown her out. *What's love but a secondhand emotionnnnn?* I meant it as a joke, mostly, but one day it made her cry, and then she didn't talk to me for a week.

####

"Where?" I demand. "Where is she?"

"Backstage." Peach slides a piece of aluminum up from somewhere in her corset and unwraps it. She feeds the long stick of gum into her mouth while she stares at Margot. "She has a set coming up."

"A set?"

"Yeah," says Peach. Margot, mouth sagging over her straw, watches Peach chew. Great. A love connection. "She wanted to do DYKE ADJACENT one last time before she exports."

"You know about that?"

"Her exporting?" Peach looks off into space for a sec, as if deciding whether to tell me something. "Yeah. We go way back." I wonder, for the millionth time, why I had never heard of X before the night we met.

"Who are you talking about?" says Margot. It's loud again, but her voice is louder, and right in my ear. I imagine seizing her by the neck and slamming her skull down on the bar. I address Peach instead.

"Can you get me back there?"

Peach has shaped her eyebrows like wedges, like Li Li-hua's, and when they lift, her jaw juts out. "You?" she asks, still chewing like a piston. Her eyes are locked on Margot's.

"I need to talk to her."

"What's your name again?" asks Peach. She's talking to Margot now.

"I'm serious," I say, touching Peach's arm. I want to squeeze it and startle her back to the present, but I only apply a little pressure. "Can you get me back there?" I wonder if she knows that I'm begging.

When Peach looks at me again, it feels like I finally have her attention back. I can't remember ever having done anything *for* her, but there has to be something, some kindness, somewhere, to convince her to do this for me.

"Margot," says Margot. She giggles.

Peach doesn't seem to hear her. "Okay," she says to me. I want to kiss her. I want to squeeze her neck until she falls into pretty dreams, drooling in the crook of my arm. "I'll take you back there. Just don't do anything weird."

Weird? This from the bitch who'll gladly take a whole fist without lube. Then again, maybe she can tell I'm on one tonight.

I did beg, after all. I'm too grateful to be annoyed. "Of course not," I assure her.

"Come on then," Peach says. The back of her dress droops into a soft *V*, like a fat slice of cake. I follow her, and Margot follows me.

We plunge into the crowd. Now that I know X is here, has perhaps even been here the entire time, my body has arrived, too. My muscles tighten, my sweat burns alkaline, my skin moves in delicate little ripples. I'm aware of my pores and my mouth and my asshole. I can smell alcohol, poppers, dirty carpet, stale cum, fresh sweat. Ahead of me, the crowd opens for then closes behind Peach, forcing me to shove just to keep up. Margot is clinging to my jacket, which is annoying, but at the same time, the pressure feels good. When she steps on my shoe and skins my heel, I don't even care. I'm suddenly full of goodwill. Maybe, after all of this is over, I'll give Margot another chance, give her the beatdown she thinks she deserves.

We're halfway to the stage when I feel a shoulder resist against me and rotate as I try to push through it. When I hear someone say my name, I turn around before I wonder if I should.

It's fucking Syd, of course. They've still got their silver rings, but this time they're in white overalls, their fingers linked with a futch wearing a pleather harness and not much else. I might've laughed if I weren't so shocked, though I have no reason to be. This is DYKE ADJACENT, after all. Syd looks just as floored as I feel, their mouth open, their forehead squeezed tight.

"Syd," I say, like a genius. But now they're looking at Margot.

"Where the fuck have you been?" Syd screams at her. The futch grabs their arm. I feel Margot grabbing mine. I glance behind me, but Peach's platinum mane moves inexorably on. She's almost out of sight now.

"Don't you talk to me like that—" Margot hisses. I consider slipping away, but Syd's eyes land on me again.

"And you!" they yell.

I should just book it. Now that I'm this close to X, I don't need these idiots. God, where's the raid when you need it? Syd's in my face, their finger shoved up right between my eyes. "You lying fucking bitch!" they scream. I'm forced back, my weight in my heels. If they swing on me, I'll duck and run.

Margot's fingers are still wrapped around my arm. "Let's get out of here," she says in my ear.

A vein throbs in Syd's forehead. "So you *are* together!" they're yelling. I've never seen them display so much personality. I didn't think they had it in them. It's sort of a turn-on.

"Listen!" Margot screams at them.

"We just broke up, and now you're with them?" Syd yells at her now, pointing at me. "You think I'm so awful, and you left for *them*? And after what happened to Petra?"

Something inside me stirs, a bad thing pricking its ears like a sleeping Dobermxn. The last time Petra and I came to DYKE ADJACENT, we were right here, dancing, drunk and flirting with each other and anyone in our line of sight. She was wearing that black skirt, open-toed heels, no bra. Now I'm yelling, too.

"What the fuck did you just say?"

Syd's head whips back toward me, a furious smile slathered across their face. "I," they spit, "am not talking to you."

"Fuck you," I say. Margot's hand tightens around my arm.

"Hey," interrupts the futch. They've wedged themself between me and Syd, their face a mask of glitter and caked-on ReflecTec. They put up their hands. One of them grazes my cheek.

####

I dream of X, and when I wake up, I keep my eyes closed. I want the dream to crystallize. I want it to stay.

These dreams are the closest thing I have to photos of her. I have a million of myself, of people I know, people I've dated, people I've fucked, people I've cruised. Faces turned to their good sides and naked bodies without heads. A gig of selfies. My Cyte archive alone would crash the dusty old desktop that the professor that Mom dated had in his office at the community college. That was the first computer I ever used. The last time I saw him, he opened up Microsoft Paint for me while he and

Mom went to talk in the hallway. I dragged the mouse around, doodling Jessica Rabbit leaning buxomly over a red convertible. As I was admiring it, the door opened behind me, and I x'd out as fast as I could. Mom looked like she'd been crying.

I wonder if X is photogenic, or if she has an unreliable face like Camille. In my dream, X's eyes were full of sorrow. Or maybe it was just her face that was sorrowful, each tender feature tightened. Why would someone like X be sad?

Maybe the sorrow wasn't for herself, but for me, and people like me. When we were together, I could see that she was anticipating something, and that that something was not for her, but for me, something as inevitable and necessary as her authority, the wrack and surge of which roared like a tidal pool in the dark.

I open my eyes.

####

Belt lurches against my gut. Arm whips around my throat. Can't see Margot. Can't see Syd. Can't see anything except colors, teeth, lights.

Someone's dogwalking me, propelling me forward like I don't weigh a thing. I twist against them and my arm twists back, and the fact that it hurts at all, in this crush of adrenaline and alcohol, tells me that it really fucking hurts.

"Leave it alone," a voice sings, breath hot in my ear. "You wouldn't want to break anything."

My face slams against the front door and it bursts open into the cool night air. A shriek of feedback all the way from the stage crawls up my spine, reminding me of my neck and the tiny little bones inside it, eensy nerves clinging to them like budding leaves. A men's size 10 slams into my ass, and the pavement connects with my shoulder, elbow, hip. Now the boot's on my head. The sidewalk burns my cheek.

"What the fuck," I moan. Stars in my eyes. Blood in my mouth. Ground smells like gasoline. The boot lifts. I hear Syd's voice, and other voices responding to them. "Get the fuck out!" someone yells. "Fuck you!" That's Syd. Other voices collide with them. "Let's go, baby," comes through soft and high, right above my head. I think about Petra.

I roll over onto my back and into the black flutter of my sight steps Mary, casually adjusting her sleeves. Her girlfriend, Tamara, as wide as Mary but two inches shorter, is beside her. I don't see Syd, or the futch, or Margot—just a bunch of strangers crowding around me and the bouncers. When I brace to stand up, my elbow touches the ground and I want to throw up. "What the fuck," I moan again, resisting the instinct to grab hold of it.

Mary just keeps tidying her right sleeve, rolling and unrolling. Tamara kneels on the pavement and leans in close, a fan of braids fainting over her right eye. "You," she says, gently stroking my forehead, "were asked to leave."

She's so dramatic. "You don't even work here!" I snap. Mary is on the payroll. Tamara just keeps her company. Lesbians.

Tamara shrugs. Like every butch, she has beautiful eyes—mile-lashed and just a little too far apart—like Katy Jurado. "What?" she asks, lifting a hand and raising her voice, as if making her case for the crowd around us. "Am I supposed to let her do all the work?"

This is probably foreplay for them. They're probably gonna go back home when Mary's shift is over and wrestle for the bottom.

"Congratulations," Mary says to me. "You're still 86'd." Her voice is as calm as her movements. She finally stops tidying her sleeve and tugs on Tamara's jersey—black, yellow, green—pulling her back to center.

"You guys can't handle a little shoving?" Gingerly, I touch my elbow with my finger. It feels like broken glass in there. Shit.

Tamara laughs. "It's like she don't even remember last time." She shakes her head. Mary rolls her eyes. They watch as I get to my feet, Mary scratching a patch of buzzed skin on her scalp.

"I really don't know how you sneaked in," Mary says.

"You need to stop looking at your phone all the damn time," Tamara teases.

Mary rolls her eyes again, but she withdraws a real cigarette from her breast pocket and offers it to me. I take it with honest gratitude, even though I know I can't smoke it here. I can feel four beautiful eyes drilling into my back as I walk away, my shoulders hunched, as if I've been defeated. I want them to think I'm leaving.

On the other side of the block, where I know they can't see me, I start a perimeter of the building. There has to be another way into Fist, perhaps through the back, where X could still be waiting. I circle around. The smoking patio is enclosed by a fence, and all the doors that I come across are bolted tight. I do three laps, carefully blending in with the crowd each time I pass Mary and Tamara, before reality sinks in: The only way into the bar is guarded by two muscle-bound sphinxes.

I loop back to the corner and lean against the wall, just out of sight of the entrance. I decide I'm going to wait right here until X leaves, and it's not a bad plan. She can't stay in there forever. I check for Mary's analog behind my ear and make a mental note to ask the next person who walks by for a light. Maybe even another smoke. Who knows how long I'll have to wait?

Now that I have a moment, I realize I've lost track of Margot. Either she wasn't thrown out with me, or she left along with Syd and the futch. I check my phone but she hasn't texted. Bitch. I wonder for a moment if she'll talk to Syd like I asked her to, but then I decide to worry about that later.

Around me, puddles shine undisturbed, reflecting the cowboy boots, threadbare tennis shoes, and galactic Pleasers of the queue. The last time Petra and I came to DYKE ADJACENT, it was right after daylight savings, and it stormed. We had gotten into an argument earlier in the afternoon, and when we

made up, we tried to play—just some needles, for romance—
but there was too much eye contact and too many silences. I
took the needles out quickly and gently, and there was very little blood. A bad omen, I remember thinking. Thunder outside.
Then there was nothing to do, so she made us drinks.

By the time we arrived at Fist, we were drunk and soaked—
Petra had forgotten the umbrella I told her to bring. We drank
more while we dried off. I didn't want to dance but Petra did,
so I went to the floor with her. I was doing okay until she
started flirting with a mint-green Mommy she knew I didn't
like. She was trying to get a rise out of me, and it worked.
We started arguing again. It got bad fast. We never argued in
public.

That was one of the last fights before I moved in with Camille.
After Mary bounced us, we came and stood not far from where
I am now, by the puddles. Petra cried, wet and puffy, while I
ordered us a car. It was too expensive, but I couldn't stand the
idea of sitting next to her on the bus or the train and watching
other passengers look at her face. I couldn't stand the thought
of spending another second with her. The thought of our bed
made me sick to my stomach.

Tonight's weather is a clone of six months ago, the Gregorian
calendar's mirror image across time. It's late, but still warm.
Balmy, even. I lean against the wall and start waiting.

####

"My fucking ex is texting me again," says Camille.

"Who?"

She sighs. She's lying on the floor, phone directly above her face. "Kim," she says. "I don't think I'll be rid of her till she dies of being a massive bitch."

For a long time after things ended with May, or Maybelline, she and I were good. We weren't friends, but we always said hi when we saw each other. Once (it was before the first wave, I think, but only just), we ended up at the same play party. I kind of panicked—it was different than bumping into her on the train—and almost left, but then she saw me, and nodded across the room. I decided to stick around. I chatted with friends and stroked the toys laid out for us by Domina Katsumi, she of the perfect feet and monster cock, doing my best to pretend that May wasn't a few feet away.

A few hours later, when everyone was putting their street clothes back on, I watched May lace up her shoes. Our arms had touched when the scene was peaking, as we both reached for the same spreader bar. It happened spontaneously, our closeness. I could smell her hair, the castor and gardenia oils. We were topping a beautiful blond laughing boy. He had a gold ring in his septum and more in his ears, as well as a pair of gold-rimmed glasses, which were waiting for him on a table by the front door. "You're so beautiful," he said to May, still laughing. Angel. He was on the floor now, on his back, looking up at her, stripped to blood-stained underwear.

When May smiled down at someone, she always looked a little shy. That's when I liked to call her Maybelline. She wasn't like a lot of other dominants I knew, me included, who had to be hard and cold and strong without fail. It was that, or else the world would end, but not for her. As her heel traced the blond boy's hairline, I suddenly realized I had forgotten what size shoe she wore. My head swam. I got that sick feeling you get when you narrowly miss getting hit by a car. How could I forget? Strong Maybelline. Vulnerable Maybelline. We might as well have never been together.

The boy's laughter, a little softer now, brought me back. You could tell he was the kind that always wanted to be good, one of those babies the scene saved from his dismal high school bedroom. His chest was scarred like an Etch A Sketch: double incision, nipple graft, razor blade, cat claw, unspooled paper clip, broken bottle, plate glass. A black heart cracked open on his left pec. Maybelline's heel lifted and dropped like a crane, twisting into the inked fissure. His skin broke like fruit. They laughed together.

Camille's eyes race back and forth, like she's watching herself play a game.

"Hey," I say. "Have you seen May lately?"

"May?" When the word is out, Camille's mouth hangs open.

"I was just thinking about her."

"May's gone."

"Gone?"

"Exported." Tendons jump in Camille's hands. "Back to France. Thought you knew."

Beach, bed, lungs. Regret feels like the tequila shot that puts you over the edge. After the scene, I had rushed for my bag so I could follow May out of the dungeon. She stood a few steps from the door, lighting an analog, her leather gloves cupped around the flame—too much clothing for the season, but that was May. The party had gone late. The moon was somewhere else. The pressure in my ears felt like a storm.

I asked if she wanted to try hanging out again sometime. Her embarrassment was worse than scorn. The blond boy came outside, hair wet from the shower, soft skin, bunny eyes, and walked over to us. I realized he and May were leaving together.

"I'm sorry," May said, and I could tell she meant it.

She went on ahead, and before following her, the blond boy turned to wave goodbye. I waved back. I wanted to rape him.

Now I regret blocking her, which I did that same night. It feels like something I can't reverse. Not that it matters now. May is gone, and I'll never see her again. I wonder if the blond boy went with her.

Camille has moved on. She's playing a game now, mouth still sagging open. It feels like everyone outside this apartment is dead and it's just me, her, and the phone.

####

"I can't remember the first time I ever did it," said Camille. She smiled dreamily. "But I remember the first time I had an orgasm. I don't know why it was different that time. I didn't use the showerhead or anything. I just touched myself there, like I always did, and then it happened. I was seven or eight, I think. After that, my mom made a rule that I couldn't go to my room between dinner and bedtime because she knew what I was gonna do in there." She laughed, delicate and dangerous, like Dorothy Dandridge.

I didn't touch myself when I was a kid. One time I asked Mom about a word—*orgasm*—that I had heard somewhere. I knew it had to do with sex.

"Christ," said Mom. As usual, she had been watching the TV in the living room from over the kitchen counter. During commercials, she would stand and write, leaning over her notebook to punch down cramped blue letters, all caps. "Christ," she said again.

When the news anchor came back from the break, the chyrons disappeared, and bursts of red, white, and blue filled the screen around him. The war update segment. Mom followed the war very closely, in an apolitical way. She wasn't invested in any particular outcome. She liked to keep track of how American imperialism was affecting the world, like a baseball geek memorizes batting averages. She lunged for the remote but missed her mark, instead ramming her finger through the left prong of a skewer that was sticking out of the ceramic jar of cooking utensils.

"CHRIST!" Mom screamed.

I ran to the bathroom for gauze, or something, forgetting my question. While she cleaned herself up, I went and opened a new bottle of wine. I decided to ask her again later, but for some reason, I never did. That was around the time when I first remember having the hardware store fantasy.

The fantasy goes like this: I'm in an empty hardware store. At first I spend a lot of time just looking at hammers, nails, clothes-pins, wood, padlocks, pullies, eyebolts, thumbtacks, staple-guns, sewing needles, wooden spoons, fishing tackle, chains, metal rulers, rubber tubing, spatulas, rope, twine, C-clamps, S-hooks, razor blades, scissors, tweezers, knives, push pins, two-by-fours, ping-pong tables, alligator clips, duct tape, broom sticks, bar-b-que skewers, bungie cords, saw horses, soldering irons. That's all I do, just walk around and look.

But after a while I start touching. I touch everything. I pick things up and put them in my mouth, running my tongue over their flavors and angles. They are bitter and hard, greasy and shiny. I know that wherever I reach my hand will find something that I desire. I know that there is no one else in the store and no cameras, and that nothing I do when I'm in there will ever be discovered or known by another person.

In the fantasy, this can go on forever. I never run out of things to touch and taste and feel. I never run out of time. And I'm never not alone.

I would usually imagine my walks through the hardware store while lying on Mom's bed, before she got home from work. I kept my eyes closed, but I didn't sleep. I didn't touch myself or anything. I would just sort of drift through the metal and wood and fabric and rope and blade, and the great beautiful capability they held. I remember my fantasy fondly, like how I imagine people must feel when they look at children they have affection for and are reminded of being young.

Like the third son in a fairy tale, I wake up with the sunrise. I'm sitting upright against the building around the corner from Fist, cold as a dog bone. My elbow aches. My neck and lower back, too. My shoes are still on my feet, and my wallet and phone are still tucked into my coat. Cooling piss beads my leather.

I jump up and race around the corner. Mary and Tamara and the line of people are gone. The lights are out. The bar is closed. I yank on the door with my good arm. Locked, it rattles.

I take a step back and look around. The street's empty, except for a few raccoons, who scurry back behind the dumpsters together and watch as I kick the door. It rattles again.

It happened back before the first wave, before I'd ever even been to New York, back when I was still going to the only gay bar in my town to cruise men. I hadn't been living on my own very long, but I was already thinking of myself as gay, even though I hadn't been with a woman yet.

That night, the guy I cruised was pretty cute, but he sobered up enough to clock me by the time we got to his place. He didn't live far from the gay bar, so when he kicked me out, I figured I had time to go back and try again.

After a block or two, I realized I was being followed. I didn't recognize the guy. He was white, wearing a baseball cap and Levi's, like me. *Faggot*, he hissed. I figured he had followed me and my cruise from the bar, and now he was following me again. A streetlight crisscrossed my face, blinding me for a blink. I looked back again. He was tall. I walked faster.

I kept going for the bar, where it would be safer inside, but he caught up to me in the parking lot. He pinned me against a pickup, and suddenly there were voices behind me, hands lifting and pushing me into the truck bed. The topper slammed shut above me.

More slamming. The voices were softer. As the pickup gained speed, they were muffled by the sound of the engine and the wind before disappearing entirely.

I couldn't tell where we were going. We would slow down, and then a violent turn would throw me against the side, my joints hitting sharp against metal. The treated steel beneath me rippled like a corrugated roof. I tried to wedge myself between the topper and the wheel well, bracing myself as much as I could. There was nothing in the bed but unwelded chains.

I don't know how long we drove. We turned too much to have been on the highway the whole time. I could have taken out my phone, but I was worried I'd drop it during a turn and it would shatter.

After a while, I heard a car laying on the horn, and the pickup screeched to a stop. I went flying into the side of the bed, slamming my head against the wall. The voices were still in the cab, but the doors didn't open. I scrabbled, curling my fingers under the handle on the tailgate. Somehow, it opened.

I knew my trick ankle wasn't broken because I could still hobble to the side of the road. I clambered over the short fence, through wet grass and dead blackberry bushes down into a ravine, the plants tearing my clothes and stabbing my hands. Leaves and spiderwebs stung my eyes, and water filled my shoes. Parallel to the road, I ran as fast as I could, my jeans soaked to the knee. Had they seen where I went? Every time I heard a car coming, I sunk down into the water, my eyes not even level with the highway.

Though I slowed, I didn't stop for a long time. Finally, in a turnout humming with crickets, I squatted on the gravel, still behind the fence, watching. I didn't know where I was. No signs, no buildings, nothing to see by except the moon, and a light from a rice mill across a big field. Was I a mile away from the gay bar, or ten miles? I pieced together the darkness with the headlights from the occasional car. Many were pickups, but none of them stopped.

When the moon began to fade, the crickets did, too. I wondered why there wasn't any birdsong. It was almost morning.

The murder podcast is on hiatus this week, so I listen to last week's episode again on my way home from work. It's light outside when I leave the office, but for the first time since the fall, an evening divides the day from darkness. I walk through the shadows under the eastern sides of the skyscrapers, catching sunshine where I can. It still feels like winter, but it smells like spring.

"I mean what else can you do but call the cops?" says one of the podcast hosts. "What else can you do? There are dangerous people everywhere. Mass shooters. Terrorists. Incels. How can you expect anyone to take that risk when, to the best of their knowledge, they're in danger?"

The host sounds indignant, maybe even angry. According to both hosts, the purpose of their podcast is to talk about murder, not politics, but sometimes what they think of as *politics*—that is, taking a stance on anything—makes it through production to the final cut.

"Are we as women supposed to just wait for someone to hurt us before we can do something about it?" she goes on. "Wait for them to keep hurting us until they do something bad enough to get arrested or exported?"

"I know you're not saying—"

"No, okay, no I'm not saying that everyone exports because they're bad. But there *are* a lot of dangerous people—"

"But hold up, let me just play devil's advocate here," interrupts the other host. "Because a lot of people say that we've given too much power to the government. And we hear—all of us, we do—about people who are being forced to leave who haven't committed a crime. And the conditions in the camps—"

"I know, I know," interrupts the other. "But you have to admit, it's a solution, isn't it? We have to be realistic. Some people export because they'd be happier somewhere else, but most of them pose a threat. I know it's probably controversial to say this, but I think it's good that some populations are exporting. Cancel me if you must." Both tittered nervously. "I think we should give ourselves some space to be proud of ourselves because this whole program wouldn't have happened if people, people like us, hadn't made ourselves heard. I know there are aspects of the criminal justice system that are behind the times, but it's served a purpose for a long time. What are we supposed to do, just destroy the whole thing?"

"We still really need the police."

"We do, we do, and sure, there are some bad apples—we talk about that all the time on here—but it takes a long time for successful police reform."

"Years and years," intones the other. "It's hard, hard, hard work—"

"And in the meantime, we work with what we have. There are a lot of good people in the system, doing the work. Do I like that there is sometimes injustice? No, of course not. But like what am I supposed to do if a very, very small fraction of people is slipping through the cracks of the only system we have in place to keep us safe?"

The silence lasts long enough to shrivel into dead air. It's unclear if the host's question was rhetorical or not. The other host finally breaks the spell.

"Well," she drawls, "I like my odds with the police better than with Ed Gein."

She starts to laugh, and the other one joins her. They sound more relieved than amused.

####

I know I'm not supposed to believe in the bioessentialist sexing of bodies, but some habits die hard. My own body, which I've paid good, nonrefundable money to have chopped up and rearranged (and for which I could now get a felony in some states), is supposed to defy "true" sex and "real" biology. And yet when I see a horse straining between a cop's thighs in Midtown, I have to look.

The palomino rises up from the lunch rush like a sandstone rockface. There are too many people around to easily get closer to it, to casually glance between its legs. I have to satisfy myself with its satiny, white-striped nose and fuzzy pink nostrils. Boy horse or girl horse?

I was never a horse girl, myself. I wanted a dog, not that it mattered. Mom wouldn't get one because she said it was against the rules for renters to own pets, but I knew this was a cop-out because she did a lot of stuff that was against the rules, like steal parking spots and smoke inside. She didn't want a dog, so we weren't getting a dog, and that was that.

There was a summer during elementary school when I started leaving out milk for a stray tabby that hung around our apartment. I would have preferred a boxer or a shepherd, but I left the milk anyway. If I got up early enough, I could watch the cat from the living room window as he warily lapped from the chipped blue bowl. He was not very trusting, for a tabby. Sometimes he saw me watching and would stare back, tail twitching, before dipping his head again.

One morning I left the front door open and sat a few feet from the entryway. I picked at the round brown fuzzies in the carpet, like bad-smelling pipe cleaners, while I waited. When he slunk around the corner of the apartment, he spotted me right away. I thought he would run, but he didn't. He kept an eye on me while he walked over to the bowl and drank from it.

The next morning, I left the door open again and moved a little closer to the sill. I sat on my hands, afraid that I'd move them without thinking and scare Maury. I'd named him after the host of my favorite TV show—Maury seemed like a nice older dad who would take you out to ice cream and the batting cages. When the cat came around the corner, with the same slinky stroll as usual, he drank without acknowledging me. A definite victory.

I decided I was going to try to pet Maury the next time he came. I anticipated the spiky arc of his forehead pushing up into my hand. "My cat," I would tell the foster kids. "That's my cat, Maury. My mom bought him for me."

I woke up early again and poured skim milk from the paper half gallon into the blue bowl, the layers of baby blue deepening as the milk eddied inside the ceramic. I set it on the ground before unlocking the door, pulling it open, and picking the bowl back up again.

I pulled cool air down into my belly. Bees flocked the crape myrtle, its pink paper flowers circled by black fuzz. Irises browned in the sunshine. The dumpsters gleamed. I took another breath. It smelled good outside, like chlorine and decomposing garbage and fresh sod.

That was the first time I found Mom passed out on the front lawn. She was wearing one of her pajama sets, as if she had almost made it to bed before deciding, for some reason, to go outside instead. Her right arm was up above her head, the fingers delicately curling in, like a Barbie doll's plastic hands. Her head was down in her rayon armpit like she was sniffing herself.

I went over to her and stood for a while, the bowl still in my hands. Her mouth sagged open to reveal her teeth, like a dog when it's on its back. I saw the pale of her belly, her hair fanning on one side and flat on the other. She looked very pretty. I considered spilling the milk on her face.

Instead, I set down the bowl and picked up her hand. She was breathing. I saw something move in the corner of my eye. It was Maury, over by the front door. He froze when he saw me turn. We looked at each other, and then he sprinted away, his tail parallel to the ground.

I don't remember how I got Mom back inside. There would be other mornings when I just left her out there, but I didn't do that the first time.

The palomino tosses its hair like an influencer. Horses look the way that people are supposed to: tall, muscular yet lean, thin-legged, big-assed, with shiny hair and enormous eyes. I wonder when rich people are going to start putting braces on horse teeth to make them less horsey.

Mom and I watched *National Velvet* a lot when she was drunk. She grew up not too far from a stable and would admire the horses when she was walking home from school. And she loved Liz Taylor. My favorite character was the horse. In fact, I was a little jealous of him. I liked the idea of a pretty girl in jodhpurs paying attention to me.

I spend more time thinking about kicking Triskit than I do working. He's licking himself again, making that sticky click-ing sound. He's so deep inside his own mucous membranes I might lose my mind. I think about nudging him with my foot, but if I do that, I might actually start kicking.

How many kicks would it take to kill Triskit? What would happen to me if he died? They'd have to fire me. But would they arrest me? I'd claim self-defense. The hellscape is such that it seems just as likely that Aisha would be fired. That would suck for her.

I look over at her desk. Her brow is furrowed and her hands are moving all fast over the keyboard. I have no idea what she could be doing. There is nothing for us to do today, and yet she is doing something.

Aisha is so boring that I wonder if it's coordinated, if there's actually a lot more to her, deep below the surface. That's what sex is good for—finding out what's really going on with people. Instead of kicking Triskit, I could kick Aisha. Pain tells you who people are. I could find out if she's the kind of person who cries passively or begs dramatically or laughs hysterically or grins and bears it or issues death threats or fights back. I see her five days out of the week, and yet I have no idea what she would do, which she would be, but knowing that she, like everyone else, must react, even by not reacting, feels good to remember. It makes me hate her a little bit less.

Petra was a good girl. She was so good, I even brought her to meet Mom.

It was after the diagnosis. At first, I listened to Mom's messages without calling her back, but Petra thought I should give her a chance.

"It *has* been a long time," Petra said. She would touch my elbow. "People can change." Stuff like that.

And maybe I had changed, too. Though I could imagine all the ways that seeing Mom could go wrong—the fights, the silences, the awful slog from first drink to bitter drunk—there was something about bringing home a girlfriend for her to meet that I actually liked. I had never done anything like that before. It was a little exciting.

I imagined it like a movie. At first there would be awkwardness. Then we would fall back into our old patterns for a while: silent resentment, passive aggression, and finally self-harm, she with her booze and me with, I don't know, fucking a straight woman for the attention? There would be a breaking point where we would yell in a moving car, or scream in the pouring rain. Our anger would hover in the air between us as the camera slowly pulled back.

And we would think that was the end of the movie, but it wouldn't be, because suddenly, somehow, we would realize that under the anger was love—that we were angry *because* we loved each other. Mom would remember that she loved me. She would love Petra, too, who was beautiful and feminine and sharp, just like Mom. Mom's mortal disease would still be a tragedy, but we would come to see it as a blessing in its own right, because it had brought us back together after years of estrangement. Nothing was ever going to be perfect, of course, but she and I would prove that you could go from being enemies to the kind of people who said, "Maybe I don't like you, but I do love you."

I began to fantasize about a real Thanksgiving, our first one ever, with Mom and me and Petra, and maybe even a few of our friends, flown out to try a holiday in the dreadful but campy suburbs. Mom would make turkey and stuffing, and I would get us a Costco pumpkin pie and deep clean the bathroom. Petra would light vanilla spice candles on the windowsills. Nino would fag out over Mom and Mom would gamely practice gender-neutral pronouns and we would all get a little drunk, but not too drunk, and do karaoke while we smoked. At the stroke of twelve, Mom would say, "Good night!" and walk into her room, eyes all the way open, to put herself to bed. No hangover the next morning, just slices of cold pie for breakfast.

So Petra and I flew out to visit her, to acknowledge her disease and, I suppose, talk about what happens next. I was feeling nervous but good on the drive into town, like I used to feel while waiting in line for a roller coaster. I drove the rental car slowly, worried I'd get lost because I hadn't been back in so long, but I remembered every exit, every stoplight. I turned the music up loud and sang along. Petra put her hand on my knee and sang with me. We were meeting Mom at a nice vegan restaurant in a gentrifying industrial district on the edge of town. I couldn't remember ever having eaten at a restaurant with Mom.

Laughing, Petra and I breezed in through the front doors. The wind blew blackened oak leaves in behind us. Mom was already sitting at the table, cupping her hand to talk into the waiter's ear.

"Lee," Mom said, standing up. The waiter disappeared. I went to her, and she touched my shoulder, then took a step back. There it was—the first awkward silence.

I remembered my antidote. "This is Petra," I said. I knew that she had chosen her outfit carefully, a black dress and stud earrings decorated with little red roses. She looked pretty but basically straight, which she almost never did. Mom and Petra smiled and shook hands, and we all sat down.

Mom's style hadn't changed much. She still wore her hair long and had on a nice blouse that was a size too large. No jewelry, except for a slender gold chain around her neck. She already had a glass of wine, which shouldn't have surprised me, but it did. I think I had myself fooled, as if through sheer force of will I could have changed what I already knew was going to be true. When the waiter came back with the bottle for me and Petra, Mom asked him to top her off.

I had expected that it would take us time to warm up to each other again, but not even the wine could make Mom relax. She was buzzing, her hands crawling the table, looking for things to touch. She pointed her head at me when I talked, but her eyes darted around the dining room.

"Yeah," she said, toying with the fork beside her plate. "Yeah."

She had no questions for us, about our life together, where we worked, or how Petra and I had met. More than ten years, I thought. More than a decade. When she did speak, it was to complain about her health and her job as an administrator at the community college, which she hated. When the waiter was at the table, she would interrupt me to flirt with him, only to then remark on his bad teeth each time he walked away. Worse still, she ignored Petra's jokes and seemed confused by her polite questions.

"I'm sorry?" said Mom.

"She asked if you were seeing anyone," I interjected, raising my voice, as if Mom merely couldn't hear very well.

"Oh, you know me," said Mom, looking past Petra to smile at the waiter from across the room. Petra took another drink.

I had never understood why men would want to be with Mom, even back when she was young and beautiful. It had been years since we'd seen each other, and the time showed. Her teeth were going translucent and her skin hung in a puddle under her necklace.

"You two," said Petra. She had broken yet another too-long silence with a little laugh. She shook her head, as if marveling. Fake. "You have her eyes, you know," Petra said to me.

Mom and I exchanged grim smiles. My head was starting to hurt. Petra was right: I did look like Mom. And I was going to age just like her, even if I didn't drink like she did. Nothing could alter genetics. I would inherit that sagging chin, that specific network of wrinkles, the coarsening of joints, the spotting hands. If I lived long enough, I was going to age like that, too, and Mom was living proof.

"I guess you do," Mom said to me. She lifted her glass up into the air and looked for the waiter. Beneath the table, Petra touched my thigh. God, could she be stupid. My headache doubled down.

Finally, our food arrived. Infinitii steaks, locally sourced root vegetables, squares of stylized pea protein with names like Mimolish and Valençiaga. The bites I could manage tasted like lukewarm dog food, but we discussed our orders at length because there was nothing else to talk about. As usual, Mom didn't eat, except to shove in a mouthful when the waiter approached so she could complain about it. After she made a scathing remark about her steak, he offered to replace it with another entree, but she waved him off, her eyes closing in a mask of resignation.

"It's fine," she said, the waver in her voice just barely under control.

We had planned to stay in Mom's spare room while we were visiting, but I started scrolling through hotel listings the minute I got in the car. Petra fought me on it.

"The hardest part is over," she insisted. "It would make things worse to back out now."

"How could it possibly get any worse?" I snapped.

"Then you admit it can get better!" she cried. She was driving, so we ended up at Mom's apartment. "Let's just hang out here for a while, and we can decide later."

Mom was sitting on the couch with a fresh glass of wine. "What took you so long?" she asked.

"Parking," I said. Petra set her purse down on the dining table, but I didn't let our bags touch the floor.

"We're pretty tired," said Petra. She touched my shoulder. "We should probably think about going to bed."

It was true that we were tired. We'd both had too much to drink at the restaurant, on top of the pills we'd taken for the flight. The spare room shared a wall with the living room and was separated from Mom's room by the bathroom. We pretended she couldn't hear us arguing from the living room.

At some point, we gave up and got into bed. Petra passed out, curled on her side and sweating booze. I could feel the frustration steaming off her. She looked like how I felt: bloated, dehydrated, greasy. I couldn't fall asleep. I laid next to her, listening to the small town quiet. After a while, I got up to smoke.

Mom was stretched out on the couch, her laptop on her stomach. There was an open bottle of wine on the coffee table. She didn't look up. "I'm winding down," she said, setting her glass next to the bottle. I hated how her wine smelled. I'd always hated it. Sweet and high up in the sinuses.

"Just going for a smoke," I said. I had my phone with me. I was going to see if there was any way we could get an earlier flight home. I was going to make up an emergency and get the fuck out of this town. Petra was invited, but I'd leave without her if I had to.

Mom turned her head to look at me. "You smoke now," she said, nodding.

"Yep," I said. I took a step toward the door.

"Wait," said Mom. "Sit with me for a minute?"

I didn't want to, but I couldn't think of a reason to say no.

"Come here," she said, pulling up her feet to make room. The wine was low in the bottle.

I sighed. I sat down.

"I'm writing," she said.

God. "What about?"

"Oh," she said. "You know. My day. I usually write in the other room, but since you're here . . ."

It seemed her notebook hobby had gone digital, though I would bet she still had the plastic tub full of finished ones in her closet. Even when I was a kid, there were dozens of notebooks in there. It would have been easy to go through them when she wasn't home, but I never did.

"That's nice," I said. I searched for something else to say. "It's nice in here," I said, gesturing at the apartment.

"It is, isn't it," Mom said.

We looked at the living room, the dining area, the kitchen nook behind the bar. The apartment was almost identical to the one I grew up in, except everything was nicer. The appliances weren't thrifted. The lighting fixtures were tasteful and delicate, not the single ugly frosted tit you find on the ceiling of every cheap rental. The ashtrays of my childhood had been replaced by a few pretty glass paperweights and hinoki-scented candles. There was another white couch across from us with a few tasteful brocade pillows. No roach traps or ant traps or mousetraps. There was that same magazine rack from when I was a kid, the magazines now inside it more compact and less shiny than they used to be, and tall, healthy plants stretched out from behind the firsthand mid-century modern furniture.

"I have a hard time sleeping these days," Mom went on. Her white feet were a few inches from my thigh. "Harder and harder, the older I get."

I nodded.

"And when I do sleep, I have nightmares."

I was nodding a lot, I realized.

"Bad stuff," she said. She was looking at her screen. "About when you were little and you were sick. You know, I thought you were going to die."

I had known that I was sick, sometimes very sick, but no one had told me I might die. Had she kept that from me so that I wouldn't be afraid? Had that been why I lived—because she protected me? Something about this possibility made everything feel a little different, as if I had been look-ing at a distant forest fire and then taken a small step to the side and then looked again, only to realize that it was actu-ally the sun setting. I thought about putting my hand on her ankle.

"You know, I get all that now," Mom said. She gestured to her own body, as if her presence spoke for itself. "Being in and out of doctor's offices and doing all the things you have to do, just to treat this disease. Just to survive."

Her pink eyes were still focused on the screen in her lap. When I thought about her blinking from a hospital bed, alone and afraid, it usually irritated me. But at that moment it made me sad. I felt my hand vibrating.

"And I just wish, you know—"

I could reach out and touch her, I thought. Her foot or her ankle. My hand would close over the old bone, skin and sock and sunspot. I couldn't imagine what she might feel like. Cold, maybe. Warm, maybe.

Her sigh was dry in her throat. She shook her head. "I just wish there was someone to take care of me in the way I took care of you, at that time."

She kept talking. I was distracted by my hand. The vibration in my fingers would go away, then come back, then go away again. Suddenly it went numb. Then it felt light and senseless, thin as paper.

"I said, could you get me the other bottle?"

Now Mom was looking at me.

I went to the kitchenette. The fridge was stainless steel, and the countertops were spotless. Nothing was out—no half-full cups or dirty plates or stray rubber bands—except for a blue notebook and a bottle of Pūr, almost full, by the sink. The kitchenette shared the same air as the living room, but it smelled different, like sour apple and bleach. I could feel my hand becoming more and more numb. Heart attack? If I looked down at it, would it even still be there? I looked, and it was. I remembered that I had been given a task. When I brought Mom her bottle, I told her I was going to bed.

"What's wrong?" Mom asked, pulling the bottle down onto her chest. Her mouth had become a little beak. Her legs were stretched out flat on the couch again. "What I say?"

"Nothing," I said. "Nothing." The bleach smell was gone, replaced by wine. It made the roof of my mouth water, like I was going to throw up.

I put my cigarettes on the desk and got back into bed. I wanted to wake Petra, but I knew if I touched her while she was asleep that she might hit me. PTSD. Sometimes I touched her on purpose because her panic got me hot, and sometimes we would fuck after. But I didn't feel like dealing with her, so I stayed on my edge of the bed and listened to her breathe.

####

When I let myself into Petra's apartment, I found her tucked in under the covers, eyes closed like a good little girl. She told me she was always asleep when I sneaked in, but I wasn't sure I believed her. I never told her in advance when to expect me.

The first time was the best. Blindfold. Choke. Smother the scream. She had roommates, which meant we had to be quiet. She fought hard, but it didn't matter. I was stronger. I held her down, shoving my fingers up into wetness. She usually slept naked, but that night she was wearing a satin slip.

"Slut," I whispered, laughing. Real things inside both of us surfaced. She was gagging when she came on my hand. I laughed more. "Oh, you're disgusting."

I considered sticking one of my wet fingers down my throat and puking on her, but she looked too pretty. Her lower lip was mushy on her face. Her tears were small, very beautiful pieces of jewelry.

"Please stop," she whispered. "Please leave."

She always knew just what to say. I shoved my fingers back inside. She fought again, twisting her hips away. I pinned her down with my weight, her legs open with my knees. Forearm heavy over cheek. I knew it hurt. Still wet down there. Still hot. I decided to make her cum again. She bit me. Blood. Backhand. With the spit and the blood and the flush and her lips, she was starting to look like a clown. Another backhand. Not so pretty now. I pulled the blindfold off and seized her chin so she couldn't look away. Squeezed her eyes shut. I spat in my hand and started fucking her again, slow, until her eyes rolled open.

"Again," I said. I wanted to shower her with kisses.

"no," she whispered. "no no no no"

I added another finger.

"no"

I went harder. I pushed. She was going to hurt tomorrow.

"no no no no"

There it was. The shaking stopped pretty fast, but she was crying so hard I was worried someone would hear. With my other hand, I covered her mouth, very gently.

"Sh," I said. "Baby."

"mffff" She coughed, tongue pressed against my palm. My hands were wet. "mhhmmmmmhmh"

I thought my heart was going to beat out of my chest. Did people have heart attacks from happiness? The idea was so romantic I couldn't stand it.

"I love you so much," I said. I kissed the top of my hand, right where her mouth was. "I love you so much I could die."

My reflection has been tricky lately. I'm still handsome, but I also look like shit. It's not just what Syd did to my face, or the skid mark on my cheek from when Mary tossed me out the front door. I look like I haven't slept properly in weeks, which I haven't.

I've gotten a lot of mileage out of my face, but I'd take a cheese grater to it if I thought it would help me find X. It's not like she cared about what I look like, anyway. I mean she could have. I guess there's no way of knowing. Doesn't change the fact that the end of the month is a little over a week away and I'm out of leads. Venus won't respond to my texts.

I know better than to try Syd again. Margot didn't text me back, so I'm going to assume that's a dead end, too.

I don't know Mason Jar's real name, let alone where they are, or how to find someone who does.

This is all assuming that my guess was correct, and that the end of the month is a date I can count on—a bold assumption to be made by a homosexual as desperate as I am.

"You're still on about that person? X?" says Camille. "Maybe you should give it a rest and find a job instead."

"I have a job," I sulk. It's true. I do have a job. Forrest won't let me forget it.

Camille is unsnapping her garters and peeling the hose down her thighs. That couple, the sports fans, has succumbed to her charms. She sealed the deal with her baseball scene, and now everybody is going steady. She has plans to meet up with them, just as soon as she's changed out of her work clothes.

"It's not a job if you're not getting paid to do it." She scrapes ReflecTec off her forehead with a disposable wipe. She uses a third of the wipe before she drops it on the floor and reaches for a fresh one. "Did you change the light bulb yet?"

I kick up off the couch and go downstairs to smoke. It's easier to ignore her than it is to fight. It's thirty-five degrees and gloomy as dried blood, but sitting outside is better than listening to Camille bitch. I stay out here, sucking my Juul dry, until she comes down for her date, glitzy with glitter, powdered within an inch of her life, pinned and pricked with words: VINYL NITRATE, SUCCUBUS, WHORE, GLAMOURPUSSY. She ignores my ignore and parks herself in front of me as she adjusts the straps on her little Versace backpack.

"Listen, I know you've had a rough couple of months," she says. She lets go of her backpack to touch my arm. I can tell she has it all rehearsed. Jesus. Just because I'm being insane doesn't mean she has to talk down to me. "But I think you need to drop it with this person, this X person. It's just making your life harder."

I glare at her. I grunt.

"I mean, you're a mess," says Camille.

"What else is new."

"I mean it," says Camille, lipstick thinning. Under the street-lights, shadows grow under her nose and eyelashes. "I don't know what you want from this person, but things are just going to get worse if you don't stop whatever it is you're doing."

She keeps talking, so I just tune her out. If she tries to hug me, I decide, I'll take a big, exaggerated step backward. Make her look as stupid as she sounds.

When she's done with the lecture, she goes on her merry way. I smoke for a while longer, then go back upstairs to my couch. I'm exhausted but not sleepy. I page through a book and don't read any of the words. I screw off on my phone. I lie there and describe every object in the room to myself in as much detail as possible, a trick an insomniac writer taught me years ago. Still no sleep. The apartment is just too quiet.

My alarm has already been going off for twenty minutes by the time I wake up. I'll be late for work again. Fifth time this week. The office doesn't have an official start time, but if you get in after Forrest does, he writes you up. Write-ups lead to warnings. Warnings lead to red slips. Then you get fired. Happy Friday.

On the train, I slide my finger across the greasy window and the reflection changes: nose goes left, cheek creeps right. If I didn't have a job, I'd have more time to look for X. Yesterday, Forrest put a meeting on my calendar for this morning, to talk about my productivity, I'm sure. Management really has the nerve to punish you for not working for free. I'll just sit there and take it. I don't have the energy to argue.

I turn around to see if the window behind me is any cleaner than the one next to me. Someone scratched something into the glass. WHAT DO YOU NEED, the graffiti wants to know. But that isn't even the right question.

I moved out of Mom's apartment when I was seventeen. It was a stupid thing to do. Looking back, I could have probably squeezed out another year with her, maybe two. Saved up before moving on and given myself a cushier landing later.

It came out of nowhere. Mom had just gotten a rehab cycle out of her system, so she was on the upswing. She was drinking again, and she didn't feel too bad about it yet because, as she kept saying, she had mastered moderation. Neither of us believed her, though we were getting along okay. I was going out on my own at that point, not telling her where I was all night. She'd always minded her own business on that end.

Things were going so good with her that I asked her to sign the paperwork I needed to get on birth control.

"What for?" she asked, shocked.

"I don't want to get pregnant," I said. Obviously. In fact, I lived in fear of it. The thought of Mom giving birth to me made me want to puke.

"Oh," Mom said. She looked like she was doing a math equation in her head. She thought I would only be having sex with girls, I realized.

I ignored that. "You just need to sign a few things," I said. "But that's it. I can take care of the rest myself."

"Oh," she said again. Her notebook was on the counter in front of her. She had closed it when we started talking so I couldn't see what she'd been writing. "That's all you need from me?"

It sounded like a leading question, but I didn't know what answer she wanted, so I just told her the truth. "Yeah."

Mom took a drink. I didn't like the way she drank water. It always seemed like a struggle to get it down. At the end of every swallow, she would grimly seal her lips, sometimes wiping them with a baggy sleeve.

"It's not a big deal," I went on.

"Are you sure I shouldn't come?" she said.

"Yeah."

"You know," Mom said. "I've been there with you through a lot of stuff."

Again, I felt like there was a way I was expected to respond, a correct answer to be given, but I didn't know what it was. I said nothing. She took another sip of water. I watched.

"What?" she said. She pointed her chin at me. "What's the face?"

"Nothing," I said. Truly, it was nothing.

"You know, you were in so much pain, when you were little. I was doing you a favor."

I couldn't think of anything to say to that, either, so I went to my room. I laid down on my bed and looked at the ceiling. I felt like jerking off. I wished Mom would leave the apartment so I could do it in her room, on her bed, with the white noise machine going and the window a little open. But she stayed in the kitchen, pacing and writing, for a long time.

I moved out the next day. I had a job, and I knew an older girl with her own place who liked me enough to share for a bit. I can't remember when I ended up getting the birth control, but I did it by myself. That was the first time I went to the doctor and remembered it the next day.

####

Forrest's office smells like his cologne, which smells like a moldy cedar chest. The vinyl chair I sit in is a little too small. Over his shoulder, in the open-floor area, I can see Aisha with her Pantene hair and linty jacket. Triskit watches me from her lap, leaning back against her, tits out.

After an initial double take, Forrest talks without looking at me. I nod my head every so often, like I'm listening. If I'd been good at school, I would have gotten a degree, and if I'd gotten a degree, I wouldn't have this job. I mean, I couldn't have this job without a degree—my résumé says I have one, but that's a lie that no one's ever bothered to check. But if I really had one, I could be somewhere else.

I dropped out of college after two years, when they jacked up tuition for the third time. Couldn't be helped. Still, sometimes I regret not finishing, even with the debt and all that. If I had a degree, a good degree, maybe exporting would be easier. I could be someplace nice right now, a place with good plumbing and no energy savers and free medical care. Like Helsinki. I could have an apartment of my own. I could travel to other countries just for fun, like rich people do.

Forrest seems to be winding down. I know it's time to go back to my desk when he nods his head and reaches for his mouse.

"How'd it go?" asks Aisha. Triskit is still watching me. He has so many tits.

"Fine," I say. I sit down and put in my earbuds, looking away from the screen until it wakes back up again and becomes too bright to be reflective. I don't want to encourage a conversation. My face is swollen almost as bad as my body was a few weeks ago, but miraculously, Aisha hasn't said anything about it.

"Are you okay?" she asks.

One time Aisha tried to invite me to dinner. She texted me during work. I have no idea how she got my number. I could tell she was watching as I picked up my phone, read the text, deleted it, and put the phone back down. I thought about blocking her but decided that it was unnecessary, and I was right, because she never texted me again. She acted as if nothing had ever happened.

"I'm fine," I said. I turned to my screen as if I were busy, but there was still nothing for me to do. I was exhausted by the idea of talking for a second longer, and it was only 10:30 a.m.

A little after five, I decide to knock off early. Forrest watches me leave from his window-walled office. I watch him right back, zipping up my coat as I march to the door.

There's an old gay bar a few blocks from my office. I rarely go because it's mostly frequented by straight tourists these days, but it's early enough to be mostly empty, and I want a drink. And since it's a gay bar in name only, I don't have to worry about a raid.

I find a barstool and lean, tenting my fingers on the bar's polished wood. When I pull my phone out of my pocket to check the time, the battery's at 2 percent. There's a message from Camille.

won't be home til late but will you stay up? need to talk.

Shit. As I compose my reply, the screen goes black. I feel a wave of relief, and then nausea. I can't get drunk now. I have to be awake and alert and ready to fight Camille over my unpaid rent when she gets home. Maybe I'll lose my job and my couch all in the same week. Now I really need a drink.

The bartender is short, stacked, and apathetically slicing a bucket of jaundiced limes. The naked ladies on her forearms dance as she moves, and when she looks up to check the soccer game behind her, the subdermals in her cheeks wink at me. The neon behind her screams TITTY TWISTERS ON TAP. Despite the shift in clientele, the wall is still covered in stickers, decals, and graffiti: the black spears of antifa, ACAB, GAY POWER, END WHITE SUPREMACY, SOPHIE'S MOON.

The bartender carefully ignores me. I slide onto a barstool and glare at the chalkboard behind her, as if the only reason I haven't been served is that I don't know what I want to drink yet. Fine by me. The longer all of this takes, the more I delay the inevitable moment of finishing what's in front of me and, with nothing else to do, thinking about X.

It's hard to believe that I didn't even know she existed a few weeks ago. That if I had walked by her on the street everything may have been different. And what about now? What if she walked in and sat down next to me? What would I do?

I finger a peeling sticker on the wall: a photo of Huey with a shotgun. He's wearing a black beret, his ammo like rolls of pennies lined up across his chest. He looks handsome and young and sad.

Guns are easy enough to get. Camille would get me one, if I asked her. Mads, too, if I hadn't lost her in the divorce. It would feel good to have one with me whenever I left the apartment, to have the final act always within reach.

As I wait for the bartender's attention, more people come into the bar, more than I would have expected so early on a weeknight. Soon it's not empty enough to feel private, yet not full enough to feel anonymous.

I wish I was in a nice, almost-empty bar where I could just chat with the barman—it's always a man in the fantasy, isn't it? Middle-aged. Any race, so long as he has a little stubble, maybe some bifocals. No hair on top. He smokes a cigarette as he towel dries glasses, nodding indulgently as you slur through your most recent heartbreak, your disappointing son, the golden retriever that died years before her time.

This bar is not that bar. Over the decades it's given up its gayness, assimilated. But it didn't go fully straight, or not enough to become the dive where everybody knows your name, homey and humble and white-bread and heterosexual. Instead, it tried to split the difference, and now it's just a sad, safe capitulation, like an oil executive who buys a mass-produced harness for a gay orgy with a hundred-dollar door fee. There's too much rainbow in here, more neon than necessary, tired slogans on the wall—LOVE WINS—and Patsy Cline on the jukebox. God, we're embarrassing.

"Ready?"

The bartender is finally talking to me. There are no more limes to slice, but her knife is at the ready, like a sixth finger. She is not the kind of bartender who wants to hear about my problems, especially the problems I'm preoccupied with tonight.

Well, I met this femdom nightmare a few weeks ago, and I can't stop thinking about her is how I might start if she were like the friendly barman you see in old sitcoms. *She's exporting soon. She might even already be gone. I need to know for sure, but I also don't want to know. I want to see her again. But I don't know why.*

Femdom nightmare, eh? the barman would say, the knuckle of a cigar poking out from under the white bristles of his mustache. A smile tickles the corners of his mouth. *I've run across a few of those in my time.* His perspiration twinkles knowingly.

I would shake my head. I would run my fingers through my hair. *I'm not even a bottom*, I explain to him. *Or a switch. But something happened. Something changed.* I would shake my head again. *I just have to find her. I can't stop thinking about her.*

And what will you do, the friendly barman would ask, his eyeglass chain sparkling in the heterosexual neon of Bushmills, Coors, German girls in lederhosen, the orange-and-blue Mets ball, *if you can't find her?*

I would take a deep breath. I would be honest with him. *If she's already gone,* I would say, *either I find out where she is and find a way to get there, or I kill myself. Or something else, maybe.*

The barman would purse his lips and nod. He would know my chances as well as I did.

"Whiskey, neat," I tell the real bartender. It's the first drink that comes to mind. When she hands it to me, I connect it to my mouth and glue my eyes to the soccer game. The drunker I get, the more fun sports are, and I have a credit card I haven't yet maxed out. Fuck Camille.

When the game ends, the bartender switches over to a nineties sitcom. I happen to be eyeing the door when they come in. They're trailing a group of people, but it's obvious they've come here alone. They're wearing black and they're not flagging, but I don't need to see a hanky: Their boots are impeccable. They shine like they're under a spotlight.

My Docs are filthy, but that doesn't matter; I can tell I have Boot Boy's attention. My fifth drink of the night taps the mahogany. In a moment, they're sitting on the stool beside me. Dark hair, white T-shirt with the sleeves rolled up.

Instinctively, I check my phone. Still dead. According to the clock by the TV, it's not even ten. Camille still won't be home for hours. I need something to do besides drinking, or I'll black out. I listen as they order their beer, sit patiently as they begin to drink it. Suddenly, I spin around in my seat. They startle, I'm pleased to see.

"Watch it for me?" I say, nodding at my glass. We look at it together. It's empty. "I'm just headed to the bathroom."

When I get up, I only sway a little. Can't remember when I last ate, but I'm good, I can handle it. The tile under my feet is checked like the Black Lodge. Behind me, the music gets louder. *I'm gonna treat you sweet and kind . . . I'll drive her right outta your mind.* More Patsy, but I'm not irritated anymore. It takes forever to get to the door with the white man shape on it.

I like the bathrooms at this bar because they have stalls as well as urinals. Two of them, in fact, one standard, one plus-size. I go into the standard to piss. As I'm washing my hands at the row of sinks, I hear the door open. I look up into the mirror. Right on time.

I push them into the stall I just used, forearm them against the wall, mouth on theirs while locking the door with my right hand. They return their mouth, but when they push into me and against my arm, I shove them down to their knees. I lift up my right foot and set it on the toilet. What's filthier, my boots or the plastic seat?

"You know what to do," I say. Their eyes are enormous. Their nipples are hard under their T-shirt.

Their tongue is out before their face meets the leather of my right boot. It slips over the darkness, dampening the dirt and something that looks like bird shit.

I have a handful of their hair, thick and black between my fingers. I pull it away from the scalp, first nicely, then hard. I can feel the follicles scream, their face pulling as they struggle against it, but they keep licking. When they reach out a finger to touch my leather, I slap it away.

"Hands off."

Obediently, their arms return behind their back, their ass out like a cat in heat.

"Now this one," I say, pushing their face away and putting a new boot in front of it.

They dig in like a starving man. Their mouth is so red, their lips pink from the friction. I wonder if they're sober. I hope they are. I want them to taste and remember everything. Want them to think long and hard about everything I've stepped in since the last bitch cleaned these things. Eat it all, then beg for more. They're moaning, squirming, lifting and lowering themself ever so slightly on their heels. It's disgusting. Maybe they'll puke.

"You're terrible at this," I say, and when they pull away, finally ashamed, I shove their head back into the leather, grinding it into their face. I hope they have a fat lip tomorrow. "I didn't say to stop. Have you even done this before?"

They try to nod, and I grind my boot again. They burrow back into it. Sick puppy. The more I think about it, the more disgusted I am. I wonder what they're wearing under their jeans. Boxers? Frilly pink panties with a white lace bow? Nothing at all?

When I get bored, I shake them off. "That's enough," I say. "You're making me sick. I'm not even turned on anymore."

I stand up and drag them with me, by the throat this time, easily because I'm too drunk to feel my left elbow, still hurt from my night at Fist. Judging by their face, you'd think I'd whipped them bloody instead of teasing them a little. I think I'm starting to really hurt their feelings. God, I hope they're sober. "Let me see that mouth."

They open up, still red, wet and rippling, the back of their throat undulating. I wish I'd strapped on before I left the apartment today. I think for a moment about taking them with me somewhere, maybe back to the apartment, and slipping in and out of their holes for a few hours, but then I decide against it. There would be too much time to think in between here and wherever I'd take them. We might have to talk. Let's not ruin a good thing. God, I need a good thing.

They're a head shorter than me and at least twenty pounds lighter. Lifting them isn't hard. Their back against the tile again, gasping for breath. I examine their face and they watch me do it, flexing themself against the wall. Slut.

"Open," I say. They open. "Wider," I say. I wind up, then let loose. Spit sprays on their face, flecks their tongue. Their eyes close. They moan again.

It takes my fingers a moment to identify what I'm touching. A jockstrap. Of course. Their hips pull away, and I let it loose with a snap, then dive back in again, holding them back with my forearm. I move it up across their throat, and their moans tremble, eyes roll, as I circle, slowly feeling out the hair, the skin, the bone softening. The wetness is pure heat.

"You're so hard," I whisper. "You licked shit off my boots and you're hard as a rock."

I press my forearm harder. The next moan rattles like a snake.

"Did you hear me?" I ask. "Pervert."

Circling, circling, pushing, and then the plunge. I miss my cock so much I want to go home and make love to it, just the two of us. One finger. Two. Three. The faggot moans against my chest like a child, panting, arching their back. Suddenly they lift their head. "Don't look at me," I say. They twist their neck away, and that's when I feel the first one on my hand, the pulsing on high. The bathroom door creaks open, but I'm not done yet. Keys jingle, footsteps slide, and I cover its mouth, flip it over, and pull down its pants just enough to get down there from behind.

"Touch yourself," I say into its ear. I don't bother whispering.

Its hand moves, darting into its fly. I pull my hand out, spit on my fingers, and go back in. I have a few of them in its asshole when it happens again, and this time it makes noises as the feet shuffle, the door slams.

Now it's time to let go. I pull my hand out again and wipe it on the seat of their jeans. I lean against the stall to catch my breath, watch them leaning forward, catching theirs. Their shirt is pulled up around their waist, and there it is, high on the right side of their ass. Two lines, four right angles, burned into their skin.

"Weather's shit," says the deli guy.

"I guess so," says the customer. He's buying a tallboy—COOL CRISP ORGANIC +50MG THC—and some swishers. Both men are wearing identical beanies. The deli smells like rice and weed. Behind me, a teenage girl with cobwebs of hickeys on her neck and a tattoo on the white meat of her left eyeball glares down at her phone.

I didn't move to New York for any particular reason. I didn't have a long-distance girlfriend or a job or dreams of hitting it big doing something important. I don't have hobbies, unless you include my sex life. I think I'm the only person I know who isn't some kind of artist with nine projects on the side.

When I decided to move here, I was twenty-three and living in a big town with endless suburbs where people sort of just oozed along. When my girlfriend Sabrina and I broke up, she traded me a little money in exchange for all the furniture and stuff we had bought together. It wasn't much, but it was the richest I'd ever been. I figured that since I was already moving, it wouldn't be all that much more trouble to come here and start over.

I had only visited New York once before, with Sabrina, actually. She was from the Bronx, and I came with her for some family event. I met her parents, nice people who didn't care at all that she was a dyke. Their niceness weirded me out, so I tried to get her out of the house as much as possible.

She took me into the city, and we walked around, holding hands, in that perfect window of good weather right at the beginning of May, after the crocus fades and just as the roses get bright. We saw all the tourist sights—Times Square and all that—but I remember the streets best. You know, dogwoods pinking, irises budding, ivy climbing, snow-white dahlias preening in kiosk windows or dead and curled in newspaper. Dogs shitting with joy, and kids running around, laughing, pushing, stealing, sitting on the train and lost in their phones and notepads and books. People talked to each other in the street and stood outside stores and subway stations eating sandwiches, bits of donut scattering on the pavement as they moved their hands. Everyone was holding a vape or a styrofoam cup of coffee. Everyone was yelling, deep into the night. Disco and cumbia at all hours, sirens, fights. Sometimes birds, when the sun was coming up, from the Japanese maples and honey locusts.

New York, I thought, as Sabrina held my biceps with her hands, had energy. New York was vital. It was flowering trees and puddle scum and mold and meth and poison and open wounds and festering wounds and healed wounds stitched up neat as embroidery. That's what everyone had always told me about New York, that it's hard and beautiful and ugly and magnificent, and I agreed. I fisted Sabrina in her childhood bed—baby-pink sheets, silk pillowcases, textured wallpaper, kawaii and neat as a pin—and made her beg Daddy to cum while her parents slept in the next room. A part of me hoped they would hear and kick us out, give Sabrina a taste of the real gay experience.

After I moved, I lost track of Sabrina for a long time. But a few years ago, a friend told me that when her dad had been deported back to El Salvador, the rest of the family went with him—Sabrina, her mother, her aunt, and her sister. They weren't allowed to sell their home. They had to give the parakeets to their neighbors.

####

PODCAST DUO MURDERED DURING LIVE SHOW, the feed said.

The hosts had been traveling across the country taping live episodes in sold-out stadiums and amphitheaters. They were in Seattle, the fourth stop of their tour, when someone opened fire from the second row. Both of the hosts, a security guy, and a woman sitting next to the shooter were killed.

The shooter died, too, of course. He fled to a bathroom and barricaded the door. When the cops burst in, the sinks were stopped up with toilet paper, and a slick of water raised the floor. The trash cans had been upended, leaving toilet paper, candy wrappers, and bloodied pads floating in the water. The killer—a man in the women's bathroom, everyone's worst nightmare—was sitting on the ground, back to the wall, face blown to bacon bits, naked except for soaked tube socks and a stopped watch.

The hosts had been telling the story of Paul Michael Stephani, Minnesota's Weepy-Voiced Killer, when they died, even though they were in the PNW, a place known for its serial killers, with guys like Ridgway, Bundy, and the Molalla River

Killer. Hooker killers, Camille calls them. She doesn't fuck with true crime.

####

Scratching and kicking, I screamed so loudly that I woke Mom up, which surprised me even more than the way the worms— eating me from the inside, exploding through my sternum and throat and lips, Princess Mononoke–style—transformed into Benji's big, hard fingers over my mouth. She burst into my bedroom, her screams joining mine, to find me in my bed, the blood from my nose covering his hands.

In less than a minute, Benji was out on the street, where he tucked himself back into his briefs and lifted his feet up high, like a cat with tape on its pads, trying to avoid the glass and loose asphalt that littered the parking lot. He wasn't wearing a shirt. The birds were awake, buried screaming in the black velvet skyline.

Mom opened the front door, still latched, to toss his car keys through the gap. "I'm calling the cops!" she declared, her breath clouding in the porch light.

I stood behind her. My fingers were on the little strip of skin between my nostrils and my mouth, rubbing the wetness there. I had the vague idea that I should get some toilet paper to stop it up. I couldn't remember where the toilet paper roll was—on the wall across from the toilet, or next to it, on the sink? Mom's legs were short and white, her ass crisscrossed with the black of her thong.

Benji said something to her that I didn't hear. Mom closed the door, deadbolted it, and turned around. We stood there for a moment, breathing hard. I wanted to look at her, but the blinds on the living room window were still up, and I was worried that Benji would come up to the window and look in, seeing Mom almost naked, and me in my T-shirt and no panties. I didn't want him to do that.

I looked back at Mom to find her watching me. "Jesus," she finally said. Shaking her head, she slid past me and back to her bedroom. "I'm never going to get back to sleep now." She closed the door behind her. She didn't call the cops.

####

When Boot Boy sees me in the streetlight, their face changes. It's subtle, just the eyebrows and some muscles around the still-red lips. I almost make a joke—I know what I look like, and I know it's not good. They should see what's going on under my clothes. It's been weeks since X, but the bruises are still there. I've started to wonder if a few of them will be permanent. That happened to Petra after a while. The softest part of her ass became discolored year-round, a perennial flower blooming blue.

Instead of acknowledging my face, I offer them a real cigarette. They remove a glove with their teeth. I don't have to explain myself to them. They're the one who came twice.

They take the analog from my fingers, which still smell like them, and I light it. They look happy now. Good. I want to keep things smooth. I light a cigarette for myself, too. I need an excuse to wait with them until their car pulls up.

We chat about the bar, joking about how straight it is these days, not that we are old enough to remember the old times. "So why did you come?" I ask them.

Boot Boy laughs a little. Cabs creep by, crunching ice and honking at buses. Every so often, a dark-coated body shoulders its way up the sidewalk. "Sometimes I get lucky. I've met some old guard daddies here that you'd never find at the *queer* places. It's like nobody told them this is a tourist trap now. But those fags will actually do stuff." They take a drag. "Not like the tenderqueers who just want to make out and flog."

Do they think of me as one of those daddies? I'd rather not know. I decide it's time to bring it up. When I do, I ensure my voice sounds casual, like I was just mulling over the big game or the newest Cyte TOS when the thought popped into my head. Totally innocent. Their phone says I have twelve minutes before the driver gets here.

"I like your brand," I say, nodding down toward their jeans. I actually do.

"Thanks."

"I take it you didn't do it yourself." I'm a little jealous, even.

Boot Boy laughs again, big this time. "Nope. Someone I don't see anymore. Got carried away being a houseboy."

I think about playing dumb but decide that's no good. Then I'd just be some nosy rando, and then maybe they wouldn't want to answer my questions.

"It was X, wasn't it?"

Boot Boy laughs some more. "Who else?"

Their analog dangles. They rub their neck like Brando. I can't tell if their voice is wistful or dismissive. I must be nearly sober now, or maybe it's just the streetlight, because for the first time I'm noticing their fancy haircut, the buttery leather of their wallet, the spare but expensive jewelry. Boot Boy is a rich bitch. Of course they wanted to get fucked in a bathroom stall.

"Yeah. I met her through Syd . . . uh . . . can't remember their last name," Boot Boy goes on. "Something with a *B*. You know them?"

"Yeah," I say. "I know them."

"Yeah. That's how we met, being houseboys together. But actually, Syd and I met before that. We went to the same summer camp when we were in high school. For like three years in a row."

"Totally," I say. I'm glad I didn't know they were this boring before I made them cum, or I might not have gotten that far. Now I notice Boot Boy's rich people skin and rich people smell, their rich people body—healthy, skinny but toned. I imagine X enjoyed permanently wrecking it.

"Syd wasn't around all that long, though," Boot Boy says. "They say they're into service, but they're not. They only care about two things." They mime something near their nose, then mime something near their ass.

"Do you still talk to her?" I ask. "To X?"

They take another drag. They seem to be giving my question some thought. "Not for a while, actually. It's been months. Since last year, I think."

It occurs to me that X and I have something in common: Neither of us, it seems, is talking to our old friends. Who *is* X talking to then? I could ask myself the same question, I guess. When Petra and I broke up, it felt like I broke up with everyone in my life. It's been months, and I still really only see Camille. Of course, she isn't talking to Petra, either.

I wonder what Petra and X would think of each other.

####

Stomachaches remind me of the hospital. Negative memory, if there is such a thing. Empty space rather than recollection.

That night at Mom's, I lay next to Petra and thought about hospitals. I was sick of them—of the ones I'd stayed in as an adult and the one where Mom was soon going to die. But I couldn't stop thinking about them. I couldn't sleep. I imagined I could hear her still typing away on the couch, her WPM slowing as she drank.

My stomachache was getting worse. The spare room was scrupulously clean, but I could smell the hospital, the bleach and the rubber and the latex and the metal. All my favorites, but bad. The drugs from the plane and the booze from the restaurant were fading, and as they did, the thing below my ribs turned over and over, as if a rodent were digging a hole in my gut.

Petra was snoring a little, I remember that. It was the last thing I remember, in fact, before the sound of the shower woke me up again. I wasn't sure how long I'd been asleep. Something heavy collided with the sink. The faucet whined. A wet foot squeaked on porcelain. Mom's voice hummed through the wall, too quiet to understand.

Who was she talking to, I wondered in that half asleep way, when even questions feel like observations. Is someone in there with her. Was someone else in the apartment. Benji. Marco.

Slowly, as if my hand were made of lead, I started rubbing my belly again. I remembered that Mom had complained during dinner about the hard water in her apartment. "Hell on my hair," she said, even though it had plenty of other things going against it—chemo and menopause and the salon. I dozed off again, the wail of the pipes summoning a conch shell I found at a Queens flea market years ago. When I held the shell against my ear, the wind inside was so loud I almost dropped it. It just kept going and going, promising an ocean that didn't exist. It cost ten dollars.

I like beaches, especially the kind you get on the West Coast. Big waves, gray and thunderous. Cold sand that burns your feet.

An arctic beach would be nice, I dozed to myself, an arctic beach on the edge of a petrified ocean. *Beach, bed, lungs.* In that moment, I wasn't thinking about how all the cold places are going away. I rubbed my belly, the howl of the conch and the idea of cold sand and wet ankles ebbing all gentle.

A grunt and a hollow burst. Mom on the front lawn, pajama set, loose hair.

I jerked awake and lifted my head up off the pillow. The water was still on. Was Petra awake? I held my breath to listen. She'd stopped snoring, but her body was heavy as a dead thing, inert as a boot. I listened and listened. The shower kept going, pouring down the drain. A waste of water. A waste. If Petra was awake, she was hiding it from me. I thought about getting up. And then I didn't.

When I woke up again, I knew it was morning, even though the room was dark. The shower was still on. The water.

I didn't knock before I opened the door. She was facing away from me toward the wall, like she was sleeping on her side. The water rained down on her back and stomach. Her hair was almost dry again, but colorless, as if its substance had been washed away.

Boot Boy wrote the address on my forearm with KOOL KOHL eyeliner. I studied it carefully, worried it would smudge before I had the chance to put it someplace more permanent. I hadn't asked them for their phone number, and they hadn't offered.

"Once or twice." That was how many times Syd had told me they met X. But according to Boot Boy, that wasn't true. In fact, Syd had been in service to X for months. Shitty service, according to Boot Boy, but service nevertheless. Syd was constantly surprising me. Who knew they had it in them.

Boot Boy told me that Syd had been doing standard houseboy stuff—little repairs, leather polishing, rope laundering—at the dungeon where X worked, the same place where Venus had waterboarded me just a few weeks ago. But then they figured out a way to start skimming off the top (or the bottom, as the case may be).

"What did they even need the money for?"

"Nothing, I don't think." Boot Boy's fillers make them look like a Bratz doll. "Some people just like to steal."

The skimming would have become a problem, they said, if Syd hadn't wandered off before anyone could figure it out. If they'd been caught, the dungeon staff would have flayed them alive, and not in a sexy way.

A black sedan pulled up.

"That's me," said Boot Boy.

Both of us tensed, but neither made a move to hug or anything, so I just watched them slide into the back seat.

The window of the train car shows a face as haggard as the one I saw in the bar bathroom. I'm sober enough now to be bothered by my ugliness, and the prospect of my talk with Camille is no longer avoidable. I wish I'd brought a flask or something.

Petra was awake. Her eyes weren't all the way open, but I could see her pupils moving below her lids. I sat down on the edge of the bed.

"What?" said Petra. She sat up on her elbow. "What is it?"

"She's in the bathroom," I said. "She's not breathing."

Petra got up and looked. I watched her from the doorway. I had already turned the shower off.

"I thought it was a dream," Petra said, her hand on the knob. The shower dripped.

They said it was blunt force trauma to the head. She had been drunk, of course. There wasn't an investigation or anything like that. She was a sick, drunk woman on the verge of old age in a slippery bathtub. What else was there to know?

You'd think that someone would care, that someone would wonder if maybe something else wasn't going on. You'd think that someone would do *something*. But no one did. She just died, and the world kept going. It turned out that Mom wasn't special—she was just like everyone else. She would have understood that, I think.

####

"Mommy issues or daddy issues?" my date wanted to know.

"Neither," I said. "I don't have a problem with *them*. They're the ones who have a problem with *me*."

I knew it was a line, but the line was a good one, and other perverts seemed to get a kick out of it.

####

After they took Mom away, I told Petra to go home without me. I'd gotten us an earlier flight the night before, when Mom was still alive, but now I had to stay in town to take care of everything. There was no need for Petra to stay for the funeral, a week away. She would lose her job if she did. And it wasn't like *her* mom died.

"I'll be fine," I said. "I really don't mind doing it by myself."

"Okay," Petra said.

I waited, but she didn't say anything else.

"Okay," I said again. I waited. She was looking out the window. A car drove by. "Okay. I'll just stay here then. Shouldn't take me longer than a few days."

"Okay," Petra said.

She was doing this thing with her jaw that I hate, this chewing thing that makes her look like a rodent. She does it when she's thinking. She's grinds her teeth when she's asleep. She has a yellow plastic retainer that she keeps by the bed but almost never wears. It can't feel good, the grinding teeth dulling themselves on each other, the tweaks of nerve spiking against each other like ice cubes. I thought about her teeth anchored in her gums, her gums limning her bone, her bones entwined with vein and blood and gore. I find this to be what my therapist would have called *grounding*.

"Fine," I said.

I watched Petra pack. She hadn't brought much with her, but she moved slowly, folding pieces of clothing over themselves and stopping every so often to tamp it all down with the heel of her hand. I was waiting for her to make a mistake, and she would. Anything can be a mistake.

When she stooped to pick up a sock she dropped, her fingers like the claw in an arcade game, my hand was already on her neck. She tried to shake me off. "Not now," she said.

"Pick it up," I said.

"I am." She looked up at me like she was looking down on me. "That's what I'm trying to do. Obviously."

A vein moved below her left eye. It was the vein that came out when we were playing or when she was angry or tired.

She shook off my hand, stood up, and stuffed the sock, un-paired, into her bag. Her shoulders were low. I took her by the waist. She slid her hips away. I put my hands on her again, and again she pulled away, but not before I felt her heat through her clothes. I thought about cutting her open and finding nothing, empty inside like a doll. White enamel, polished clean, completely dry. The trees outside the window were red and orange and trembling in the wind, the sun a golden ball beyond them. I thought about blood the color of the trees or the sun, hot and tasty like soup. Hands in her black hair, warm on her skin.

"What is wrong with you?" She pushed me away again. I was standing up, but it felt sort of like falling. "Jesus." She took another step away. I wished she was wearing a skirt. I pinned her against the wall. Behind her was the bathroom, and behind that, Mom's room.

"Aren't you going to miss me?" I said, brushing her ear with my lips. A whole week without Petra. There were so many things to do. The estate. Packing up this fucking apartment. I wondered if I was going to get money. If I did, I could buy something nice for her. Maybe a ring.

"I need to finish," she said.

Her hands were on me. I pushed my nose in her hair. She smelled like girl.

"I said to stop."

Now her push was hard-heeled, square in the shoulders. Her bag was behind me. I tripped and fell on it, landing flat on my back like a Marx brother, feet briefly up in the air. My tailbone would bruise, I knew.

"Oh," said Petra.

I was too surprised to say anything, or even get up. From the floor, I watched her line up her lips, push a hand through her tangled hair.

"Well," she said, red-eyed. She picked up another sock. "It's almost time to go."

####

When I get home from the bar, the apartment is quiet. Keys: thrown. Coat: hanging from one arm, dragging behind me on the hardwood.

"Camille?"

Nothing. Silence, except for the fridge and its noises. I sit down on the couch. It doesn't smell great. I plug in my phone and wait for it to turn on again. I keep my eyes glued to the screen. A few minutes of zen as my head swims. When it glows, it glows empty: no messages or calls. I guess I shouldn't be surprised. I don't get many of those these days.

I take a picture of the address on my forearm and look at it for a while, trying to commit it to memory, because like what if something happens to my phone. Stick my finger in my mouth and smear the eyeliner with spit. Now it looks like a demon incantation. But I don't need to conjure a demon all the way from hell—the address is right here in Brooklyn. I could go right now. Go find her, after almost a month of waiting. Fuck Camille.

But I can't move. Don't know why. Maybe Camille and I can have our fight and then I can get her to come find X with me. Maybe we'll work everything out, and then I'll at least have someplace to come back to.

I ponder the likelihood of booze in the kitchen, something to keep my buzz going until Camille gets here. No groceries because I've overdrafted and I'm saving my last line of credit for a real emergency (like getting wasted and fucking some twink at a fake gay bar), so if there is something to drink, it's probably Camille's, and I have to consider the Optics of the Situation: her coming home to find me slurping her last FATBURNER ACAI COCKTAIL is not going to put her in a generous mood. As of tomorrow, I'm three months behind on rent. Gonna need all the goodwill I can get.

Fine. I won't drink any more, I decide. I look in the corners and under the couch cushions for green instead. Fingers crossed she doesn't come home while I'm smoking, or I'll have to explain that, too. But maybe she won't even come, I think, as I pull the couch away from the wall. There's one. I reach for it. Maybe she'll find someone to go home with tonight, or go find that couple she's been seeing.

I clean a little bit—*see, I'm helping*—dump the ashtray in the garbage, shove some mail and ancient Juul cartridges in my backpack to get them off the coffee table, swipe the table for crumbs. I pincer a pair of socks back to the laundry basket in Camille's bedroom. When everything is looking a little tidier, I tear the weed up with my fingernails and pack a bowl. I'm deep in my third inhale when I hear a pair of size 8 platforms outside the door.

Keys: hooked. Purse: dropped. Coat: hung. But Camille isn't going for her first highball. She just stands there, looking at the living room. I turn to look at it with her. It's clear that my tidying has only made things worse. Just moved the crap around, exposing lines of dust and gum wrappers.

I look back at Camille, trying to read her face. Bongsmoke clouds the rhinestones woven through her hair and stuck on the tips of her lashes. In this light, and from where I'm sitting on the couch, she still looks pretty, dewy, sparkly, hard as a rock, even after a double. Do I look pretty? The black of the broken flat-screen confirms that I am still ugly. My eyes used to sit up high in my cheeks, and my cheeks were once less sunken, and the bruises were on the people I fucked, not me. I watch as one of my hands appears in the flat-screen to slide over the scab under my eye. It hurts. When was the last time I washed my face? When was the last time I took a shower? The smell again, even worse now that I'm floating in the depths of a deep, dank high.

I would kick me out. Who wouldn't. I brace myself for yelling. But Camille's voice is normal.

"I ran into someone tonight. Mads. At the club. I hadn't seen her in forever."

Mads. When I open my mouth to say her name, smoke burns my throat. I cough, sinuses burning with tears. I try again and cough more. The hand with the lighter in it is on my heart. I can feel the plastic through my shirt.

Camille's not looking at me. "She told me what happened to Petra," she says.

More coughing, though it doesn't appear to bother her, which is good, because I can't stop. "I don't—" I begin. The itch tears up the roof of my mouth. Belly hurts.

"Do you remember that time you came and stayed here when you and Petra got in that big fight?" says Camille. It's like she's talking to herself. "And then you and I got in a fight, too? When I got back here later on and you were gone, I almost called her to warn her. But I didn't. I was like, 'Don't be stupid, Camille.'" Delicately, she touches the heel of her hand to her forehead, then pulls it away, rolling her eyes. "Because I believed you." Now she's looking at me again. "But now I think that *that* was stupid." She laughs.

I think about Ariana. I want to tell Camille about what happened on that table, right over there, the same one where she and I sat and drank coffee and smoked analogs when she said,

Are we gonna talk about all this or what? and I said *No*, and about how it was me that texted Ariana, not the other way around, that I invited her over and kept her drink full. I think about the dog noises she made when I was inside her. How she turned away from me after to belt her pants again.

Camille just keeps on talking. In the moment, it's hard to believe. I push the edge of the lighter into the crack between my nails and their beds, driving the blood away, whitening my fingers.

"But I was thinking about it on my way home. Like I was really trying to be real with myself. And I think I thought I believed you before."

Her hands are on her hips, toes angled in slightly, knees touching. I see the version of Camille from twenty years ago, a little person who was too young for 9/11 and still had her original nose. She didn't know that she was going to grow up to have me living on her couch.

"But after what Mads told me," she said, "I realized that maybe I was lying to myself. Lying for you. And you know why?"

When Camille walks toward me, I want to lean away, but I can't go any deeper into the couch. Nowhere to go. Her eyes come tired out of her perfect face. Her eyes remind me of the blood under her skin, working away.

"Because I was worried you might hurt yourself if she left you." She shakes her head. "I protected you. I let her stay with you."

She sits down on the couch. Sweatshirt says WE RECRUIT. Bong twinkles. From this angle, she looks kind of like Mom.

"I can't believe you didn't tell me what happened with her," says Camille, and for just a moment, I think she means Ariana.

No. Not Ariana. Petra. My throat burns. "I didn't," I begin, but I start coughing again. It's true that I didn't tell her, but that's because I don't know what happened to Petra after I moved in with Camille. I made sure not to know. I am going to keep talking, I think, but then I don't, even when the coughing stops.

"No one told you?" The shock softens her eyes. "Nobody told you what she did after you left?"

It's unbelievable, but I think Camille believes me. I shake my head. She looks like she feels sorry for me, but it doesn't feel good.

"I can't believe you can listen to that," Aisha said.

She happened to see the murder podcast on my phone. She was actually disdainful, which was unlike her. It made me hate her a little less. Aisha couldn't be all that stupid if she hated true crime. Only perpetrators and victims like it, and most people think they're victims, even though most people are perpetrators. Like SM, true crime is just the fantasy of victimhood, and it's a fantasy because it can't be real. It isn't true. We're all bad. No one is good.

If Aisha is smart enough to get that, I don't know why more people aren't. And really, it's a lot more reassuring than the alternative.

####

I take my backpack and my duffel. I leave the books, the stuff in the fridge. When I get downstairs, I plug the address into my phone and start walking. It's wet and cold. More wet than cold, really. It's dark. The duffel isn't heavy, but my elbow hurts, so I can only carry it on one side. I won't be going back. I'll have to figure out something else.

For a long time, I walk. When I reach the water, I get as close as I can without falling in and head south, keeping it on my right. As I walk, it gets colder and less wet. I don't see hardly anybody. The water looks like nothing. At some point, I notice that I'm sober again. The cold helps.

I'm not far from my destination when the sky starts to turn colors. Since the murder podcast no longer exists, I've been listening to old episodes. They still have the archive up. Downloads have skyrocketed since the hosts died. Brand-wise, they couldn't have made a better move than getting slaughtered.

The host's voices, reanimated in more than one way, are almost too quiet to hear, but I don't turn up the volume. It's not like they're telling me anything I haven't heard before.

####

You see the graffiti everywhere: BE STUBBORN WITH ME. STAY ALIVE. Stuff like that. HARD TO KILL. Wouldn't it be nice to be easy, though?

I don't know why I didn't I kill myself after Petra. I thought about it. Who doesn't? But there are always reasons to stay, aren't there. There are people here that I care about, or there were back then.

I'll admit that knowing that some people want me dead is energizing in a way, and while defiance isn't the worst reason to stay alive, it's not mine. If I had any single reason, it was probably Mom. I used to hate the idea of her at my funeral, bored and waiting to drink.

She couldn't do that now, of course. I decided not to have a funeral for her, but not in a bitchy way. I just don't think she would have wanted one.

Petra was a good girl. She was so good that she bruised better than anyone I'd ever met. I rarely touched her face, saving it for special occasions. It wasn't smart for her to be seen at work that way.

The night we got kicked out of Fist was a special occasion. I knew Petra wouldn't like it in the moment, but she would like staying home from work with me the next day, stroking my hair in bed. The sooner we fought, the sooner we could get back to loving each other again.

I watched Petra watch Mary go back into the bar, then caught her by surprise. By the time our driver pulled up, I was holding her, and she was quiet again. He didn't say anything. I don't even think he noticed her face. Five stars.

The apartment was as we left it. There was the sheet on the couch with a cotton pad for the needle stuff we had been doing earlier. There was the red sharps container on the coffee table. Next to it was the plastic jack-o'-lantern where we kept our stash of sterile needles and scalpels and razor blades. The drawn blinds clicked when I threw her against the wall. Hand squeezing her throat. Hot and wet and hard. I hadn't wanted to fuck her this bad in forever.

Her inside felt so good. When was the last time it had been this good? When I spit in her face, she caught me on her tongue. Her lips shaped *thank you*, like I trained her. Squeezing harder. Our favorite: me fucking her standing, her hands around my wrist, my other hand inside her. When was the last time?

If her feet hadn't come out from under her at the angle she was at, I don't think I would have known. Her weight pulled her out from me, and then I fell, too.

I had hurt her. I could have really hurt her. She was crying loudly now, and wouldn't stop. That was when I started crying, too. Mouth open, realizing how drunk I was. Apologizing. I kissed the socks on her feet, the ground under her socks. Never again, I told her. Never again.

She went to Mads's house for what was left of the night. I stayed at our place. I was lying on the couch, still crying, thinking about Petra's tears, and then I was touching myself, thinking about her in her sleep, the way she looked when she looked dead. About what people look like when they look dead.

Eyes closed for a while and then eyes wide open. A moment between me and the ceiling, a long one. *Beach, bed, lungs.* Petra was never going to tell me to leave, and she was never going to leave herself. No matter what I did.

So I will keep her safe, I thought. I bagged up my stuff and called Camille.

That was the last time I saw Petra.

####

The app tells me that where I'm headed is around the corner. If I had something on me, one of Camille's pills or powders, I'd take it, but I don't. The moisture deadens noises, numbs distant traffic. There's an apartment building and black SUV idling out front, exhaust curling over the curb and into the trees above. Everything is wet.

She's not. She's under an umbrella, a suitcase by her boots. I'm just a few feet from her. She's slouching, toe out, head turned away from me. Something lit flutters to the ground. Skin in the dimness catches light.

Does she know I'm behind her? When she sees me, will she recognize me? I consider making a noise, then decide not to. Seconds, seconds. A loud singsong blinking from the SUV— open door. With a click, the trunk pops open. In the headlights, the street address, the same as the one scribbled on my arm, beams brass across the brick. My arteries roar in rhythm with the blinking. I feel like I'm being emptied, eviscerate bailing from my body in great, sweeping movements.

Now she's walking toward the SUV. Now it's time! The trunk has opened wide, and she's lifting her suitcase. I open my mouth to say her name, but another voice, one coming from the apartment, beats me to it. She turns toward me, and then I can see her, and now I'm silent. It isn't X. She has hair and other eyes and different fingers. My throat catches. Tricked again, a trick of the light.

The other voice again—a name that isn't hers—and she says something in response. Someone is coming out of the apartment, holding another bag, and she takes it, and they talk for a moment and then they hug. The other person notices me from over her shoulder. The woman I thought was X does not.

She gets in the SUV and it goes away. Another ghost. Ghosted again. Maybe she's exporting, too. Just like X.

Everything is wet. It's a new day and a new month. I could stay here outside this building all day, but I don't want to wait anymore. There's a bench by the bus post. I set down my bags and sit. There's enough light around the horizon that I can tell it looks like rain.

####

My coat isn't waterproof. The rain wasn't heavy, but it stayed long enough to drench me. Now I'm colder and cleaner. It's for the best. I have to go to work soon, if only because there's nowhere else for me to go. I wonder if I'm going to get fired today. I wonder what I'll do if I am.

My backpack isn't waterproof, either, so I open it to check my things. On top is the mail I stuck inside when I was cleaning Camille's living room, still dry. A bill, a Shen Yun coupon, a reminder that meat is murder. Last is a spammy-looking envelope with tiny black print. I'm about to shove it back down into my bag when I see, above the P.O. Box, that the return address says FLECC. The coupon glides to the pavement and darkens there.

There's no need to open the envelope, so I just sit with it in my hand. The light changes. My forehead warms. The clouds are breaking. When I look up, it's all red.

Acknowledgments

Thank you to my agent, Julia Kardon, for understanding, and to my editor, Alicia Kroell, whose patient insight found the good in this manuscript.

Thank you to Charlotte Shane, whose artistic integrity inspires optimism. To Morgan M Page, Torrey Peters, and Gretchen Felker-Martin, among the first to read this book, whose support and example have meant everything. To Tyler Ford, for championing me.

Thank you to Amanda Whip, for taking care.

Thank you to Elizabeth Harvey and Marie Sefton, who gave me a safe place to think. To Sophia Hoffman, Julia Race, and Jack, who gave me a safe place to work.

Thank you to Kitty Davies, for being my friend. To Dahlia Snow and Bambi Katsura, for being my family.

And thank you to Jade, for being mine. It's a damn slippery planet, but heaven hurries.

© Elle Pérez

DAVEY DAVIS's first book, *the earthquake room*, was released by TigerBee Press in 2017. They live in Brooklyn.